NO HARM DONE

An absolutely gripping British crime thriller full of twists

JUDITH CUTLER

Fran Harman Mysteries Book 4

Originally published as *Burying the Past*

JOFFE BOOKS

Revised edition 2024
Joffe Books, London
www.joffebooks.com

First published as *Burying the Past* by Severn House Publishers Ltd in Great Britain in 2012

This paperback edition was first published in Great Britain in 2024

Cover art by Nebojša Zorić

ISBN: 978-1-83526-629-8

For my dear husband Keith, who brought the sun into my life and makes it shine brighter every day

PROLOGUE

Holding Fran's hand, Mark presses back towards their new house. They're right up beyond the eaves, on the scaffolding platform installed by the roofers. Despite the guard rails — the builders are as safety conscious as one could wish — his legs want to fold till he's foetal. But he forces them straight. He focuses on the horizon and tells himself it's been worth the effort to get here. Maybe it has. Here he's monarch of all he surveys. Co-monarch with Fran, of course; she's returning the pressure on his hand, not, he's sure, with terror like his, but with love.

Caffy, one of the all-female firm, Pact Restoration (for 'Paula And Caffy's Team', he thinks), is on the other side, short, slight, but defying all efforts to think her small and vulnerable. She grins with triumph, as if it was worth giving up a Saturday-morning lie-in just to get him up here.

Forget the word 'up'. And 'lie-in' for Caffy — does she ever rest?

Held in the palm of the Kentish countryside, the rectory garden's like a relief map, with ghostly flower-beds at one end, what look like the foundations of an ornamental fountain, and then a kitchen garden. It will take years to complete their project, but in the short term a motor-mower backed up with a strimmer should work wonders. 'What a wonderful place for our wedding reception,' he thinks.

He's said it out loud. There's a huge silence.

'You're so good together I thought you'd been man and wife for years.' Caffy is an expert at filling silences.

'With or without the benefit of the clergy, we'll be together for many more years,' Fran says, falsely jolly and pointedly ignoring what he said.

'I can't back out.' His smile feels stiff. 'Not now we've got a witness. Fran, are you OK with this?' It might be a decision about staffing. Where the hell is loving eloquence when he needs it?

She clutches his hand and nods. She's been ghost-pale; now she blushes, rosily, as if she's a coy girl, not, like him, well over fifty. It's hardly surprising, considering how often and how hard he's snubbed her marriage hints in the past. She's worn that sort-of-engagement ring for ages, just to silence any police colleagues who might have baulked, even in these liberal days, at any unofficial relationship. Would he have backed out even now but for Caffy's presence? No. Surely not.

Again Caffy fills the silence. 'Me — a witness? At the wedding?' she says, with a worrying edge of joy to her disbelief.

He curses himself for using the word. All he meant was that he'd proposed in front of someone else. He ought to correct the mistake, but Caffy's still speaking.

'No, you don't mean that. You'll want an old friend. Family.'

He makes a desperate grasp at common sense. 'I guess we'll be married quietly at St Jude's in Canterbury. We know the vicar there. So we may not need witnesses in the register-office sense. But nothing would give me greater pleasure than for you to be my best woman.' All this formal conversation on a roof. He wonders if he's stepped into the world of Lewis Carroll.

The women envelope him in a triple hug. Fran is shaking, as if with cold. Whatever their thoughts, they all stare at the garden. Yes, he was right: it will make a grand setting for their wedding reception. He must just think about that.

He and Fran manage a wry sideways smile. She looks as if someone's just switched a light on inside her — but also as if she's afraid they're about to switch it off again.

Caffy speaks again. 'Sorry to bring you down to earth, as it were. This new job of yours, Fran, that Simon Gates was talking about. It's looking at dead cases, right? Just how dead does the case have to be? Or rather, the body?'

How can she mention his name so casually? Simon, a protégé of Fran's and now Kent's Deputy Chief Constable, heaven help them all, has been stalking the girl, not to put too fine a point on it.

She's pointing at the far corner of the vegetable patch, where the weeds and grass grow with far more energy than anywhere else in the plot — anywhere in the garden for that matter. A strip, two or three feet by six or seven. A few canes, weathered grey, suggest it was a runner bean row.

Narrowing her eyes, Fran says, 'It's meant to be cases we have on file but have never solved. I suppose it could be any sort of body. But I wouldn't want one on my own patch. Literally,' she adds with an amused glance at Caffy, who responds with the broadest of smiles, a lick of her index finger and a mark in the air.

'The omens aren't good, are they? Nothing like a decaying body to raise the nitrogen levels so spectacularly.' He squeezes Fran's hand: together they can deal with whatever problems come with this new situation — both new situations.

Caffy says, 'All may yet be well.'

Pretty much an autodidact, she's read more than the average professor of English, so no doubt she's quoting something he ought to have read years ago. But he doesn't know what. So he just says, 'I'd say we need to get our colleagues and their clever thermal imaging equipment in here.'

Which means that somehow or other he has to get down again, doesn't it? If only he can make his legs work without thinking about the space below.

'One rung at a time,' Caffy says.

At last on terra firma, Mark feels more assertive. 'Now, Caffy, your plans for this evening — this "date" that Simon's talked you into. I really am not happy.'

'Are you talking as a top cop or as the bloke I'm best womaning for?'

'Both. I want you to stay at home with a box of chocs and your feet up and let Simon and his dinner go hang.'

Caffy looks straight at him. 'In the circumstances, not a good choice of verb.' Her face softens. 'To use that horrible cliché, I hear what you're saying. But I've given him my word, and that's it: although he may not always know a hawk from a handsaw, he's still a human being.'

'And a good cop,' Fran admits, biting her lip. 'But he's been stalking you. It's an offence.'

He nods, glad that Fran's called a spade a spade.

'Yes. But I'm not going to press charges. I just want to spell it out to him that any romance is in his head. No more, no less. OK? OK. Unless someone in a white coat gets him sectioned, dinner goes ahead.' Suddenly, she flips into something like hostess mode. 'Now, would you like to see how the work inside's going? We've done our best to make some of it habitable for you even if it's not much more than a glorified bedsit.'

'So long as we can just camp there — we've got to move out of the cottage on Thursday, whatever happens.'

Caffy shakes her head doubtfully. 'We still need Sparky Smith to come along and do all the wiring . . . It'll be a damned close-run thing,' she concludes.

CHAPTER ONE

Detective Chief Superintendent Harman needn't have been supervising the operation at all — indeed, she was virtually paid to stay away from such interesting events. These days her life revolved around endless acrimonious meetings as she desperately defended the tattered Kent CID budget. This was the only reason, she told herself, not necessarily truthfully, for not retiring tomorrow — after all, she was doing her pension no good at all by staying on beyond her thirty years' service.

In fact, she really shouldn't have been here, enjoying the fresh air, fascinated by the clinical approach of the team in front of her. She'd already officially declared an interest in the rectory crime scene and could take no part in any of the decisions regarding the investigations. Possibly. Certainly not officially. Just the odd word of advice, perhaps. As she'd told Caffy, now at work with the rest of the Pact team on the lovely old house behind her, she hadn't officially started her new role reviewing cold cases, so given a possible corpse, she might as well continue her old role running CID and, in Caffy's words, generally solving murders. Not that Caffy was half as naive as she claimed to be, not with all that reading under her belt. A former drugs user, she had once been trapped in a relationship with her pimp, which only his violent death at someone else's hands had ended. And now she had another death to deal with — that of Deputy Chief Constable Simon Gates.

'Any developments with your body?' It was Paula, whom Caffy always grandly called the *prima inter pares* of Pact Restoration. Goodness knows where she'd learned about Latin feminine nouns. And remembered how to use them.

One of Paula's many gifts was to be able to materialize apparently at will, much like a serious-faced Cheshire Cat. 'Sorry — didn't mean to make you jump.'

Oh, no? 'Not yet. How's Caffy?'

Paula said flatly, 'At work. As usual. It's been hard getting any details of this Simon's death out of her. Is it true that when she told him to stop harassing her he just dashed off to his room and jumped?'

'Pretty well.'

'In other words I've got to wait until all the details come out officially.'

''Fraid so.' Details of how he'd filled the hotel room with roses; how two bottles of champagne at a hundred and fifty pounds a pop had been chilling. If only, in his desperation, he had recalled the Hippocratic Oath — in Fran's younger days, she had always quoted to her colleagues: 'Do no harm' — or her warnings about putting themselves in harm's way. But he had come to hate her, and no doubt her platitudes too.

'Poor devil,' she added. 'And poor, poor Caffy.'

'Why didn't Mark put his foot down? I mean, he's an assistant chief constable. Surely his word would count for something.'

'Don't think he didn't try. But Caffy was adamant . . . and the chief constable overrode Mark.'

Paula shook her head. 'Not good. Duty of care. But on the other hand, human rights,' she conceded tersely. 'Hell, Fran, whatever happened to good old-fashioned common sense?'

'Quite. But Caffy's OK?'

Paula nodded in the direction of the house; Caffy was now halfway up some of the scaffolding that had scared Mark witless. 'And how are you? Caffy said you'd helped Simon when he was one of your underlings.'

Fran nodded. Simon had been one of the many young officers whom she'd tenderly mentored, though one who'd become decidedly unlikeable. 'It's always tough when one of us dies,' she said, non-committally. But she had an idea that that didn't deceive Paula for a moment.

'Especially for management,' Paula said ironically. 'But standing in the sun talking isn't going to get your house fixed, Fran. I'd best be off.'

Fran nodded. In her way, Paula was as hard to read as Caffy. Meanwhile, she should be working too, planning the new cold case team for a start. Some people she'd worked with before might volunteer. A few more would be dragged in later, resentful at being in what they saw as a backwater. Any sign of a mutiny, though, and she'd make sure the waters were too choppy for comfort.

The trouble was, thinking didn't look like work. Just in case anyone was watching, she'd better look official. So she pulled on a pair of light gloves — vinyl, since she'd developed an irritating allergy to standard issue latex. Then she looked for something to lean on while she watched. Nothing. But she could imagine herself here in a few years' time — maybe even a few months' — becoming a tentative gardener, for the pleasure of leaning on a spade handle and looking around. She didn't want a plastic-handled spade; her father had used an old-fashioned wooden-handled one, the grain polished to a fine silky sheen by the years of use. She wished she'd claimed it when he died, but future gardening had been far from her thoughts then. As for digging, for the near future any that was considered necessary would be professionally done — and not, of course, by gardeners.

At last she found a low wall that had crumbled to just the right height, so she could sit and watch the show. It might have been an episode of *Time Team*, with the archaeologists wearing not their usual eclectic clothes, but the familiar white garb of crime scene investigators. White tape marked off segments of the ground, and a serious pair of sturdy young women marched backwards and forwards with some scientific instrument the TV *Time Team* presenters, if not the actual experts, referred to casually as geophys. They were checking for irregularities in the subsoil — or something like that. Everyone knew that these days you couldn't just go and dig where you thought there might be a body. But to wait so long before a single clod was turned almost had her jumping up and down in frustration.

She'd already spent a weekend playing a waiting game. In the past, at the merest sniff of a murder, CID and crime scene investigators would have flooded on to the site, raking in overtime hand over fist. They'd have been halfway to solving the crime by now. But in these new bean-counting days, you had to acknowledge that if a body had been *in situ* as long as this had been — always assuming it was a body, of course — it might as well wait till the much cheaper working week before the team of forensic archaeologists started to exhume it.

The slam of a car door disturbed her reverie. Automatically, she stood: time-wasting was one thing, but to be caught out in it was another, even — perhaps especially — by a delivery driver with more material for their house. However, it was a police car, unmarked, but one she recognized from the pound. The driver wasn't the person she was expecting, her deputy senior investigating officer, who'd phoned in to say she'd be held up by dentistry to a broken front tooth. DI Kim Thomas, new to the Kent CID team after a spell in Gloucestershire, had had an off-duty argument with a drunk trying to urinate on a war memorial. So DCS Harman had declared, unilaterally, she was at very least entitled to a couple of hours' police time having it dealt with. Nor was the driver Harry Chester, the DCI to whom Kim Thomas would answer, as soon as he was back off sick leave following gall-bladder surgery.

No, it was top brass. Topmost brass. At the wheel was Mark, who no doubt couldn't keep away from the site either; his passenger was no less than the chief constable himself. Both completed their shiny braid-and-buttons ensembles by donning protective footwear like her own — a complete waste of time, she privately considered, given the general state of the area. Perhaps they simply meant to keep their highly-polished shoes pristine.

Just in case their arrival had attracted the attention of the officers on site, she greeted the newcomers formally, even though she was going to marry one of them — yes, the word 'marry' still felt strange, making her heart beat faster and a silly smile spread across her face — and felt subtly indebted to the other for having supported the relationship between two senior officers that might well have raised eyebrows in some circles.

The chief always indulged in verbose preliminaries, and today was no exception — he touched on the beauty of the location, the elegance of the house, the potential of the garden. But then, abandoning the verbal bonbons as if he was sated, he said, 'I didn't want you to hear this from anyone except me, Fran. I'm retiring. My resignation's operative from today.'

'But—' Fran stopped short. The chief was an institution. He *was* Kent Police. On the other hand, she'd imagine that that was one reason why he'd chosen to go now.

'I can't have a senior officer topping himself on my watch, Fran, and that's the truth. Whatever the outcome of the enquiry. The hotel room he jumped from is being treated as a crime scene, of course, and we're not supposed to go anywhere near it till Devon and Cornwall Police have given it the going over of its life. But even if they find me lily-white pure, I'm not happy with what happened and my part in it. How's the poor young lady, by the way?' He dropped his voice as if a Victorian maiden had been sullied. 'The one with the unlikely name? Caffy? What sort of name is that?' he added with sudden tetchiness, as if embarrassed that he'd been unable to refer to Simon by name.

'It suits her,' Fran said mildly. 'Anyway, she's at work today. There she is.' She pointed to the overall-clad figure at the top of a ladder. 'We expected her to take a few days off, but Paula — she's the woman in charge of the team — says she's better where she is.'

'Up there? Dear God. She can't . . . Not when a man killed himself for love of her less than forty-eight hours ago.'

'Caffy doesn't do hand-wringing. And why should she? Her take is that Simon was clearly unbalanced. She compared him to Hamlet — brilliant but unhinged. What if she'd continued the relationship — which she says never was a relationship except in his eyes — and he'd decided to take her life instead, or even as well? But I must admit, her calmness disconcerts me,' Fran added.

'It probably disconcerts even Paula,' Mark said, 'but if anyone could deal with Caffy should she suddenly have some sort of crisis, it'd be Paula. Do you want a word with her?'

The chief shook his head emphatically. 'I mustn't be seen to do anything that could be construed as interfering with a witness. I'd best be off to clear my desk.'

Mark and Fran exchanged a glance; no, neither was going to try to argue him out of his decision. They turned with him, one either side, to walk him back to the car.

He held his hand out for the keys. 'I'm sure you can rely on Fran here for a lift back to the office, Mark. You might want to discuss what we were talking about earlier,' he added with a discreet cough.

Mark shook his head. 'With respect, Adam, I shall stick to what I said then. It's one thing if they insist on my acting as a stopgap until they find a proper replacement for you, but as for applying for your job at my age, forget it. No, they want some young thrusting alpha male — or, *pace* Paula over there! — alpha woman, of course. And I wouldn't want to take on anything extra at the moment anyway.' He turned slightly to mouth at Fran, 'I told him.'

Her face froze, more rictus than smile. She knew what was coming — could feel it in her water. This precious tiny wedding was going to grow of its own accord, wasn't it? Though how Mark could tell Caffy she'd been dropped as best woman she didn't know.

The chief produced his kindest, most avuncular smile, odd in a man not more than eight years her senior. 'My dear, I am so glad that you are about to enter the married state. And nothing, believe me, would give me more pleasure than to give you away, since I understand your father is no longer with us. On the other hand,' he added quickly, 'I can't imagine that you need to be in any sense "given". So would you do me the honour of letting me accompany you down the aisle? I understand that Mark is already equipped with a best man.'

'A best woman,' Mark corrected him. 'Look: she goes up and down those damned ladders like an old-fashioned monkey-on-a-stick toy.' He looked away quickly. Clearly, his trip to the roof hadn't cured his vertigo, which even seemed to afflict him second-hand, when someone else was scaling heights — or, in this case, descending from them briskly.

'Will you be having a big wedding? A police guard of honour is always a fine sight. It would look well in the Cathedral Close. Imagine that.'

He must mean Canterbury Cathedral! 'I think we might rattle round a bit in a building as grand as that,' she said, trying to sound diplomatic. Infinitely better than poor ugly St Jude's, of course. On the other hand, a pretty country church . . . 'But I would like to be escorted, wherever we end up. Thank you.'

'Good. That's settled then,' he said, suddenly gruff. He swallowed, and continued: 'Do you have any other family, Fran? I know Mark's having trouble with his daughter . . .'

That certainly wasn't an issue Mark would want aired just now, so she gabbled, 'I've a married sister in Scotland. She keeps an eye on my mother, whose ambition is to take over and run the care home she's in. But I should imagine she'll be physically too frail to come down, and I don't know that my sister would want to leave her in case she causes an insurrection.' Not that she'd want her sister anywhere near her, for all she was fond of her clergyman brother-in-law.

The chief laughed.

'I'll say this again, Adam,' she said, keen to change the subject, 'I really shouldn't be involved with this investigation. I've told you: there may be real clashes between me as an investigator and me as the householder. And Mark's not exactly disinterested, either.'

He looked at her under his eyebrows. 'I'd trust you with my life, my dear — and if you imagine my eventual replacement will have time to concern himself with anything involved with day-to-day crime fighting you must be living not here but in cloud cuckoo land. You've got some good DCIs — trust them if you're in any doubt, though they must be up to their ears carrying Harry's caseload as well as their own. And didn't I hear that one of them is on maternity leave? Otherwise, do what you do best, with the rider that you must save money while you're doing it. Think cuts, Fran, think cuts.' He might have said more, but, looking anxiously at Caffy, who was fast approaching, he let himself into the car and, with a general wave, set off more quickly than was wise given the state of the track.

Caffy, arms akimbo, stared. 'Was it something I said?'

Mark shook his head repressively. 'Police business.' But his face softened. 'Maybe he didn't want to meet the person who'd got the job he really wanted. Best whatever.'

'He's going to give me away instead,' Fran said quickly. 'Which will suit him much better than organizing Mark's stag do.'

Caffy looked enigmatic, something she did remarkably well. 'It's all in hand — what a good thing you didn't let him usurp me, Mark.' Her eyes followed the retreating car. 'He didn't want to meet me because of Simon's suicide — something to do with protocol, right?' Clearly, she wasn't going to give them a chance to offer more condolences. 'No problem. Oh, there is, isn't there? Don't tell me he's decided it's all his fault and he's got to pretend he's an ancient Roman and fall on his sword. Simon was mad, that's all there is to it. If you want to make it sound romantic, mad with love. OK, a weird, possessive and entirely unrequited love. So it's not the old guy's fault, any more than it was yours. Hey, don't you two go resigning! Not till you've paid us!'

'Quite,' Mark said. 'We can't have Pact going bankrupt.'

'You mean you couldn't face Paula doorstepping you till you coughed up. Who could? She's a real pussy-cat, but crossing her is not something I'd recommend. Not that you would. Not that anyone does more than once.' She added, 'I only came down for a wee, anyway.'

Fran laughed. 'You came down because it looks as if the recovery team is about to start work and you wanted to see what they were up to.'

'I came down to say you can see much more from my ladder. But I don't suppose you want to come up, do you, Mark? No? Now what's going on?'

All three watched. There seemed to be a lot of gesticulation towards the rectory.

'My God, they can't want to make that part of the crime scene,' Mark gasped.

'They won't find much worth looking at,' Caffy said flatly. 'Not after all the work we've done. And had done by subcontractors who believed in brute force and ignorance. You want to tell them that every single floorboard has been replaced, downstairs at least, and joists too, so there's nothing hidden down there. And we've had a very good look under those in the upper floors, remember.'

'And found not so much as a bent penny,' Mark agreed. 'Unless there's something you haven't told us?'

'Oh, yes,' chirped Caffy, 'like the bag of gold sovereigns we've flogged to pay for a joint holiday in the Bahamas. It's funny — you'd have expected more, really. It's almost, as Paula says, as if someone gave the place the spring-cleaning of its life before they moved out. Ironic, isn't it, given the total chaos it fell into and which we, to be fair, have exacerbated.' She pointed to the approaching car. 'More of you lot?'

Fran drifted the three of them towards the marked police car, wearing her least intimidating expression. After all, it was bad enough to be late on your first day in action; to find your DCS chatting to the Assistant Chief Constable (Crime) must be pretty terrifying. DI Kim Thomas, wearing a ridiculously elegant suit given the nature of the case, unfolded herself from the car, pulling down the pencil skirt with embarrassment. She looked straight out of school and was certainly no more than thirty-five. Her stance, all six foot of it, was as rigid as her poor mouth. 'Sir. Ma'am.' She saluted them both, as smartly as if she was in uniform. Fran supposed that Mark's fancy dress, if not her muddied trousers, merited it.

He responded with what Fran always called his friendly salute.

'Good morning, Kim. How's the poor tooth?' Fran asked, with a sympathetic smile.

'Temporary crown, ma'am.' Or the nearest approximation to the words the frozen lips could form.

'We're still at the forensic archaeology stage, as you can see,' said Mark affably, 'so the whole investigation's a bit hypothetical. Fran and I are here only because we want to see what's going on in our garden, and Caffy Tyler is one of the team working on the house restoration. Caffy, this is DI Kim Thomas, who'll be in charge of the investigation—'

'Assuming it actually becomes one, of course,' Caffy said, cocking a bright eye at him.

'Quite. Fran and I ought to head back to HQ, Kim, but I'd have thought Caffy could find you a cuppa to defrost that poor mouth of yours and fill you in on how we've had the rest of the crime scene destroyed before we even guessed there might be a problem.'

'Sir!'

Caffy, ultra-casual, nodded. 'I'll find you some more sensible footwear too,' she said with a sudden stern glance down. 'We might mess up crime scenes, but we absolutely don't allow stilettos on site.' She raised a hand. 'Before you two go, I should warn you that Paula's just had some more thoughts about your move.'

'Why doesn't that surprise me?' Mark asked. 'Rhetorical question, Caffy.'

As always, her grin lit up her face, making it almost beautiful. 'I thought it might be. Now, Kim, what size shoes do you take . . . ?'

CHAPTER TWO

'A word, please.' Paula appeared again, brandishing her mobile. As they paused, hands on the car doors, she continued: 'It's not good news.' She nodded back at the rectory. 'There's one van missing, as I expect you've noticed. No?'

Like recalcitrant children, they shook their heads. Paula would have made an excellent prime minister, Mark always thought. Or Secretary General of the United Nations. Aged — possibly — in her forties, she exuded both calm and purpose. Today her eyes, her best feature in an otherwise unremarkable face, flashed with anger, though she kept her voice low and controlled.

'The electrical contractor's van is missing,' Paula continued. 'And it's not his fault. His yard was robbed last night — he's lost every last centimetre of cable. When I suggested he should let you people and his insurance company worry about that, and go to his supplier — any supplier — and get some more, he told me what I expect you know already. No? I'd have thought CID, Fran, might have been interested to know that every electrical wholesaler we've contacted had the same visitors last night. Quite a heist.'

'More copper?' Fran groaned.

She had the excuse that all metal theft nationwide was now being dealt with by the Serious Organised Crime Agency, who didn't always communicate with their local colleagues as swiftly as they might have done. Mark's excuse — well, the chaos the chief had spoken of. All the same, he felt, and Fran looked, foolish.

'As you know, he was going to pull out every stop to finish the work here by Thursday. As it is . . .' Paula shrugged. 'No can do. The place won't be habitable. Sorry. Can you delay your sale?'

Fran shook her head. 'It'd mean letting down the friends we're selling to. And everyone else in the chain. Everything, absolutely everything, is in place. So we have to move in here.'

Paula shook her head. 'I really do not recommend it. Health and Safety would have a fit.' She looked ironically at Fran. 'And for once I couldn't blame them. It's not on. Even if I tell Sparky to go to suppliers further afield, he'll lose a day's work. You can move in this time next week. With luck.'

'But—'

Paula had already turned on her heel and was stalking towards a knot of men who might not have been working as hard as she expected her subcontractors to work. Even her approach galvanized them into action.

'Shit and double shit,' Fran said. 'How come I didn't know? You might as well have my notice as well as the chief's.'

Mark's face was serious. 'If you've ignored a call from SOCA, I might ask for it. But I can't imagine your phone's switched off?'

She waved it in front of his face. 'But the coverage is poor round here. OK, let's head back and get things moving.'

He picked his way through the ruts while she made a series of staccato calls. If she was displeased with herself, she was even more displeased with the colleagues who'd left her in ignorance.

'So where does that leave us?' he asked as he negotiated the crumbling pillars that once supported wrought iron gates and pulled into the lane hardly wide enough to merit the name. 'You're right — we can't afford not to move out now.' He shot her a sideways look. 'Do I imagine it, or is there a great fat elephant lolling on the back seat?'

'You tell me.'

'Two large elephants, in fact. My house, and Sammie.' Suddenly, his face looked unutterably weary.

She braced herself. 'I know she's your daughter, not mine, and I know I'm about to be a traditional wicked step-mother, but we may have to act on what that Rottweiler of a solicitor suggested and require her to leave your house. She's squatting. She's changed your locks. You can't get into your own home. You can't get at your clothes, your books . . .'

Mark murmured something inaudible.

'You paid enough for Ms Rottweiler's advice, after all,' Fran reminded him, but wished she hadn't. Mention of money in a family context made her feel petty.

'I still think it'll look bad in the press, a senior police officer — possibly acting chief constable by the end of the day — throwing his daughter on to the street. Literally.'

'It's fortunate Caffy didn't hear you say that. *Not* literally, Mark. You've told Ms Rottweiler that you can provide her with an allowance, cash if she wants, for which she signs a receipt, enough to rent a suitable place — heavens, I've never seen so many "To Let" signs. Then you simply go back and live under your own roof.'

'I suppose we could move to a hotel.'

Fran winced. How could a man she'd seen risk his neck to save strangers' lives be so supine? It wasn't just Mark's possessions locked behind Mark's front door; there was stuff of hers she couldn't get at. She said nothing — didn't want to whine. But buying the rectory for cash — at their age no one would give them a mortgage on such a doubtful property — and paying for all the repairs meant that two well-paid, comfortably-off people had a serious if temporary cash-flow problem and as from Thursday nowhere to call home. And moreover they were dealing with a matter of principle: how could a man let a daughter throw him out of his own house?

It hadn't been quite like that at the start. Sammie had originally taken refuge with her father claiming she'd been battered. To give her and her two children privacy, Mark had moved into Fran's tiny cottage. One day he'd gone back to find Sammie had changed every last lock.

Mark negotiated the turn on to the main road. 'I suppose, with the chief going, this could be a good day to bury bad news . . .'

She sucked her teeth. 'It won't be entirely buried whatever the day. Not with Facebook and Twitter.'

He groaned.

'At least you've got that press statement that Ms Rottweiler prepared for you. She was right: Sammie's not your responsibility. After all, she's still married to a man who's the proud possessor of a well-paid job. Whatever Sammie's relationship to Lloyd, he's legally, not to mention morally, responsible for maintaining his offspring.'

'What about paying for her to stay in a hotel?'

She suppressed a sigh. 'Do you think she'd really stay just the one night? She'd squat there too and refuse to shift. She'd milk you dry. No, like Ms Rottweiler said, she must go back to her own place in Tunbridge Wells if it's not yet sold. Or she can always live with you, as your daughter.'

'Live with me? Not us?'

'You need to build bridges if she stays, and my presence would preclude that.' There was no need to remind Mark of all the hysterical abuse Sammie had thrown at her: she was used to tolerating foul language and venom when she was working — usually, but not always, from lawbreakers — but not when she was at home. 'I can find a hotel.'

'I wonder what state the place is in,' Mark said.

He was wavering, obviously, so she gave a verbal push. 'Only one way to find out, my love. But I'd take the locksmith to the back door, not the front, if I were you. Less publicity. Actually,' she added, 'I'd take up Ms Rottweiler's other suggestion that you find a negotiator to go with you. I'd hate her to start throwing things.'

'Especially if they were mine to start with,' he agreed with a rueful smile. 'But I can't act now, Fran — we've both got to get back to hear the chief drop his bombshell officially. And then for a week I can't see me needing to sleep anywhere except on my office floor. Can you?'

'I can, actually. And I'd say you needed somewhere quiet to sleep. But if you can't face any more pressure, phone Ms Rottweiler and ask her to initiate Plan B. The stern final warning letter. It'd certainly be nicer if you didn't have to get your hands soiled.' Even if just one of Ms Rottweiler's letters would cost a day of Mark's not inconsiderable salary. Anything, anything, just to have a peaceful home for him to go to. Stress wasn't kind to men of his age, and although he exercised and ate a well-nigh perfect diet, she never lost the niggle of fear for his heart that she'd experienced ever since they got together.

'Plan B it is. I'll phone her from the car park,' he said. 'Then, Fran — into battle. I can't blame the chief for resigning, but I can't help feeling a lot of the shit he might have fielded will now be the responsibility of yours truly.'

Fran put her head on one side, Caffy-like. 'Haven't you mixed a metaphor or two there?'

* * *

Paula was the sort of woman Fran would want beside her when the last trump sounded — or was it last trumpet? Caffy would know! — calm to the point of stolid, as she had been when she'd broken the bad news earlier. But when she phoned Fran an hour or so later, at precisely the time that all the senior officers were doing headless chicken impressions, she allowed a hint of exasperation to seep into her voice.

'Fran, this DI of yours — is she for real?' With Paula, you never got preliminaries, polite or otherwise.

'It's her first day at school,' Fran said.

'Ah. In that case, you'll have to give her detention. She's being totally unrealistic in her demands. She wants all work on the house to cease forthwith. I tried reminding her who the house belonged to, but that seemed to make her all the more determined to play by the book.'

Fran remembered her own green days. 'It would. Have they dug up that bean row yet?'

'Nope. Talking of the bean row, now Caffy's worrying about misplacing her copy of Yeats — some poem she wants to quote. She didn't lend it to you, did she? No? It must be one of the plasterers. I had to tear her from that DI's throat when she suggested all the plaster would have to come off, by the way.'

'All this for what might not even be a body. OK,' Fran said with a sigh, 'I'll try to get someone to drop by and have a word with poor Kim. Not sure when. I certainly don't see me doing it. It's chaotic here—'

'I'll bet it is, with the boss throwing in the towel. Mind you, I don't blame him. As I'm sure you know, the press are going wild. I hope they don't know where you live, because sure as God made little apples, they'll sit on every senior officer's doorstep till they can get a comment.'

For an evil moment Fran felt like leaking the Loose address so they could drive Sammie out of the house; on the other hand, Sammie might spin some hideous tale about her father's cruelty.

'And Fran — have you found anywhere to stay yet?'

'I still wonder about the house—'

'No.' Paula cut the call.

* * *

'Kim: try to forget what's convenient or not for the ACC and me,' Fran told her, doing the work a more junior officer should have been doing. Since there'd been a nasty murder on someone's doorstep only a few hours ago, the already depleted DCI team had more pressing matters than Fran's to worry about. And — to be honest — she simply enjoyed being out at the rectory, after the horrors on the pensioner's doorstep. These days she found herself getting less, not more, inured to the sight of blood and brain tissue. And the smell . . . 'Think budgets. If you strip the house down to bricks again, it's going to cost the service an arm and a leg. The grounds — well, you can see there's nothing to worry about there. Uproot every last weed with my blessing, but watch the trees — some of them have preservation orders on them. Start small, and then move the enquiry outwards.'

Kim's face remained stubborn, and it was hard for Fran to believe that this was simply the result of the anaesthetic. She'd hoped that, in the absence of DCIs, there'd be some experienced sergeant around to support the young woman, helping her develop skills and confidence, just as she always had mentored all the officers in her various teams. Caffy had referred to the late Simon as her protégé; she sometimes felt she'd peopled the senior ranks across the country with youngsters she'd nurtured — she didn't need a shrink to know that they'd become her surrogate children. To pursue the analogy, perhaps Kim was going through the belated terrible twos, or whenever it was children started to argue with everything their parents wanted. Of course, Fran could simply remind her who was boss by giving a direct order, but that would soil their relationship from the start.

'Then, if you really think the case merits it, of course you can order work on the house,' she continued, feeling as spineless as Mark in the face of his daughter. She regrouped immediately. 'But remember that the chief was emphatic this morning that we had to count every penny. Paula's already told you that the house has been gutted once. Believe me, had there been anything slightly amiss, those women would have summoned us. Don't forget it was one of them who pointed out the present problem.'

'Even so, ma'am—'

'Quite. By the way, did Paula tell you we should be moving in on Thursday?' she lied.

Fran's possibly innocent smile must have reminded Kim of a crocodile's: paling visibly, the young woman said swiftly, 'Paula said something about the place having been unnaturally clean of evidence. Do you think the owner knew what was in the garden and made sure they left nothing that would be any help to anyone coming across it?'

This time Fran's smile was genuine. 'If I were you, that's exactly the line of enquiry I would be pursuing. I can start you off. We bought it from a charity I'd never heard of, which was left it in the last owner's will, though for the life of me I can't recall her name offhand.' Hell, was this what they called a senior moment? 'They could do what they liked with quite a lot of land that lay with it, but they couldn't sell the house for ten years.'

'Weird or what?'

'I'm afraid we wanted the place so much we hardly registered that anything might be dodgy. In the ensuing years, the place became pretty well derelict: it's looking good, now, in comparison. We wanted to awaken Sleeping Beauty, as it were — but we might have poked a stick into a hornet's nest, mightn't we?'

Kim nodded. 'But it's odd you weren't curious. What was the charity?'

'Something to do with preventing the culling of badgers: I've got all the details back at the office, so it should be easy enough to find who left it to them — who is obviously our prime suspect. As for the charity . . . Ah, Don't Badger Badgers, that's what it's called. It didn't have much to spend its funds on, of course — until recently, I should imagine. Now it's probably busy organizing protest meetings in the south-west, where dairy farmers have got the go-ahead to shoot them on their land.'

Looking up from the notes she was making, Kim said, 'I've always thought of badgers as *Wind in the Willows* characters, I'm afraid. What farmers ought to be doing is inoculating the cows, surely?'

Warming to her at last, Fran said, 'Since I don't like guns in anyone's hands, I couldn't agree more. But I'm not a farmer, of course. Nor an archaeologist — apparently, badgers do huge damage to as yet unexplored historic sites.'

Kim nodded grimly at the figures in the vegetable patch. 'We'll just have to hope they haven't been busy here, then.'

Fran shook her head. 'I can think of two damned good reasons to hope they have — my home and my budget. Don't look so shocked, Kim! You must admit that a body that's lain there for at least twelve years — the charity found it couldn't shift the place when the bottom dropped out of the housing market — is probably of less interest to us than one that's just appeared.'

'That Chinese illegal that turned up by the OAP's bungalow at two this morning?'

'Exactly like that. Just one thing, Kim. On my watch we don't call them "illegals". It's a term that seems to diminish, to de- humanize people. And for all I'd rather not have a skeleton in my bean row, if we do find remains, we'll treat them with absolute decency, even reverence. Won't we?'

'Of course, ma'am.' She was pretty well at attention again, poor girl.

Fran sighed. She'd picked up rumours that youngsters — and a few old lags — were inclined to find her intimidating. But she rarely meant to be. Oh, when she put her mind to it, she could draw tears, male as well as female. Now all she'd meant to do was remind the newcomer of the CID ethos — OK, her ethos — but it was clear she'd overdone it. Perhaps it was a generational thing. Perhaps it really was time to retire. But not quite yet. Not if it meant letting Kim plough on unrestrained.

'Look,' Fran said, 'they seem to be having some sort of chinwag. Shall we go and put our three penn'orth in? Or rather, Kim — your three penn'orth: you're the one in charge here, in case *I'd* forgotten,' she added with a grin.

Kim managed to respond with a hint of a smile, while not quite dropping a curtsy. Roll on the return of that nice malleable DCI, Harry Chester; with luck, having your gall bladder fished out didn't require much time off.

Fran's phone rang; expecting gossip from HQ, she was surprised to see the caller was Janie Falkirk, the vicar at St Jude's, Canterbury, whom Mark had mentioned upon their scaffolding the other day. Janie was a tough, laconic Glaswegian, currently based at one of the ugliest churches Fran had ever seen.

'Fran — sorry to disturb you, but I've got a problem. Serious. But it needs a wee bit of sensitivity. Any chance?'

With all the problems at HQ, and just when things were kicking off here! But she ought to give Kim a freer rein, ought to let her find her feet. And in all the time she'd known her, Janie had never asked for a favour. 'How urgent?'

'About as urgent as it can be.'

CHAPTER THREE

In its way, not to mention in its day, the Edwardian vicarage next to St Jude's, a viciously Fifties concrete bunker on the east side of Canterbury, must have been as grand as their rectory. It sat within its own grounds next to the church; together they made a decent and potentially highly profitable site should the church ever be declared redundant. Fran could imagine some rapacious developer sidling up to the Church Commissioners and rubbing his hands in glee as he saw the tiny congregation dwindle further. As for Mark, a fervent admirer of the Reverend Janie Falkirk's sermons, he always thought she was wasted where she was and nursed the hope of hearing her in a grand cathedral pulpit.

Janie, on the other hand, greeting Fran with a smile that couldn't disguise the fact that her face was lined with anxiety, always said she was where God had planted her, and no doubt He'd transplant her when He was ready. 'My study,' was all she said, heading Fran off from the kitchen, where she was usually entertained.

She didn't respond to Fran's raised eyebrows till the study door was firmly closed. Fran didn't need to be told to sit; she moved a heap of papers from a chair the room might have been built round and prepared to make herself uncomfortable.

'There's a lass in the kitchen thinks she's killed someone.'

Janie could still surprise her. 'Thinks?'

'Man broke in to her flat and raped her in her bed. She had a knife to hand — this is the bit I don't like, Fran — and stuck him between the ribs. He left, with the knife in place. She came here.'

'Because?'

'Trust issues with you people, of course.'

'So she's not been medically examined? Of course not. But she must be — you must make her see that. If she has knifed someone, there's got to be a damned good excuse. If she's killed someone, a watertight reason would be better.'

'Hand herself in?'

'No! Report the rape! She's the victim, assuming she's telling the truth. The Sexual Crimes Unit people are the ones who should be dealing with this.'

'I don't know them. I know you. If I tell her I'd trust you with my life, maybe she'll do as you say. Maybe.'

'You want to talk to her alone first?'

'You can edit my sermon while I'm away.' She patted an elderly computer.

* * *

But it was Fran's mobile that took all her attention. After twenty long minutes spent handling a torrent of calls and texts, dealing equally with the chief's departure, the Chinese murder and the cable thefts, Fran was finally summoned to the kitchen. This was Janie's sanctuary, the beating heart of the vicarage — it was, as Janie always said dourly and almost certainly truthfully, the only room in the house she could afford to heat, which was why her sermons were getting shorter. At one end of a much-scrubbed table hunched a young woman the height and build of Caffy; the main difference was that this girl had *victim* written all over her, with *drug-user* as part of the palimpsest.

'Just tell me what happened,' Fran said, accepting a mug of tea, which both she and Janie knew she'd never drink because it was so strong and stewed.

'He came in and raped me. I was asleep, miss, and he raped me. No condom, nothing. Does that mean I'll get pregnant?'

Janie said, 'We'll make damned sure you don't, lass.'

'Aids! I could get Aids!'

'If he's carrying it, it's always a possibility — so we need to address that quickly too,' Janie said. 'As I was telling you a wee while back, Fran here's not just a policewoman, she's a top policewoman, the sort that makes things happen. Now, one of the things she's done — this is right, isn't it, Fran? — is set up a team of women, police officers and medics, who specialize in sexual assault. They'll take your clothes and bedclothes and make sure they get any evidence.'

The girl said, with a mixture of worldliness and terror, 'They'll want more than that, won't they?'

'They'll want a full statement — and because you'll be talking to women, you needn't be embarrassed,' Fran said.

'I don't mean — you know what I mean.'

'Of course I do. They'll ask a woman doctor to examine your insides and take swabs. It won't be a bundle of laughs, but having a smear test isn't anything you look forward to, is it? But it's as necessary as that. And a good deal more urgent. What's your name?' Fran smiled. 'Janie's so good at keeping secrets she hasn't even told me that, you see. No? Let's not worry about that yet then. May I phone one of my colleagues? The one who's an expert? Jill. She's a really decent woman. She's got kids of her own — her daughter's a bit younger than you, I'd say. So nothing'll shock her. And she'll drive you straight to the place where you'll have your swabs, and then you can have a nice shower and put on some clean clothes. People often say they feel dirty all over when they've been raped.' She smiled again.

'But going to court—'

'Let's cross that bridge when we come to it. We don't want you getting pregnant, and we don't want you getting

Aids or any other STD. May I phone Jill? I'll make the call here if you like so you can hear everything I say.'

'But what about killing the bloke?'

Janie put a warning hand on the girl's wrist.

'But I might of! I stuck him in the ribs, miss. And he ran off.'

'With the knife still stuck in?' Fran kept her voice calm.

The girl nodded.

Fran held up her hand. 'We're going to have to talk about this, but not now. Let's deal with the crime committed on you first. And then we'll look into the problem of your assailant — the guy who attacked you. I don't suppose — did you know him?'

'In the dark? Wearing one of them woollen hood things? Not a hoodie, it covers your face too.'

'Balaclava,' Janie put in.

'Whatever.'

'Was there much blood?' Janie asked.

'Not a lot. Not what you'd call a lot, anyway.'

Fran held up her hands. 'I'd much rather we didn't talk about this now. I'd much rather concentrate on you. Is that OK? Can I make the call?'

The girl grabbed Janie's hand convulsively.

'Yes, it's fine for Janie to stay with you — if it's OK by you, Janie?'

Fran had hardly cut the call to DCI Jill Tanner when another call came in. 'I'm sorry — I have to take this.' She stepped out into the hall, cool to freezing even on a pleasant day like today. 'Kim?'

'I thought you'd like to know, ma'am, that the archaeologists are about to excavate the bean patch. Just that, for now.'

'I'll be over as soon as I can.'

'Don't worry — if their progress so far is anything to go by, they'll still be here at midnight.'

Perhaps she might just warm to Kim after all.

* * *

With Jill Tanner now officially in charge of the girl, who still hadn't given her name, Fran could indulge herself again before an urgent meeting about metal theft. Indeed, every visit to the rectory, scaffolders and now archaeologists notwithstanding, was an indulgence, come to think of it. Perhaps retirement wouldn't be so bad, not with that house to care for, that garden to tend — not to mention that view to feast her eyes on when she and Mark, with their end of the day glass of wine, sat on the terrace she planned to revive. Just the two of them. Man and wife. Bliss.

Except she really did not want to be married in poor St Jude's. The whole fabric had become permeated with the despair of its parishioners — and even more by the smell of their sad, unwashed clothes and bodies. All the perfumes of Arabia, as represented by nuptial roses, carnations and lilies, would be unable to disguise that. But how could she confess that to the living saint that was Janie? Or to Mark, whose idea it had been? The poor dear man didn't really want to marry at all, so surely she should allow him the choice of venue. She was pretty sure the chief wouldn't get his, of course — she'd bet her pension that the weddings in the Cathedral were the option of only the most select few. An acquaintance had managed to arrange hers in the crypt, but celebrating so life-enhancing an event in a place more properly the domain of the dead didn't appeal either.

Which thought brought her, physically as well as mentally, to the garden, which was probably the province of the dead too. The policewoman in her didn't like one scrap. The thought that someone had not only buried someone in her vegetable patch — probably killed whoever it might be there too — but had also systematically denuded the house to prevent any sort of detection. It was the work of someone who believed in forward planning — or retrospective planning, if there was such a thing. What vibes could such a person have left? Common sense told her none — not after Paula and her colleagues had done their work. It was her dream — a brand-new old house. All the pleasures of new equipment set in the most beautifully proportioned kitchen, for instance, like the rooms elegantly decorated in what Caffy would ensure were authentic styles and colours.

But Kim had noticed her arrival, so she waved, got out and walked over, looking officially purposeful.

Where once there had been a straggle of canes — she could see they'd been removed and bagged as possible evidence — was the standard large tent. Within was something that looked like a newly-dug grave. Newly undug it might have been, but its occupant had been there some time. She looked down at the skeleton of what even she could tell was a strapping man. A strapping man with a deep concave dip in his skull.

CHAPTER FOUR

Though the top brass were dashing round like toddlers on a sugar rush, at the level CID worked it was business as usual, as Fran found out when she sought refuge from all the politicking in the safety of the familiar briefing room where the meeting with a team sorting out the major metal thefts was just about to kick off. The latest news was that some enterprising bastard had stolen the earth cable from a substation. The resulting power surge had ruined the computers and TVs of most of Folkestone and wreaked havoc on Eurostar's timetable. The Serious Organised Crime Agency were supposed to be sharing information with her and her equivalent in the transport police. But there was no sign of Alan Burbridge. He'd taken the train from Ashford, had upbraided a man for putting his booted feet on a seat and been stabbed for his pains. It was touch and go whether he'd survive. And him with his first child due in a week.

But the show had to go on. Quickly taking the chair, although the SOCA superintendent clearly had his eye on the position, she announced a time limit on each agenda item, before texting a brief message to her secretary. By the time they'd dealt with matters arising, there was a knock on the door, and trays of sandwiches and coffee appeared. But she wasn't a total softie — while her colleagues were eating, she was volunteering them into all sorts of tasks they'd never have put themselves forward for.

'Well done, Fran,' said one of the SOCA team as the meeting ended. 'We'll miss you when you go. What are you and Mark planning? A round the world cruise?'

'I'll send you a postcard,' she said with a grin. Inside, however, she was stone cold. Thinking about retirement was one thing — having others think it for you was absolutely another. Meanwhile, however enticing the prospect of checking up on the progress of Jill and Kim's cases, she must resist temptation. There was a whole tray of paperwork awaiting her. On the other hand, however, she needed to find when Kim's team would be ready to report, so she called a briefing for five thirty, just after the update on the Chinese murder — which was fortunately now in the hands of her most experienced DCI. He would be liaising with the Met, who had a series of such killings on the go. All she'd have to do was balance budgets and leave him to run the show. Balance budgets, and wonder if the PM on the skeleton would throw up anything more useful than the injury that had clearly killed him.

* * *

At the late-afternoon briefing, she found that Kim had augmented her team by a rather beaky young man with a charming smile and eyes that radiated a fearsome intelligence. Did they also presage a huge bill for professional fees? But Fran wouldn't raise that very salient issue just yet, and certainly not publicly. Let her have a bit of glory: it would do her ego good.

'This is Dr Valentine,' Kim told her team, stepping back with the air of one producing a highly attractive rabbit from a hat.

'It's a bit late for a doctor,' someone at the back quipped, rather too audibly for Kim, who blushed to the ears. Valentine merely offered a sardonic grin — he'd no doubt heard all the available jokes before.

'Dr Valentine's a forensic anthropologist,' Kim said quickly. 'He'll be working alongside us for a while to discover what the skeleton can tell us.'

'I'd have thought we'd need a psychic for that,' the same wag observed.

'And it doesn't take a medic to tell us he's dead,' said a mate, encouraged by the general laughter.

'I'm not that sort of doctor,' Valentine said tolerantly. 'I'm an academic. But before you ask, I don't spend all my life in an ivory tower. I get as muddy as you do, but not quite as muddy as an archaeologist — who, as you know, isn't a medic either.'

He embarked on what Fran feared would be a lengthy PowerPoint presentation, but the computer went into tantrum mode, refusing to give more than half his first screen. He shrugged the problem off with a cheerful sangfroid that made her warm to him. 'No matter. All I wanted to say is that people like me regard a body as an archive. It records all its activities, whether it wants to or not. Once, remember, it was the core of a living body. The bones can reveal what this body ate, if it suffered diseases and where it lived. When it lived, of course. With luck you won't see much of me — I hope this one will yield up its secrets quickly so I can get back to Libya, where I've got some more work to do on yet another mass grave.'

There was a rumble of approval; clearly, if a man could deal with decomposing bodies, there was something to him.

'Meanwhile,' he said, 'I ask you to remember one thing: knowing what happened to the dead affects others' futures.'

As an exit line, it went down very well. Fran's exit, not his. Her phone was summoning her to yet another meeting. But she had a nasty feeling that if anyone's future was going to be affected it was Mark's and hers, so she called Alice, her new secretary — who was as yet unused to her ways and needed instructions where her predecessor had anticipated her every whim — to send her apologies and stayed put. After all, she had useful information to share.

She shook hands with Dr Valentine as he went off to listen to the bones, and then took centre stage herself.

'Mark and I bought the house from a charity calling itself Don't Badger Badgers. Sorry — you can choose the house but not the vendor,' she said as the team collapsed into predictable laughter. 'At least they can't badger them on the patch of land down in Devon the charity spent all its money on before it packed up.'

'So the charity's defunct?' Kim asked. 'Shit! Why didn't it exercise a bit of forethought and save some cash to fight the proposed culling?' she wailed.

Fran shrugged. 'At least we've got the trustees' names on all our legal papers. I'll pass them on the moment I can contact our solicitors. Then can someone follow them up and get all the paperwork dealing with the bequest? Good,' she said, acknowledging the hand that had shot up.

Kim said, 'With luck they won't all be dead. Someone check with the Land Registry? Thanks. But with our luck it'll be some dear old lady who couldn't lift her fork to her lips, let alone wallop someone over the head with something hard enough to shatter his skull. Not to mention heaving the corpse into a grave.'

'An unusual dear old lady, I grant you,' Fran said, aware that some of the kids present, all with their degrees and postgraduate qualifications, probably saw a dinosaur on a Zimmer when they looked at her. 'But sometimes even someone who's frail will find strength from somewhere. A name. That's all we want. And we start from there.'

'I suppose the budget won't run to fast-tracking the guy's DNA?' someone asked.

'As I said to DI Thomas this morning, I simply can't justify the expenditure I'd willingly authorize for a contemporary crime.' Her pager vibrated. 'Sorry — I'd better see what this means. Remember to pace yourselves — this is a pretty dead case, so going at it all guns blazing isn't a financial possibility.'

Kim held the door for her as she left the room and stepped outside with her. 'It's a bit tricky, isn't it? Until we know when our victim died, we can't really check the missing persons records and dead cases records either.'

Fran shook her head. 'Has that dishy doctor of yours given us any idea how long ago he was killed?'

'Not yet. If we could get a glimmer of an idea who he might be, we could check dental records — apparently, he'd got what must have been quite painful impacted wisdom teeth.'

'Not something you'd want to hear at the moment, Kim! How is your mouth, by the way? Has it thawed out now?'

Kim nodded. 'It feels very strange — the crown must be a different size from the tooth he smashed.'

Fran pulled a face. 'You did well there — I've seen the CCTV footage. He was a big bloke, wasn't he? But I dare say all he'll get is a bit of a telling off. Mind you, I can't see what a custodial sentence would do for him either. At least the budget cuts mean they're trying to keep folk out of prison who shouldn't be there in the first place.' Before she got into her verbal stride, she remembered why she'd left the room. 'It's the chief's number,' she said. 'But is it the old chief or the new one?'

It turned out to be neither, just Sally, the old chief's PA, throwing an ad hoc farewell party that evening and wondering what she should do about organizing a presentation. Fran could hardly say that she was really only interested in who was going to hold the fort in his absence, but came up with the neatest solution she could think of as she waved goodbye to Kim — who made a tiptoeing return to her team that reminded Fran startlingly of the cartoon version of Pink Panther — and headed for the secretariat.

'Make sure everyone you invite knows this is only a preliminary party,' she told Sally, 'and that there'll be a proper lunch or dinner to which the chief's wife and senior officers' spouses, etc, will be invited. That gives some poor sap time to organize a whip-round.'

'I was rather hoping you'd offer, Ms Harman. You see,' she continued primly, 'I'd normally ask an ACC or the deputy

CC, but in the circumstances one won't be able to help and the other will only ask you, won't he? And since I was going to ask you to organize a collection in memory of Simon . . .'

'I'm not sure it's a happy combination. I'd like to do something for Simon, since I knew him before . . . all this, but I'm not sure if protocol permits. Could you have a word with Cosmo Dix and get his opinion?' She prayed Cosmo would know she was beyond her ears in work and suggest someone else should do it. 'If he gives the go-ahead, I will. It's a horrible business, isn't it?'

'You're quite sure you can't do both?'

'Absolutely. I wouldn't know whether to approach people with a smile or a sad frown.' Distantly, her memory clanged that there was an apposite quotation, probably from Shakespeare. Caffy would no doubt be able to come up with it immediately. 'Tell me what's going on about a replacement for the chief.'

Sally looked furtively around the empty office. 'Looks like it'll be an outside appointment, with a temporary replacement drafted in, since Mark wasn't keen. I'm dead peeved, Fran — he's a nice man to work for, your Mark. And now we're on to the subject of Mark, what's this about wedding bells? No, he's said nothing, but the chief's been touching the side of his nose and muttering, "Nudge, nudge; wink, wink," and humming "Here Comes the Bride".'

'Bastard! Oh, Sally, he's making a takeover bid for the entire ceremony, I'll swear.'

'Let him run it: he'll be bored to tears after three days of retirement. He'll need a project. Your wedding will do fine. The Cathedral, I gather.'

'You gather wrong. Look, Sally, just organize someone to open tonight's booze and keep quiet about this, there's a dear. I've got two bodies on my hands. Possibly three. And I reckon a corpse in my own bean row is the outside of enough. Now, I've got to make a few calls—'

'You'll have to keep them short, then — champagne corks pop at seven sharp.'

* * *

Fran always preferred face-to-face, so, hoping Jill Tanner, another officer she'd taken under her wing, was still on the premises at six thirty, she dropped into CID to see her. She trapped Jill as she grabbed her coat with one hand and bag with the other. Presumably, Jill was regarded as too low in the pecking order to be invited to the drinkies.

'Car park? I'll walk with you,' Fran said. 'How's things?' she continued as they strode off together. 'Family?' A while ago she wouldn't have risked the question; now they were trying — cautiously, sometimes, and Jill, it seemed, always aware of their difference in rank — to repair their friendship.

'Fine. Rob's talking of getting an apprenticeship his Gran's found him; he still prefers her to us. Natasha's glued to her iPhone, but they're predicting good exam grades, so I suppose I can't argue. You took a risk speaking up for me for this job,' Jill observed, holding a door for her.

If Jill didn't want to mention her spell on antidepressants, Fran wouldn't either. 'Nonsense. You were the obvious person. How did you get on with that kid this morning?' She kept step for step with Jill as she skipped down a flight of stairs. 'Does she have a name yet, by the way?'

At last the pace slowed. 'Sinned.'

She couldn't believe Jill had mispronounced Sinead. 'Sinned? As in *peccavi*?'

Clearly, Jill hadn't done Latin A level. 'Cynd, as in Cyndi Lauper. Cyndi Lewis. We got her to the unit: she's been swabbed and given all the drugs she might need, but she obviously won't know about the Aids issue for a bit. The problem is, while the medics can see she's had sex, and there's plenty of evidence to show it was rough, there's still the small business of the stabbing. What sort of girl keeps a knife under her pillow? And uses it after sex, not before?'

'Do we have a stab victim yet?'

'No. Nor any reports from any hospital in the whole of the county. But there *is* someone else's blood at the scene. She says her assailant — she says he's white, by the way, twenty to twenty-five, apparently his breath was really bad

— was wearing a leather jacket, so perhaps the knife stuck in that, not his flesh, and he's decided that in the circumstances he won't make a complaint. So I really want to find him, not as a victim, but as a suspect. After all, being raped in your own home, be it ever so humble, etcetera, is traumatic, and I want to find Chummie and stop him doing it again to someone else.'

'Absolutely. Throw everything at it, including the kitchen sink. I suppose there's no record of any other similar rapes? Lesser offences?'

'Nope. Nothing to go on. Precious little new to go on, semen and other samples apart. And, of course, checking them takes time. And — before you say it — money. There was evidence of forced entry, by the way, though it's not absolutely clear when, so probably the story holds together. Possibly,' she conceded.

Fran picked up the element of doubt. 'CCTV?'

'No one in a balaclava and leather jacket within three streets. Mind you, I suppose you wouldn't wear a balaclava on a warm night for fear of attracting attention.'

They shared a laugh.

'And, of course, a leather jacket could go in a backpack . . . Assuming you get the guy, is she up to a trial?'

Jill sucked her teeth. 'Touch and go. Unless she has to be in the dock herself because she really did kill the guy.'

'Pray God it doesn't come to that. God and the Director of Public Prosecutions, of course. They seem to be getting more sensible about taking folk to court when they've killed intruders into their own homes.'

'I'll get Janie Falkirk to tackle one aspect of the case while I do the other. Hey, you're not really going to be getting married at St Jude's, are you? It's such a tip. Right in the middle of the red-light area, too.'

Fran grabbed handfuls of hair. 'How come everyone knows more about this bloody wedding than I do?'

Jill ignored the question. 'Did you know there's a nice bridal-wear shop just opened in Canterbury?'

'Oh, spare me a meringue outfit!'

'Fran, *they're* all size zero, as far as I could see,' Jill said with a chortle, letting herself into her car. 'But there are some cracking mother-of-the-bride outfits, which would be just the ticket for you, and they make them to measure, apparently.'

Fran said something she'd never imagined she'd say. 'Jill, if we ever get ten minutes to spare, would you come along with me to help me choose? Once we've found a church and set the date, of course.'

'Of course. But you will get that splendid woman Janie to officiate, won't you? See you tomorrow!'

CHAPTER FIVE

Apart from the fact that they had a fixed rule not to talk shop at home, there wasn't much in the way of a home for Mark and Fran to go to. Each room was already stripped down as far as they could manage, before the removal men came in on Thursday, when the buyers would move in. So after the drinks party they stopped off at a pub, only to find as they sat down and reached for a menu that they were joined at the bar by a pizza delivery man, who handed over his burden to an embarrassed barman.

'You know you're supposed to come to the back door,' he hissed. 'Sorry,' he said, addressing Mark. 'Chef's night off, and this is what he feeds his face on so he doesn't have to cook. But I can rustle up something plain if you like. I do a pretty mean steak, and my mum reckons my chips are better than the boss's.'

'Two steak and chips it is, then, please. And a large jug of tap water.'

As they sat, they had their usual bicker about who should drive; eventually, Fran gave way more speedily than usual — a glass of red wine was becoming a pressing need.

'Not a bad send-off for the old bugger,' Mark said, sinking back against the squabs of an ageing banquette that still smelt of long-dead cigarette smoke. 'Better than the proper one will be, probably. Though he does like a bit of pomp, doesn't he? A few speeches and toasts?'

'And he'll lead me down the aisle beautifully,' Fran agreed. 'But I don't see us at the Cathedral, Mark. Unless you really want to—?' she added quickly.

He said nothing, eyeing her glass of wine. She pushed it towards him, and he drank absently. Goodness knew where he was. But he was probably at least as tired and twice as stressed as she was, so she said nothing until the barman, who'd brought their cutlery, rolled in proper linen napkins, left them on their own again.

'In fact,' she said bravely, trying to sound as unconcerned as possible, 'there's no point in even thinking about it while everything's up in the air like this. But I'm so proud of you for turning down the chance to be chief.'

For the first time he smiled. 'No-brainer, that one, Fran. It's going to be bad enough being picked over by Devon and Cornwall Police, not to mention the Police Standards people, when they investigate Simon's death, without taking on the pressure of being chief. A heart attack at this stage is not on my agenda, believe me. Ironic, isn't it, that Simon was once in the rubber-heel brigade himself? What must it do to a man's psyche, always to be sniffing out his colleagues' mistakes? I bet you forget what it's like to have a friend.'

'Which is possibly why he became so infatuated with Caffy and saw no way out but to end it all. I wish she wasn't so phlegmatic sometimes. I know, I know, I'm sure it was the way she learned to deal with being a prostitute, but even so.'

'Thank God for whoever it was that sorted her out. She's got an amazing mind, Fran — she ought to be more than just a decorator.'

'You know she's more than just anything, Mark. She's been on every course going about restoration and period materials and so on. I just wish she could find a nice bloke: she must be thirty at least, and the old biological clock must be ticking.'

'You old romantic.' He took her hand and smiled with great affection. 'I'm glad I've got you.' He kissed the hand, in what she always found the most erotic of gestures, and played briefly with her ring. Her actual engagement ring, no longer just a pretty jewel. Perhaps the wedding was still on. 'Actually, rumour has it she did have a bloke, a cop with the Met, but he couldn't hack her past. Or maybe she was just too overpowering in other ways. I wonder what her idea of a stag night will be. What if it involves that pop star that adopted her? Todd Dawes?'

She smiled nostalgically. 'I had pictures of him all over my bedroom wall when I was a kid. God, he was so sexy. Look, he'd be wasted on mere stags. My hen party, on the other hand—' She broke off as the barman approached with their food, wishing she'd had a moment more to check he really was prepared to go ahead with the wedding. Really, truly. Cross your heart sure. But he was talking about it all with something like amusement.

'I didn't think you'd be frozen veg people so I did a couple of salads. The dressing's my own recipe,' the young man said, putting a jug in front of them, 'but I shan't be offended if you want a packet of salad cream. Not everyone likes balsamic vinegar and virgin olive oil.'

'We do. And—' Mark sniffed like a Bisto kid — 'garlic!' He waited till they were on their own before saying, 'Now, tell me about our skeleton.' Before she could point out that a corpse might not be the best company for supper, he added quickly, 'Has it put you off the house? Do you want to pull out?'

'It's a bit late for that, Mark. But I take your point. If you really wanted, we could always do it up and sell it — though probably at a huge loss, the way the market's going.' Her heart hurt as she made the offer.

'Hideaways in Kent will always fetch a high price in one area of the market,' he pointed out with a quizzical smile. 'Come on, we both know there are more criminals lurking in remote Kent houses than you can shake a truncheon at.'

She returned his grin. 'No one shady shall buy our dream home,' she declared. 'Even if we have to have ghosts exorcized, I draw the line at that. Truly. All houses have secrets and sadnesses, especially old ones. Who knows who suffered what in my cottage?' She stopped and tucked into her salad. No point in reminding Mark that his beloved wife had actually died in his house. Not to mention what was going on there now. She bit back the question she was desperate to put: had he contacted his solicitor to start proceeding to evict Sammie? She flushed, but for another reason. 'I'm sorry — it's *our* cottage. You're not a visitor, for God's sake.'

'It won't be yours or mine soon,' he said soberly. 'Has Paula said anything more about the rectory wiring?'

'She wasn't on site when I went to look at the skeleton,' she said. 'But truly, Mark, with or without electricity, I can't see it working. Not if young Kim wants to strip it down to its bones again. And even if she doesn't, there'll be no comfort anywhere. I know we could shower and eat at work, but I don't fancy using the Portaloo in the middle of the night with only a torch to guide us. It'll have to be a short-term let.'

'A bottom of the range, tiny short-term let? It's all we can afford with the wedding coming on too.'

'Bugger the wedding!' she said, not meaning it at all.

'Bugger the grotty short-term let, too. Or rather, instead. I've been chasing round like the proverbial blue-arsed fly all day but I did remember one thing — I phoned the Rottweiler. The letter will be in Sammie's hand tomorrow.'

'Oh dear.'

'But I thought you wanted her out!'

'Of course I do. But I don't think she'll take it lying down. Do you?'

'Not really. Which is why I had a word with Cosmo Dix.'

'Cosmo! But he's Human Resources, not PR!' And had told her she wouldn't be organizing the collection for Simon, not if she took his advice.

'A wilier old bird you'd never find. He says — and I think he may have something — that, for all its horrors, camping at the rectory would be a better deal as far as the media are concerned. Who could argue against people wanting their own place back if they're living in a tip? And it'll have the added bonus of stopping Kim undoing all the Pact team have done. How's about that? After all, we do want to hold the reception there, and the sooner all this is sorted the sooner we can reclaim the garden too.'

It all seemed too good to be true. Perhaps it was. Because then he said, 'Or we could always accept retirement and run. It'd make financial sense, what with the lump sums and all. It's what the chief's advising.'

'He's what?' She repeated, more quietly, 'He's advising what?'

'Actually, he suggested a sideways move for me — to Bramshill, to teach there. Assuming they'd have me. Failing that, some university with a criminology department might want me.'

He sounded so appalled by the prospect that she said briskly, 'I doubt if that would wash. The Grove of Academe's been deforested. Even worse cuts in higher-education funding than we've got. If they need staff, they'd want someone young and part-time and cheap. You'd be far too expensive. Tell me, just assuming the chief or his successor can dispose of you, what are their plans for me? Before or after he's given me away, that is?'

'He'd still like you to take over cold cases. But not at your present salary. More as a part-time consultant.'

'Blow that for a game of soldiers. Cancel the old bugger's wedding invitation,' she added with a laugh, but not a happy one.

'It's just his way of trying to tie up all the loose ends before he left. And, poor man, he's got absolutely no say in what happens next. But I think cuts and senior staff reductions'll be very much what his successor wants. Needs! Retirement — or even redundancy — would certainly ease our cash-flow problems, and there's no denying our pension provision's not bad. At the moment. There is a case for jumping ship.'

'In my book it's the rats that jump first. Losing one chief, one deputy chief and one ACC at a stroke—'

'Exactly. Not to mention a pretty sound chief super. Not good for morale. And there is something else: I can't see you moving out until you've sorted out our skeleton.'

'Quite. Plus the cable theft, which I'm also inclined to take personally. Oh, and I've got a rape and a stabbing now, too,' she said, leaning forward to share the details.

* * *

'Thanks to you giving permission to question your solicitor, we have a name for the previous owner,' Kim told Fran the following day. As in the classic TV movies, they met in the women's loo, but by chance, not design.

Fran had just emerged from yet another bruising budget meeting, which had managed to last till almost noon. She had almost forgotten about the real world as opposed to the world of figures. She was washing her hands, as if, like Pilate, to absolve herself of responsibility for bad decisions. And this was before the new round of spending cuts the government had just threatened. 'I'm only sorry I didn't have time to wait for an answer myself. Anyway, name?'

'Marion Lovage.'

'Lovage? How very herbal,' Fran observed. 'For real, Kim?'

'According to the Land Registry,' Kim said huffily. 'And we have other information too. She was a headmistress. *Dr* Lovage. She ran a junior school in a village not far from yours — what will be yours, I mean, when you move into the rectory.'

'Someone with a doctorate running a tiny school? Weird.'

Kim didn't seem to think so. 'She did very well there, too, according to the present head. Got it out of special measures, whatever they are. She did so well that some government minister came to congratulate her. It made not just the local but the national news: they've still got the fading photos up in the head's office.'

'Good for her. What happened next?' If Fran was hoping that Dr Lovage had suddenly left the neighbourhood, leaving everyone in the lurch, she was to be disappointed.

'She worked there till she retired — a couple of years later. Then she told the staff she was going to take the holiday of a lifetime, and shut the rectory up and left it. Well, it's so off the beaten track that vandals might not notice. Or squatters . . . But she told the school secretary she'd put some of her best pieces of furniture in store. Just that. Not where. I've got someone on to it. It'd be nice to see if she reclaimed them before she died.'

'It would indeed. And you have a year of death?'

'It fits in with what you said about the house not being sold till ten years after her death and the market going flat — March, thirteen years ago.'

'Excellent. Where?'

'Hammersmith. Sheltered accommodation. She bought her apartment outright, lived there a couple of weeks, talking to the warden every day, and then just died. Phut. Heart, according to her death certificate. She had a minimalist funeral, ashes scattered on Dartmoor. Near those sodding badgers, maybe.'

'Is her solicitor still alive?'

Kim blinked.

'I just thought that putting a ten-year moratorium on the legatee selling something as lucrative as a house might be a bit unusual — he or she might have tried to talk to her about it. Sometimes solicitors are just as nosy as the rest of us — might have wanted reasons.'

Kim retired to a cubicle. Fran blasted her hands with the drier until Kim emerged again, to use the basin next to Fran's.

'You've got the team working well, by the sound of it, Kim, not always easy for someone from another force. Is anyone trying to be too clever by half? You're sure there isn't? Good. Remember, if anyone plays you up, come down on them like a ton of bricks.'

'Thanks. But you won't like what I've got to say next too much, Fran.' She wrinkled her nose and rubbed one leg against the other, like a schoolgirl. 'I'm afraid there was no trace of any ID on the skeleton, and, more to the point, no trace of a murder weapon. So it looks like we're going to have to give your garden a bit of a going over.'

'As I said, the garden's not a problem. In fact, we'd be grateful to have it dug for us,' she said, laughing.

'But you still don't want us to touch the house itself, even though from what that Paula woman says, you can't move in for a bit anyway?'

'Money, Kim, money,' Fran said. 'Twenty per cent cuts. If you don't cut some expenditure, you cut either front-line staff or the back-room people we all depend on. Last year I had to watch them sacrifice a whole team; this year there'll be more. If we get extravagant on this investigation, there'll be less to spend on the next. What if we have to skimp on the investigation of a current murder just so we can say we've crossed all the T's and dotted all the I's on this? In fact, rather than dig up the whole patch, I'd get a metal detector run over it. Maybe find a keen amateur detectorist — the heritage officer might be able to recommend an honest one. No nighthawks, thanks very much. But I'd bet any possible murder weapon disappeared years ago, wouldn't you?'

'If the garden's like the house, yes, I suppose so.' Kim shook the excess water off her hands but didn't attempt to dry them.

Fran held the door open for her, and they walked into the corridor. 'This Dr Lovage. She sounds a very capable woman — very thorough, very meticulous in her planning.'

Kim came to an abrupt halt. 'You're still thinking of her as the killer, ma'am? But she's tiny. You can see in those school photos. Five foot four at the most. Slightly built.' This from a woman who was probably a mere size eight for all she was nearly as tall as Fran herself.

'Might have been whippy. And nothing like needs must for finding a way to do something. Tell you what, Kim, when

I've got a moment, which may not be for a few days with the house move coming up, I'm going to try a nice informal chat in the village pub with the locals. After all, there'll be a lot of folk interested in this new couple daft enough to try moving into a building site. I'll report to your team as soon as I know anything — meanwhile, let me know when you've organized the post-mortem.' She couldn't imagine it throwing up anything more than they already knew, but she could hardly skip it, not with such an inexperienced officer as Kim at the helm of the investigation. Only bones, at least. No guts or gore to spoil her day. 'I might not be able to get to all your briefings, but I'd like to be kept in the loop, and not just for personal reasons, either. Nor,' she added with a grin, 'merely to see how much of my budget you plan to spend. I hope that nice Dr Valentine won't cost the earth.'

'He's my sister's partner. I'm pulling in a favour.'

'Uh, uh. Favour or not, we pay him.' Remembering the red column on her much-loathed spreadsheet, she added, with a smile that in her youth would have been called impish, 'But ask him for a family discount. You're doing well, Kim, especially as your DCI is conspicuous by his absence at the moment.' She added with a grin, 'It'd be nice if you'd got it all done and dusted before he came back from his sick leave. Good for your CV.' Fran waved Kim on her way as she headed back to her office.

Meanwhile, how was Jill's investigation getting on? If she knew Jill, she'd be too busy to think about breaking off to eat; Fran would make that decision for her. She'd even make it sound official; instead of popping her head round Jill's door, she got Alice to make a formal phone call asking Jill to present herself.

So Jill looked both puzzled and apprehensive when she arrived five minutes later.

Fran grinned. 'Eaten yet? About to? Gotcha! Canteen, or sarnies here?'

'Canteen. I don't suppose we'll have it much longer. Cuts . . .'

Fran didn't contradict her. She held open the office door and they headed for the canteen.

'I'd have thought you'd be eating with Mark,' Jill said, at last, looking for a quiet corner.

'We used to. When we were "courting".' With no hand free, she inserted the quotation marks with her voice only. 'But now we're living together, there's less need. Though we still stick to our no-shop rule once we shut our front door. Goodness, I'm so hungry. We're moving out on Thursday, and breakfasts tend to be a matter of polishing off whatever happens to be left in the fridge or the cupboard. We take another lot of stuff to the self-store tonight, if only Mark remembers.'

'And you're still moving into the rectory? Despite the body?'

'Skeleton. Actually, that describes the house as much as the corpse. It's stripped down to the bones. We would have moved in despite that, except someone stole our electric cable.'

'Part of that huge sweep over the weekend? Shit.'

'Quite.' She tucked into her salad. Perhaps it would be more filling than it looked.

'You can't move back into Mark's place?' Jill split her baked potato to help it cool. 'Or is his daughter still acting up?'

'If by acting up you mean squatting, yes. But that's between you and me.' She suppressed a shudder: Sammie should have had the solicitor's letter by now giving formal notice to quit. 'Now, how's your waif? Cynd?'

'She'd been going to stay with a friend — we'd not finished with her flat, such as it is. Teenage squalor and poverty — not a good combination. And I wasn't impressed by the friend's place either. Think Rob in his drug-taking days. Squared.'

She must be better if she could speak of him as casually as that. Possibly casually. But Fran knew better than to make any comment about it. She limited herself to saying, 'Cynd's not your responsibility, Jill.'

'I know, but all the same . . . She'd never worshipped at St Jude's, apparently — just got to hear of Janie via some *Big Issue*-selling friends whom Janie provides with soup and sandwiches.'

'Why aren't I surprised by that? What a good woman she is.'

'Quite. Anyway, I had a word and Janie had a word, and now Cynd's actually moved into the vicarage, thank goodness.'

'Or God.'

Jill ignored her. Pointedly. 'I gather she trails Janie like a duckling after its mother.'

'Well done you. Any news of Cynd's assailant — or victim, depending on which way you look at him?'

'None.'

'In that case, are you thinking what I'm thinking?' Fran laid her cutlery down, as if that would make her think more clearly. 'That she gave a false description? For whatever reason?'

'Like—?'

'Like she was so scared of the real assailant she wanted to put us off the track? Would that wash? But then there's the problem of the stabbing — why confess to killing the wrong person?'

'Doesn't make sense.' As if was the end of the speculation, Jill started eating.

'No, it doesn't. But what if someone else stabbed the victim? If Cynd doesn't have a police record, and was clearly a victim, then she might get away with it. Shit, Jill, I don't want to harass a girl we should be cosseting, but we need a few answers.'

It seemed as if Jill wasn't enjoying her potato — she pushed her plate away. 'Won't do it. You drew up the code of practice yourself, Fran. Don't even think of asking me to go against it.'

'I wouldn't dream of it. Eat while I think. Go on. My salad won't go cold like your spud.' She pressed her temples.

‘I reckon I could stretch the budget to speeding up the DNA tests on the bedlinen at least. And on her vaginal swabs. And we pray there’s a match on the database. How about that? It’d probably mean a proportionate reduction in your overtime, though.’

‘Maybe we wouldn’t need so much.’ Jill smiled hopefully. ‘Thanks, Fran. Now, before we hit the shops, what sort of wedding outfit did you think of?’

‘I was wondering — hell, is that the time? Another bloody meeting!’ She grabbed her apple and ran.

CHAPTER SIX

'Retirement would mean more time for sunsets like this,' Mark observed, slowing to admire the view from the hills guarding what he thought of as their valley. The rectory, still bristling with scaffolding, was centre stage. To its right was the village from which it had somehow become separated years ago — or perhaps some moneyed rector of Great Hogben had decided he didn't want his parishioners inconveniently close to his glebe land. The sun just caught the weathervane on top of the stocky church tower.

'It'd mean more time to worship at our parish church,' Fran observed, 'where I'd bet the congregation's better heeled than at poor St Jude's.'

'The patron saint of lost causes,' Mark murmured. 'Speaking of which, Ms Harman, soon to be Mrs Turner — no, you'd stay as a Harman, wouldn't you? — shall we make ourselves even later home by dropping down to see what they've been up to?'

'Paula and Co or Kim and Co?'

'Both, I suppose. And then catch a snack in our new local?' He didn't manage to stifle a terrific yawn.

'It's tempting, but we've still got stuff in the freezer we ought to eat. More of my unlabelled meals. You can choose some at random while I deal with the utility room.'

'What about the self-store? We said we'd take a preliminary load?'

'Tell you what, we're paying the removal people enough. Let them deal with everything, not just the furniture. If you could just scout around on the Internet for a hotel . . . A week, I suppose, to allow time for Mr Smith to get his cable and install it. And we must make damned sure we label the stuff we need,' Fran said.

'OK. I'll get busy labelling while you microwave our feast.'

'Excellent. If we're good, we can treat ourselves and take a look in tomorrow morning. Both of us. That'll scare Kim. I've held you up as a monster of official miserliness, by the way. So don't worry if she hexes you and backs swiftly into the excavations.'

* * *

'What the hell? You don't get traffic jams in the country! Especially not at seven thirty in the morning!' Mark beat the steering wheel in exasperation.

'Farm plant — you know, those mega-tractors or combines or whatever. Or maybe even a Bulgarian driver with an insistent satnav. Look, there's a gate. Why not turn there? We'll get off work early tonight — by which I mean while it's still light — and come and see the house then instead.'

'Nope. Farewell drinkies with the neighbours, remember?'

She squeezed his hand affectionately. 'Never mind, I'll contrive an official visit here during the course of the day and update you. No, that's not good enough, is it? You want to hug it yourself. Well, you'll have to ask yourself for half an hour's lunch break.' When he didn't laugh, she looked at him harder. 'OK, what's up?' Hell, he'd not got round to checking hotels, had he? And he didn't want to confess.

He completed his manoeuvre carefully and set the car in motion before replying: 'Sammie.'

She managed to stop herself screaming. 'Ah. The letter. What did she say?' And why had he kept quiet for twenty-four hours?

'Nothing. Nothing that I know about. I'd have said, wouldn't I? Yes, I would, Fran — I know I tried to keep you at arm's length, but not now. I need your savvy, apart from anything else.'

'What savvy?'

'The bit that got me on to Ms Rottweiler. Maybe I should phone her later — assuming I have time.'

'That's one hell of an assumption, sweetheart.' As was the assumption he'd have the will to do it. But she didn't want him to see how anxious she was getting — not just about somewhere to lay their heads, but about him and his inertia. 'See — my phone's active already. Hell. I'd forgotten that disciplinary panel I'm supposed to be chairing. Thank God we got stuck in traffic — I like excuses with the foundation of truth.'

* * *

Released from a bleak committee room four hours after going in, Fran wanted to cry with frustration. In her youth, when she'd made stupid mistakes, she'd stood to attention in front of her sergeant — at worst, her inspector — and ridden out the bollocking. Occasionally, she'd have muttered an apology in the hopes of stopping the tirade, but it was only when the guv'nor was ready that she'd been sent out with a flea in her ear. And she'd done the same in her turn. Now it was all official and minuted and — God, she hated the whole time-consuming, paper-generating farce.

Not to mention the fact she'd missed the skeleton's autopsy and had to respond to the load of calls that had stacked up during her meeting. People who knew her made a point of leaving only brief messages, so she wasn't surprised when Kim's voice snapped, 'Phone me urgently.' Belatedly, she'd added, 'Please, ma'am.'

She was, however, a little surprised to find a text saying much the same thing; she wasn't used to getting reminders. But then Kim was a newcomer to her team, so perhaps she should forgive her. She texted back that she was in a meeting

— well, she might well be — and would respond as soon as she could. In other words, as soon as she'd checked the other messages to see if they made equally urgent demands. She rather thought the summons to meet the new acting chief constable might, in official terms at least. Not in terms of genuine importance, of course. However, as long as she was a team player, she'd better play by team rules.

* * *

Mark arrived at the conference room just as Fran did. As he held the door for her, he hissed, 'It's Wren — that guy from Hampshire who's flitted onward and upward and never let his feet touch the ground.'

'Never! That little guy?' she hissed back. 'And don't you mean twig, not ground?'

Shit! Any moment now, he'd get the giggles. For the duration of the meeting he must not catch her eye in any circumstances. This in itself would be hard, since he would be standing like some sort of overgrown page boy at the new acting CC's shoulder and leading the applause.

Fortunately, it fell to the chairwoman of the police committee to introduce Paul Wren. Since she was only five feet tall, it was possible for her at least to look up to his new boss. Mark knew he was being illogical — no, worse, despicable — but he didn't want always to be peering down at this young-old man, who in his and Fran's early days would have been lucky to land a job as an office boy. He'd certainly never have been accepted as a cadet; not in the days when you had to be five foot ten to get in.

But Paul Wren obviously used the gym, as you could see from the movement under his shirt — he'd opted for the more casual uniform shirtsleeves look as he pulled himself up straight, tucking his elbows and his tummy in as if he were about to pose for the centrefold of some ladettes' mag. Actually, he looked more like a pouter pigeon than a wren. Hell, if only he'd had a less prejudicial surname. Do not laugh. Do not let your mouth twitch. Dear God, twitchers are birdwatchers, aren't they? Bloody hell.

Above all, do not look at Fran. Do not speculate what Fran might be thinking as Wren trots out his spiel to his new colleagues.

The Big Society seemed to be at the heart of his statement of intent. And it was wrong to blame him for that, of course. It had been put there by the Prime Minister, no less. Had the Prime Minister spoken about citizens' journeys, of community-based and -orientated decisions? Probably. He'd almost certainly spoken about increased accountability, which was fine by Mark. He'd seen too much policing involving nudges and winks to people who should have known better than to nudge and wink back. So accountability was fine, as was the idea of scrutinizing perks — he'd never indulged in demanding personal cars driven by official police drivers or anything else remotely like a freebie; he wouldn't have been surprised if he'd started to sport a halo. He liked the idea of restorative justice, in theory, though how it would work in practice he didn't care to think. Reducing bureaucracy — huge tick for that. Perhaps the little man was growing in stature as he spoke.

Or not. For now he was talking about cuts. All the senior officers present smiled in anticipation of the promise that Mark would have given first, had he been in Wren's position — a total, all-out fight against cuts in staffing at whatever rank and in whatever function, officers and civilians. But it seemed that cuts were to be embraced. An army of special constables was being recruited countrywide, Wren declared. They would bring untold expertise to the incompetent professionals that were Mark's friends and colleagues — and they would do it all for free.

If Mark had been delivering this address, he wouldn't have liked the silence that greeted that section.

Now Wren was talking about prioritization of resources. It seemed he wanted to take a leaf out of the Met's book: that if officers thought there was no chance of getting a result, they shouldn't pursue investigations.

Fortunately, it wasn't Fran who interrupted, but someone he'd always suspected was a bit of a yes-man. 'Might one ask, sir, what sort of crime we might not investigate? Are we to have official guidelines?' There was so much irony in the man's voice that Mark was surprised it didn't drip all over the floor. Amazing how one's opinion of another could be changed by two sentences.

As he stared at the floor, he mentally reviewed all the cases he'd pursued just because he wanted justice to be done. Sometimes it was impossible to bring the miscreant to court — perhaps a witness was too old or frail. But at least the scrote that had committed the offence knew that the Law was after him, that the police had him in their sights. Not to investigate? The words of his resignation letter began to shape themselves in his head, arranging themselves into well-ordered clauses, not management-speak clunking phrases either, the sort that must have George Orwell spinning in his grave — except Orwell would have hated that cliché too.

Now Wren was talking about meetings to establish priorities. Mark had a terrible fear that long-unsolved crimes, Fran's cold cases, would not be high on the list. Meanwhile, people as angry as him were firing off notional crimes — domestic violence and rape, for instance, both types of violence with poor conviction rates. Or drunken assaults. Or—

Wren declared, in a tone not admitting any more argument, that talks would involve colleagues from the Crown Prosecution Service and other police services.

By now people were definitely looking at Mark. Were they expecting some support — which he would have liked to give — or some bland welcome? The silence grew. There were mutters.

Stepping into the breach time, then.

'Thank you, Mr Wren, for a most interesting synopsis—' (he wouldn't use the word summation wrongly, not for anyone's money) — 'of the policies our masters would like us to consider. I'm sure we all look forward to detailed discussions with you as you settle into post.' Looking round, he gathered up familiar eyes and led the politest round of applause he'd ever heard. Too late it dawned on him that the people the eyes belonged to might be regarding him as a figurehead in their all too obvious rebellion.

Fran might have been reading his mind. She contrived to hang back as his colleagues streamed — or possibly steamed — from the room. It was unlike her, as was the way she tucked her arm into his. 'Didn't Wat Tyler come from Kent?' she murmured as they drifted slowly along the corridor.

'You expect me to march on London?'

'Maybe not. Poor Wat didn't have a happy ending, did he? But at least you'll be able to keep the brakes on this Happy Chappy's little schemes.'

'Possibly. Fran, I've never been keen on trades unions and strikes, but my God, I can see why we need them. Sack all the highly-trained, efficient, experienced people we utterly depend on and bring in squads of unpaid do-gooders? I thought community support officers were policing on the cheap. But this!'

She brought him to a stop. 'It's not exactly news, Mark.'

'I know. But to hear the man embracing it! Dear God! All my life I've fought crime, and now it seems I've got to fight management. I know it involves you too,' he added belatedly. 'At least you've got real cases to tackle. You can still make a difference, as we always wanted to do. But all I shall be fighting is this runt of a civil servant.'

'Sweetheart,' she said quietly, 'you don't have to. There's the R option, remember? Think about it: in the course of your career you've been shot at, bottled, had ribs broken, lost a few teeth — all in the course of duty, you'd say. Same as I would. But having a heart attack or a stroke as a result of the stress that this is likely to cause — that's not heroism, it's folly.' She looked around, either to check no one could overhear or to try and blink away the tears he'd seen gathering. His Fran — tears? 'Do you remember bollocking me once, when I'd put myself at risk? And you said you didn't know how you'd survive without me? Please, please don't take yourself from me now.' The pressure from her fingers was almost painful. Forget the almost.

He gripped them back. 'First anti-stress move. Let's book ourselves into a good hotel, not a cheapo one, and worry about the expense later when we get our credit card bill. Incidentally, I had a call from Ms Rottweiler. Apparently, she's had a letter from Sammie threatening counter legal action. She says we can discount it because it wasn't from a solicitor — anyone in her profession would just have simply advised a client to grab all our offers with both hands and to run. But it's clear Sammie isn't about to cave in. So, we have two immediate options: we send in the bailiffs, as Ms R suggests, or go in ourselves.'

She grabbed her hair and tore at it. 'Oh, Mark. Let's just make a decision and stick to it! We've had enough faffing round. We're in the most awful shit, for God's sake. Hell, we've been on enough decision-making courses. Let's decide now.'

Just the moment for his pager to have a tantrum. Feeling, probably looking, guilty, he checked it. 'Sodding emergency meeting. Now.' Feeling as if he was handing over a giant packing-case, he said, 'Fran, can you make a decision for us? I'll accept it. God knows when you'll have time, of course. But I promise I won't moan whatever it is.'

Raising an eyebrow in an expression that made him long to kiss her, she expressed all the cynicism she was capable of in two syllables. 'Oh, ah.'

'Promise. Finger wet, finger dry, cross my heart and hope to die.'

All the fun drained from her face. For a moment he thought she was ill. 'Do — not — ever — even — say — that. Please.'

'I'm sorry. You know what I mean.'

'And you know what I mean. Go on — off to your meeting.' She turned first. Surely that wasn't a sob she was suppressing? Not his Fran.

CHAPTER SEVEN

So many people stopped Fran to ask why Mark had refused to stand in as acting CC that by the time she had reached the sanctuary of her office she was ready to scream. If Mark's stress levels were through the roof, hers were at least ceiling high. She was the one to make a decision, was she? OK. But after she'd dealt with all her phone messages.

Kim. She'd phone Kim first. But the number was unobtainable — she must be out of mobile range. Perhaps she should go out there. Even an argument at the rectory was better than a further barrage of enquiries, though she was afraid she wasn't likely to deal kindly and patiently with what she saw as silly box-ticking on Kim's part. It didn't make it any better to know that a perfunctory enquiry was just what Wren would applaud.

But even as she headed out of the building, her phone rang. She'd have silenced it, except that the call was from Janie.

'There's a lot this lass Cynd's not told you, I reckon. And for all that Jill's a decent woman, I reckon you'd do better.'

'Janie, how would Jill feel if I came barging in? Have another talk to Cynd yourself, maybe?'

'Do you think I haven't been talking to the poor lass?'

'And you've got a parish to run. I'm sorry. But I'm in the middle of a fight now, and I just can't do this evening. I can't miss my own farewell drinkies, can I?' she pleaded. With a sigh, she added, 'Tomorrow morning, half seven? Before the removal guys come?'

'Fran, chick, you expect a teenager to be up at that hour? I'd forgotten your move. I'll maybe have yet another wee talk to Jill myself. How about that?'

'I've said it before, and I'll say it again, Janie Falkirk — you're a saint.' Fran closed the phone and stowed it. She could do with a bit of Janie's sanctity herself, couldn't she?

And a cup of tea. She'd have made Mark sit, and for once she'd take her own advice. What was there that a phone call couldn't fix? Cheaper than petrol, she reminded herself. So she headed back to the canteen, found a quiet corner, and sat and sipped. The green tea Mark favoured didn't press as many of her buttons as dear old builders', but she found herself unable to swig nice dark brown brews anymore. Soon, at least, she felt able to try Kim again. 'I'm sorry I didn't get back to you earlier, Kim. And there's no chance I can come out. I've been in a succession of meetings, including one with the acting chief constable.'

'What's he like?'

What did she expect? 'Short and sort of — I know it's an old-fashioned word — dapper. Oh, he does weights, you can see that.' She clapped a metaphorical hand over her mouth. All the things she wanted to say about Wren — that he was a manager, not a cop, that he used meaningless strings of words and other people's ideas — were not the sort of things to share with a junior officer, especially one who considered you lax in your practices. 'He brought with him very bad financial news, the implications of which will no doubt be communicated to us all formally in the fullness of time. In the short term, he's reining in budgets on all enquiries, which will certainly affect us.'

'But this is a murder enquiry!'

'We may have to skin our cat a different way, depending on what the boffins tell us. Any news from them? Tell them if we don't get something soon the case may be closed without a proper resolution. Yes, Kim, blackmail them, for goodness' sake. Play as dirty as you like. OK. Now, what's the problem?'

'It's those women . . . I'd call it total non-cooperation, ma'am.'

'In other words, Paula won't let you get the plaster off the walls without a directive from the Vatican?'

'From you, at least, ma'am.'

'I hate to say it, but the new chief wouldn't permit it, even if I wanted to. I'm in a difficult situation here, Kim. I told the old chief about my conflict of interests, which could possibly be resolved if Harry Chester were back. As for the new chief, even at my level you need two weeks' notice to speak to him. And Mark's not exactly disinterested, is he? Impartial,' she added, suspecting that Kim might think she meant *un*interested. 'Anyway, have you managed to find a detectorist to scan the place?'

'Early this evening.'

'Well done. Now the bad news. I want you to get back to HQ to set in train every bit of paper enquiry you can. Fingers are cheaper than feet, Kim. I want everything, absolutely everything, that you can find about Marion Lovage's past. Past address, past jobs, relatives, friends — assuming any are still alive. I want a full picture of her. And chase the boffins, remember — we need a date of death first thing tomorrow.'

'I want to be back here when the detectorist comes,' Kim said, with a note of defiance.

'Bloody hell, of course you do. I wish I could be. OK. First thing tomorrow you're on the paper-chase.'

'Very well, ma'am.'

If only she could be there for the detectorist herself . . .

Almost certainly the Pact team would still be on site. She speed-dialled Paula.

'First off,' she said, adopting Paula's own manner, 'you can tell me what's up between you and Kim.'

'She's one of those women who have to be right, isn't she? I told her, we'll go to court as expert witnesses to state that we found absolutely no artefacts, incriminating or otherwise, in the house itself. We drew your attention to the suspicious patch because of our expertise. Actually,' she added, with what in anyone else would have been an evil chuckle, 'I've pointed Lady Muck in the direction of another suspicious patch near the old midden.'

'Isn't a midden just a heap of shit?'

'How appropriate. Actually, this one's a slightly odd shape — as middens go. So perhaps I really am helping the police with their enquiries. Meanwhile, since, for all your years of making life-changing decisions, you two couldn't organize a piss-up in your own brewery, we've borrowed — this is what's really got up Kim's nose — an old motor-caravan for you to sleep in here until we've at least finished a bedroom and a bathroom. OK?' She didn't wait for an answer, perhaps because it wasn't a question.

Fran stared at the phone. It seemed that a decision had been made.

* * *

'Are you sure about this motor-caravan?' Mark asked, after the farewell party, collapsing on to the bed in their denuded bedroom. 'I thought we'd agreed on a luxury hotel?'

'We did. But we hadn't told Paula. Do you fancy calling her and saying no thank you? No? I thought not.'

'I wonder who they borrowed it from . . . Hey, what if it's Todd Dawes?'

Fran sat bolt upright and then swooned back.

Pointedly ignoring her, he asked seriously, 'Is this Todd guy the sort of person we should accept loans from?'

'According to Caffy, he's a Good Man, who saved her life. He also saves others' lives — he and his wife have set up a foundation which, while not as large as the Gates', does impressive fully accounted work in Africa. Todd—'

'I don't like the way you say his name! You sort of breathe it, reverentially,' he complained.

'You should hear the way I speak your name! I practically salute as I say it. And that's just while I'm cleaning my teeth.'

'Glad to hear it. I like a bit of respect.'

'Is that all you like? Since it's our last night here I thought you might like . . .'

CHAPTER EIGHT

Fran was just stowing their toilet bags and her make-up in a carrier bag, which Sainsbury's supermarket had promised would last a lifetime, when her phone announced the arrival of a text. Another bloody meeting on a day off she'd booked the moment they knew the removal date. Three-line whip, according to the secretariat.

She began to text back, envying every kid a quarter of her age who could press their thumbs apparently at random and produce something intelligible, if not to people like her, at least to each other. At last, she deleted the whole garbled message and dialled the direct line back. There were times when speech was better than abbreviations, especially with the removal lorry due any second.

'This meeting — no can do. Mark's already en route, but one of us has to supervise the removal men. And there they are at the door. Oh, grovelling apologies, if you wish, but the answer is still no.'

Cutting the call, she hurtled down the stairs, cursing the impulse that made the removal team hammer on the door as if trying to awaken the dead. She flung it open furiously — to find herself confronting not Mr Pargetter or any of his team, but a young man whose face was strangely familiar, though she'd have sworn she'd never met him before.

He had the ultra clean, ultra smart look of a man about to sell her religion in some American form. So she wasn't surprised by his light US accent or by the manner of his speech, though the content disconcerted her — momentarily, at least.

'So you're the painted Jezebel I've heard about,' he said flatly.

Unable to detect any irony in his tone, she hoped her eyebrows didn't rise too much. 'I may well be. Or the Whore of Babylon.' She didn't point out that her garb of jeans and T-shirt scarcely suggested an intention to seduce anyone. 'But you have the advantage of me,' she added coolly. Hell, she knew this guy from somewhere, didn't she?

He fished with a well-manicured hand in his inside jacket pocket, producing a visiting card with a flourish that convinced her he knew he was putting her at a disadvantage: such small print called for reading glasses, or the stretched-arm squint of those whose eyes were already benighted by the long-sight of middle-age. What did they call it? Presbyopia, that was it. She supposed it was something that her brain still threw out useful bits of information.

David L. Turner. Financial Advisor.

Trying to take in the whole situation, again her brain threw up something she didn't want — didn't you spell *adviser* with an *e*? But she'd seen it both ways. And she shouldn't even be reacting to such trivia.

'You're Mark's son?' she managed eventually, adding more lamely, with a beam she didn't think was forced: 'We didn't expect you, Dave. Or is it David? How lovely to meet you again! After all those years . . . Well, you were only a child . . . Welcome to the cottage, such as it is.' She threw open her arms to embrace him, but since he didn't step forward, converted it to a gesture inviting him inside.

He gave no sign of having heard her and ignored the invitation. 'I phoned my father when I flew in last night.

Got some message about his voicemail being full.' Sounding aggrieved, he added, 'I tried emailing too.'

He'd flown over, no doubt, in response to some hysterically urgent communication from Sammie. But she must not put words into his mouth. This wasn't her battle, not yet. Not until she and Mark were man and wife — and she had, in the face of his neat correctness, a sudden surge of relief that they really were about to marry.

'I'm afraid our computer's in that box over there,' she said, pointing and raising her voice slightly over the rumble of the removal van inching as close as it dared to the gate. 'And although he's got his laptop with him, it's so chaotic at work I should be surprised if your father gets a moment to open his personal mail. Look, I wish I could offer you a cup of tea, but, as you can see, the removal men are just about to empty the place.' She waved to Mr Pargetter — dressed, as always, as if he was heading for a day at a particularly respectable office — and his strapping team.

'Starbucks?'

'Nothing like that in the village, I'm afraid. And our tea shop doesn't open till ten. No! That's to go in my car!' she yelled, digging in her pocket and zapping open the doors for the youth carrying her Sainsbury's bag. 'And that box!' she added as his mate headed off with her kettle and tea bags. Where was their common sense? And this young man's, thinking he could turn up unannounced and expect a welcome, and still be standing with an evangelical smile on his face? 'Let me phone your father,' she added, trying to sound gracious. 'I can make it sound official.'

'It wasn't my father I wished to see; that will come later. Isn't there some place we could sit down?'

As if on cue Mr Pargetter emerged from the living room, carrying her favourite armchair as if it was no heavier than a deckchair. He was followed by the lads hefting the sofa. They made it quite clear that they did not like being wilfully obstructed.

She edged him on to the tiny front lawn. 'I'm sorry. This isn't the way I'd have wanted to renew our acquaintance,' she said, retiring behind slightly ironic formality. 'I always hoped we'd meet again before the wedding, but not like this.'

'Wedding?' His bland expression gave nothing away. Unless, perhaps, his eyes narrowed slightly.

If only she could take the words back; if she knew Mark, he'd not quite got round to updating his son. She couldn't entirely blame the police for that, of course, but she'd try. 'Mark's deeply involved in a major reorganization — he's been working fourteen, sixteen-hour days recently.'

'So the decision to marry is a recent one?'

'The intention has always been there.' She used her thumb to jiggle her ring, so that the stones glinted in the sunlight. 'It's just a matter of choosing the time and the location. Our boss — ex-boss — fancies Canterbury Cathedral,' she added flippantly, instantly regretting it as he asked:

'And what does your marriage have to do with him?'

She stepped aside to let a mattress through. 'Long story.' Years of practice meant she could take a deep breath without it being obvious. She took one now and tried a different approach, with a smile she hoped appeared genuine. 'Your father calls you Dave — hell, I always called you Dave. You were Driver Dave when you played with your train set, weren't you? But the name on your card is David. Which do you want me to call you?'

'Dave's for family.' Which didn't, from his tone, include her.

She was within an inch of retorting that in that case he could address her as Detective Chief Superintendent, but bit her tongue in time. Instead, she put out her hand, choosing to ignore what he'd implied. 'Then welcome, Dave — though a poor one it is. We seem to have arrived at an impasse. I can't leave the cottage. You don't want me to call your father. I can't dispatch you somewhere convenient to bring back coffee. All I can hope is that Mr Pargetter has a spare mug so that when he breaks for a brew we can join him.'

He ignored her hand. If only she could read his inscrutable features. He was as unlike Mark as Sammie was, and resembled Sammie not a jot.

'May I suggest something else, then? That you nip over to Loose and spend the day with Sammie, and then join us in our new village for a pub supper this evening? Great Hogben, the Three Tuns. Any problem, call me — my in-box is empty. Here.' She found her bag and fished for a business card. 'I wish I could offer to feed you, but as you can see . . .' With an ironic smile she pointed to a box marked POTS AND PANS in Mr Pargetter's hands. God knew what Mark would say when he found their promised quiet evening on their new territory, if not in their new house, hijacked this way.

'I might just do that. Go to Loose, that is. But don't bank on my seeing you again this evening.' There was a distinct emphasis on the pronoun. 'It seems everything my sister says about you is right.' He turned on his heel and left, stowing the card in his jeans' back pocket.

She wanted to run after him, desperate to tell him she was doing her best in the most trying of circumstances, when two of Pargetter's lads emerged with the frame of their bed, the sight of which appeared to confirm all that David had said — that she was a scarlet woman, seducing their father from the paths of righteousness.

If ever divine intervention was needed, it was now — but all she got was a phone call from Kim, which she took, since she could see what she presumed was a hire car driving away.

'I'm sorry to trouble you, guv'nor, when I guess you've got more than enough on your hands, but I thought I should update you.'

Suddenly weak at the knees, Fran retired to a garden bench she'd promised to leave for the new owners. 'Fire away.'

'That strange looking compost heap: we thought we should take a look in it.' Fran knew it was at Pact's suggestion, but let that pass. 'And we found a wheelbarrow in it.

You know you said that even a small woman might move heavy things if she was desperate? Well, what if she had the assistance of a set of wheels?'

'What indeed! I know we're cash-strapped, but get it checked for blood, DNA, anything you can think of. Well done — and thanks for letting me know. Did the metal detectorist find anything else? Like the Staffordshire Hoard?' she added hopefully.

'What would they be doing down here?'

Fran didn't feel up to a long explanation. She just wished Caffy or Paula was beside her. 'So the detectorist found nothing at all?' she prompted. 'No broken tools?'

'A couple of Victorian pennies, a table fork that might be quite old, he said — just two prongs. A few odds and ends. We've bagged everything up as possible evidence.'

Blast: she'd have loved to pick over items, however trivial, that connected her to previous owners. 'Have we got a decent guess at a year of death?'

'About fifteen or twenty years ago, they say. Shall I email the complete report?'

Surely, Fran detected — at last — a tongue in cheek joke? 'All couched in impenetrable jargon, no doubt? At your peril, Kim. Just fillet out the best bits. And remember I'd like the most detailed biog you can get on Lovage as soon as possible. Go back to her weight at birth, if you can — no, only joking. But, as I said, her family, relationships — anything relevant and irrelevant. No chance of an ID on the skeleton yet?'

'With the extra cash you freed up, we're looking at Monday. And we'll get the DNA analysis, so we can go for matches. Better than three weeks' time. Thanks, guv.'

She smiled. 'My pleasure.' And it was. How could she do relationships with strangers but not with her putative family? Stepfamily. It looked as if already she was doomed to be the Wicked Stepmother, despite all her determination to do better.

She'd still not told Mark what was happening: if the voicemail had been full last night, it probably still was, so she phoned Sally, the old chief's PA. 'I really, really need to speak to Mark — it's personal, but vital.'

'He's with Mr Wren and some bods from Police Standards, so I daren't interrupt him now, Fran. Daren't. As I told a previous caller,' she added, meaningfully.

'Would you not tell him about the previous caller till you've got him to phone me? I wouldn't ask, Sally, but it's family politics, as you may have gathered.'

As she cut one call, another came through, this one from Janie. 'How much longer will the removal men take?' she asked without preamble.

'No idea. No idea what the time is, even. Hang on, I'll go and ask Mr Pargetter . . . He says they'll be clear by noon — so say twelve thirty.'

'So where would you like your picnic? There, or at your new place, or somewhere neutral?'

If she knew Mark he'd make a big thing of their arrival together at the rectory. Or perhaps she just wanted him to. 'I really, truly don't have time.'

'The removal men will be stopping for lunch. You can too. Thirty minutes max, if you insist. Twenty. Somewhere on your way.'

She supposed it made sense. 'Somewhere neutral. The new place is a crime scene, remember. Not very user-friendly . . .'

'Grafty Green. Where the Greensand Way heads south. One o'clock.'

'No problem — hang on, why don't I treat you to a pub lunch?' But she spoke to a dead line.

* * *

There was no time to get sentimental over leaving her cottage, although she had loved living there, mostly alone and latterly with Mark. Good times, by and large. She gave one final sweep of the kitchen floor, chasing a couple of spiders that had taken up residence behind the fridge freezer, probably on the day it had been installed, and, which, from their size, had never deemed it necessary to find a new territory. Only when, still clutching the broom, she locked the door did she find a sob rising, very painfully. But she put her shoulders back and reminded herself that the money popping into her bank account within a very few minutes would enable them to pay Paula for the huge amount of work that Pact had already completed.

Even as the Pargetter team drove away, the new owners' van drove up. It was time to scoot. She scooted.

CHAPTER NINE

There were a dozen places Fran should be, none of them here, on her own, wasting time.

Just as she was about to give up and fume off, however, Janie's surprisingly chic Ka appeared — a gift from an occasional member of the congregation who had decided to emigrate. It was only when Fran saw the second figure in Janie's car that it dawned on her that the reason for a picnic was Janie preferred not to have their meal recorded on any sort of CCTV, though of course their journeys would be. Smile for the camera! Half of her was angry that Janie had gone against her wishes and brought Cynd to see her, undermining Jill's authority. The other half was interested to hear what Janie or Cynd had to say.

Janie and Cynd emerged with a couple of carrier bags, Cynd looking around her as if a green space was an entirely alien concept, even though if ever a city nestled in countryside, Canterbury did.

Fran fell into step with them, saying nothing till she felt she was cued in. By this time poor Cynd, carrying the most enormous bag on one crooked arm, as if she was some Hollywood celeb, had trodden on endless prickly plants that had somehow eluded the older women's more thickly shod feet. At last, fishing three empty carrier bags from her pocket, Janie announced that this was a perfect picnic site and they were to sit on the grass and eat. The sandwiches — cheese and pickle — were home-made, but that was about all that could be said for them. Perhaps if you were a *Big Issue*-seller you could feed them to your poor dog. The water might have come in bottles, but it was from a tap — about which Fran had no complaints at all, though she did wonder, when Janie passed it over, whose lips had drunk from the bottle before her own.

'Cynd's had all her tests, and we're awaiting the results,' Janie announced, as if she too had pressures on her time. 'We know she's not pregnant. But she has had some problems with her memory, Fran — shock, probably, I'd say. Wouldn't you?' she prompted.

'Like Hillary Clinton, she misremembered something?'

Cynd blinked, as if the word and the name were equally strange. 'He wasn't quite like I said, miss,' she told Fran, as if she resembled a half-forgotten teacher.

Probably, she did. But she tried to wipe every shred of threatening authority from her voice as she replied: 'It's hard to be clear in such awful circumstances, isn't it? But I'm glad your memory's coming back, because the CCTV didn't show anyone like you described near your flat. So why don't you just tell me quietly what you remember now. Take your time.' Should she mention the knifing? Or the DNA tests? On the whole she thought not. Not yet.

* * *

There was a light scratch on the door, and Sally put her head round. Mark suppressed a grin — she'd never have interrupted the old chief's meetings like that. Her arrival was greeted with a mixture of exasperation and relief, depending on whether you were Wren or a normal human being. How many hours had they been talking? He wouldn't have minded if they'd been using English, but it was all management-speak

— worse, it was Whitehall-speak, polysyllabic pap, although the Police Standards people were all serving officers like himself. None of them seemed upset by Simon's death, for all they'd once been colleagues. Did that say more about them or about him?

He was hungry and thirsty — Wren's first economy had been to axe mid-meeting refreshments, though surely their old instant coffee and bottom of the range custard creams hadn't been an extravagance. He was also so stiff about the jaw and shoulders that he'd have a migraine, if he wasn't careful. Or a heart attack. That was what Fran was afraid of. For him, not for her, though he'd read somewhere that women of her age with stressful lives like hers were candidates too.

By now Sally was tiptoeing across to him. 'Could you spare a moment outside, Mr Turner?'

He caught Wren's eye, as if asking for permission, but since he was already on his feet it was clear he was leaving anyway. Shutting the door quietly behind him, in the freedom of the corridor, he couldn't help releasing a theatrical sigh.

Sally's smile suggested that what she had to say wouldn't be good news. Panic-stricken thoughts about no-show removal vans and motorway crashes replaced the tedium of the previous three hours.

'Everything's fine. Fran's fine. But Fran wanted you to phone her before you did anything else. Anything at all. I've waited all this time, but you'd better do it now. Now, Mark, before I say the next thing.' She returned to her office, ostentatiously closing the door.

She'd have made a good oracle, with her strange gnomic utterances, wouldn't she?

Blast and bugger it! He couldn't reach Fran. Bloody Kentish mobile coverage. And by now the cottage landline would have been cut off.

He shrugged his way into Sally's office. 'What was the next thing? I can't get hold of Fran,' he added, like a kid whose dog had eaten his homework.

'I think there may have been a connection between what she wanted to say and what I have to tell you. No, there's nothing the matter with Fran. Nothing, I promise you,' she repeated, as if she saw the fear he knew must still lurk in his eyes. 'But there's a young man waiting in reception claiming to be your son. He says he won't leave until he's spoken to you. But I think,' she said, getting to her feet and pushing him gently backwards until he had no option but to sit on one of the visitors' chairs, 'that I'll get you a cup of tea before you go and see him. And there are some of those custard creams somewhere.'

Dave. What the hell was Dave doing here? No reason why he shouldn't be in the UK, of course, and no reason why he shouldn't want to see his father. But why today, dear God — why today? Because of Sammie, of course. Hell, when had his thought processes got so slow?

There was a light touch on his shoulder. His tea, with a couple of biscuits in the saucer, hovered a few inches away.

'Thanks, Sally. Just what the doctor ordered. Tell me,' he asked, realizing belatedly that all these proposed changes would affect precisely the sort of people like her whom the Home Secretary dismissed as non-front line, and thus expendable, 'have you heard anything about your own future? Now the chief's gone?'

'The chief is dead, long live the chief,' Sally responded with a rueful grin. 'I work for the organization, remember, not a particular person. I go where I'm put. These days a woman of my age has to be grateful she's got a job — all this anti-age discrimination's a lot of theoretical tosh, if you ask me. I'll just have to get Mr Wren trained, assuming he's appointed long-term.' She nodded home her point, before adding, 'Are you feeling better now?'

'Much, thanks. Maybe I'd better try Fran again before I go and beard this stranger, though.' Stranger. How about that for a Freudian slip? Caffy would love it.

But stranger he was, his lovely firstborn, the kid he'd never quite had enough time for — the kid whose birthday parties he'd turned up late for or had to leave early. The kid he'd left to Tina to discipline and cuddle better: she might as well have been a single parent. Perhaps that was why Sammie had turned out as she had; he didn't even know how Dave had turned out, did he?

Observing him via the CCTV screen, Mark was shocked. He'd have passed him in the street, with that American business suit and aggressive hair cut. He was tapping away at the latest phone, occasionally flicking a fierce glance at his wristwatch, though surely the phone would have told him the time in every continent, every time zone, even.

Mark found himself checking for biscuit crumbs, squaring his tie, pulling in his stomach, though thanks to Fran and her insistence on exercise for them both, he was trimmer than most men his age. And at the thought of Fran, he was suffused by a simple but profound desire — to have her beside him literally holding his hand when he confronted Dave. Turning from the reception area, he dialled her, just in case.

* * *

Although she'd have said the place Janie had chosen was quiet to the point of peaceful, Fran had to bend her head close to Cynd's to catch the words.

'It was a punter, miss. That I knifed. I do it for me fix, see.'

Fran could almost feel Janie willing her not to mention at this juncture the possibility of coming off drugs. But she didn't think she would have done anyway.

'Did you know the punter? I mean, was it the first time he'd been a client?' Hell, this was all too heavy. These days interviews like this — any interviews, for God's sake — were conducted by officers with special and regularly updated training. In something as delicate as this there should have been a team watching, waiting to advise — interrupting if necessary. Meanwhile, Cynd's trust was ebbing away quite visibly.

'Sorry, Cynd. I just can't stop myself interrupting. Why not just tell me what happened and I'll try to keep my mouth buttoned.' With her left thumb and forefinger, she literally pinched her lips together, hoping the bit of silliness would undo some of the harm her earlier tone had done. Meanwhile, time was ticking on, and she was supposed to be at the rectory.

Cynd stared at Janie, as if asking what the hell she'd done to agree to talk to the daft old bat again.

'That's fine. Just tell her what happened,' Janie said.

Fran's phone rang. Her instinct was to kill it — but she checked. Fatal to her interview — her *talk* — with Cynd. Possibly. Possibly not? It was just what Cynd would have done herself.

It was Mr Pargetter. 'Don't like the thought of taking the van down that lane of yours,' he declared.

But he'd never been meant to! 'Go straight to the self-store,' she said. 'I'll phone ahead to tell them to let you in.'

'Doesn't work like that, Mrs Harman, does it? You have to be there to unlock your units. You've got the keys to the padlocks.'

'So I have.' She'd put them on a chain round her neck so she wouldn't put them down somewhere and lose them in the chaos. 'Have you and your lads had lunch yet?'

'We don't do lunch, Mrs Harman. We work straight through. And we finish when we've done the job. Which we can't till we've unloaded at the self-store. Where we'll be in — say — twenty minutes.' He cut the call.

Meanwhile, Cynd was bickering with Janie. And she'd managed to brush her hand against a nettle.

Her phone rang again. 'Mark! Thank God you've called. Any chance you could meet the removal men at the self-store? I'm in Grafty Green.' Fingers crossed he wouldn't waste time by asking why.

'Not unless I can take my son there too,' he said flatly. 'And you're the one with the keys.'

'So I am. Son? Oh, shit! I did try to phone you. Love you!' She cut the call and scrambled to her feet. 'I'm sorry.

I've got to be in Maidstone. Now.' She wouldn't make it in twenty minutes, but maybe thirty.

'Wouldn't mind a lift,' Cynd said. 'See my cousin.'

Perhaps Janie had been praying on her behalf for just such a suggestion, so that Cynd could speak in private; a driver's eyes fixed to the road sometimes made it seem like a confessional for the passenger.

'We have to run,' Fran said doubtfully, eyeing Cynd's flip-flops. To her chagrin, she was easily outpaced. On the other hand, she was finding Mr Pargetter's number and calling him as she ran. But she also felt she saw the appearance of writing on the nearest wall. Approaching old age, it said, in shaky letters . . . With an extra turn of speed, she told herself she'd erased it.

* * *

'You just have to go on the game,' Cynd said. 'Either that or burgle or thieve. I mean, you've no idea how much it costs.'

Fran had a very good idea of the street value of most illegal substances, but took advantage of an awkward bend to do no more than grunt a prompt.

'And we look out for each other, mostly. Word goes round — watch this one, don't go with that one. But this was a new punter. Came to my place, didn't he, without a by-your-leave. I thought he was a burglar. Maybe he was. What he thought he'd get in my place, God knows. I thought I heard voices outside, like he'd come with his mates. Anyway, he rapes me, like I said. And then he gets up, calm as you like, and gets his hands on my gear. So I told him to piss off out of it. And then he said he'd have another fuck, and to shut up and lie down, and I saw red. Really red. And I saw a knife in me sink and let him have it. And that's the truth.'

Except it might not be. It sounded too pat, too rehearsed. For a grim moment Fran suspected Janie might have edited it.

'Have you told Jill yet? Because she's still looking for someone who doesn't quite exist. And now she could start checking the CCTV footage for someone who does. What does he look like? Black, white, Asian?'

She could feel Cynd tense beside her. She'd gone too far, hadn't she? So she rewound a bit.

'How hard did you stick him, Cynd? Really hard? Because when I saw you the first time, you really wanted to tell us you'd killed him.'

'I must have done. I mean, it was a bloody sharp knife, and for all I'm thin, I'm strong. And he was white, miss. But he had a funny accent and smelt weird. Real yuck, his breath.'

Anyone could be strong in that situation, propelled by fear or in self-defence. Possibly Marion Lovage had been, with a wheelbarrow to assist her. But ribs — and a precise placing of the knife . . . She had a strong feeling that Cynd and the guy who was supposed to have raped her were not the only ones in the flat. Thank God for DNA and the clever things Scene of Crime officers could do with chemicals and light and photography. Maybe one day she'd send herself on a course to find out what was going on, instead of funding everyone else. No, it was too late now. In the meantime, she really did not want Cynd to know about her storage solution — quite illogical, but she'd always done her best to ensure her colleagues' privacy and didn't see why she shouldn't have the same rights.

'Whereabouts in Maidstone do you want me to drop you?'

'Like, anywhere.' It seemed she wanted privacy too, for herself and possibly for her dealer. She lapsed into silence and didn't seem inclined to go over her narrative again.

So all she'd got out of this, Fran reflected sourly, was a nasty hurried lunch, an itchy wrist, zero information and a horrible conviction that she'd compromised her rule never to be caught on CCTV with a suspect or a victim. Funnily enough, Cynd seemed to have the same opinion of the cameras and slouched down in the seat, her face sunk deep on to her chest and mostly obscured by her hands, well covered by the sleeves of her top. Neither managed a smile at the invisible eyes.

Relieved that the drive was over, Fran pulled into a convenient bus lay-by and, once Cynd had sloped off, called Jill with the latest information.

CHAPTER TEN

In the event, it didn't seem too silly an idea to take Dave along with him to the self-store. It got them both away from Headquarters and the far from remote possibility that there would be yet another three-line whip meeting, just as tedious and pointless as the last. As for him and Dave, they could scarcely do more than chat lightly about Dave's wife and children, after all, while Mark was driving. And he had, of course, been somewhat duplicitous to imply to Fran that she was the only one with keys to their units: he'd made sure he'd kept the duplicates. In his head he turned over the two words, *duplicitous* and *duplicates.* The syllables gave him the sort of pleasure he imagined young Caffy must get from the words she insisted she was still discovering. What would the tightly respectable Dave make of her? He hoped the experience would be beneficial: if anyone could penetrate the shiny carapace of his firstborn, Caffy could.

Dave had been notably tactful about recounting his meeting with Fran, but the very set of his lips suggested that something had offended him. Or perhaps that was the way his face fell these days — it had something of Sammie's smug defiance about it. If only he could ask him about Sammie, but he didn't trust himself to be tactful.

He found Fran surrounded by cardboard boxes — literally surrounded, as if they'd closed like a brown tide around her. Pargetter and his crew were ferrying the furniture into the first of the storage modules they'd hired; the second was to accommodate the cardboard boxes, all of which were supposed to have the contents written on the top and on all four sides so it should be possible to extract the right one with the minimum of fuss, before they were stacked in a giant Rubik's cube. Their system seemed to have gone wrong, however — it was quite clear that Fran was searching quite frantically for something.

'It isn't in the car, is it?' he called, by way of greeting.

She slung him her keys. 'Check. I could have slung the Crown Jewels in there and never noticed.' She paused long enough to give Dave a brilliant smile. 'Hi again — I still can't offer you a seat, I'm afraid.' She pointed at Pargetter, carrying two kitchen chairs, stacked seat to seat. 'You're looking for a box marked KITCHEN.' Her voice cracked ominously.

He dug in the car; nothing doing. But he knew his Fran, and he emerged to shout, 'What about the carrier bag with the kettle? Would that do?'

'Uh, uh. And we need the bathroom box too — loo rolls and towels. And the scales,' she added mock-threateningly.

He'd have given anything for Dave to shrug off his jacket, roll up his sleeves and start rooting alongside Fran. Anything. But he stood coolly aside, watching them as if they were ideal jet-lag entertainment.

Bent over a row of boxes, he asked, over his shoulder, as if it made it a casual, not a significant, question, 'Where are you staying, Dave? With Sammie?'

'The Hilton.'

He hoped Fran had picked up the flatness of the three syllables. She was good on nuances.

'I wish we could offer you a bed,' he said truthfully. 'But we're staying in someone's motor-caravan. And our new house is — well, both a building site and a crime scene. Take your pick. Neither conducive to comfort.' He was talking too much — he could tell from Fran's quick glance. 'But we'd love to shout you dinner — at your hotel if you like.' Except he felt as if he'd moved mountains, and Fran looked as if she had.

'Perhaps that would be better than the Three Tuns,' Fran said. Why the Three Tuns? He was horrified at how slowly he realized she must have suggested supper earlier. 'We could meet you there,' Fran continued. 'We really need half an hour to settle ourselves in — hang up clothes and so on.'

Dave tossed his head back as if he might have taken offence.

'We've been up since before five, Dave,' he said soothingly, 'and I'm sure you could do with a nap after your flight.'

'We have to pick up my car, remember — it's still in your car park.'

Shit. So it was. And if he knew Fran she'd have wanted their arrival at the rectory, even if it was to camp in a motor-caravan, to be something special. Whether he could carry her over the threshold . . . but he'd try, and she'd pretend. It would be important to her. Funnily enough, he didn't want a third party around, either — and somehow he could trust Paula and Caffy to be tactfully out of sight.

He inched over to Fran. 'I'll sort out Dave's car and see you back here. OK? Then we can go in convoy.' It was only a peck on the lips, but it would have to do.

* * *

For some reason — was there a connection? — Dave seemed to have decided to grasp a couple of nettles, though Mark wasn't at all sure that an edgy drive in Maidstone's early rush hour was the moment to voice intimate and controversial matters. He knew he differed from Fran, who said she liked the impersonality of non-eye contact conversations. She seemed to pick up tonal nuances; as he got older, he relied far more on visual ones. Maybe Fran was right, and he should get his hearing checked. The ear drops she'd been assiduously applying each bedtime — Caffy would have remembered, as he always did, the dumb show in *Hamlet* — hadn't been noticeably successful.

'So now you're planning to marry this woman?'

'Fran and I have always intended to marry,' he said, fairly sure that this was the line Fran would already have taken. 'It was just a matter of when and where.'

'So what's this Chief of Police got to do with it?'

'Old Adam? Nothing. A joke between the three of us. The catalyst, if you want one, was a sudden realization of mortality as I stood at the top of our scaffolding.' It wasn't wholly true, but he thought the more prosaic truth might not work. 'Fran's always been a good friend: come on, surely you remember the times she babysat you. No? You always were a sound sleeper, Dave. And when your mother was ill, she took a huge amount of work off my shoulders so I could spend time with her. Precious time.'

'In other words, the woman always had her eye on you.'

Mark almost ran into the car in front. He took a deep breath. 'Don't make her out to be some predatory female, Dave. I've an idea my suggestion we have a date took her totally by surprise. Since then . . . Look, after your mother, I couldn't have imagined anyone I'd want to share my life with. Now I can't imagine spending it without Fran.' Did he sound angry? Why not? He felt it. He'd almost have preferred a nudge-nudge, wink-wink approach from his son, though he wouldn't have liked that either.

The quality of the silence told him to say nothing more yet, but to wait for the reaction.

'She's a gold-digger.'

'On the contrary, she's brought more in cash to the relationship than I could.' Why on earth was he offering such spurious information? Why hadn't he made a simple flat denial?

'Cash. With your salary?' Perhaps he reflected on how his birthright had been spent, on his education and Sammie's.

'I wasn't going to raise the matter, Dave, but since you have, I can tell you that we wouldn't be able to afford our new marital home had she not sold that cottage of hers and stripped out her savings. So Fran is literally penniless at the moment. And until I can sell the Loose house, I can't help out.' Again, he stifled any further words, though they would have come tumbling out had he let them. But Dave said nothing, so he added what he should have said earlier: 'And were Fran a beggar maid to my King Cophetua, she'd never be a gold-digger.' He liked that sentence. Caffy would too.

'So you're saying this is all Sammie's fault?'

'Saying what? What's Sammie's fault?' Perhaps he'd seriously misheard, because Dave's question seemed to have come from nowhere.

'This rushed marriage of yours. And if you had your house back, it'd be OK.'

There was a tailback of people leaving the car park, but only him wanting to get in. He ID'd himself, the huge barrier admitted him, and he pulled into his marked space. He eased himself out of the car before he spoke. 'Dave, I've not the slightest idea what you mean. I want to marry Fran because we want to spend the rest of our lives together. In our jobs, that might not mean very long. As far as the Loose house is concerned, I want access. It's not just my property locked in there, remember. There's a lot of Fran's. And yours. It's not Sammie's house to occupy. When I die, it'll be shared between you and Sammie.'

'I thought you wanted to sell it.'

'For God's sake, don't take things so literally. I need to sell it now. But you'll have equal shares eventually.'

'Uh, uh. She'll have first claim.'

'She?'

'Your new wife.'

'I think we have such things as wills, Dave.' In case Dave thought he was talking in philosophical terms, he added, 'Bequests. You'll be legatees. Now, let me take you through to your car. Will you remember the way to your hotel or would you like me to lead?'

'Satnav.' Suddenly, he sounded like the sulky boy who'd been made to tidy his room.

'Very well. We'll see you there in the bar at eight? Maybe a bit later? How's the jet lag?' Maybe everyday questions would take some of the poison from the air, he thought as he signed Dave out and walked through to the public car park. As he'd always done, he patted the top of the car in farewell and waved till Dave was out of sight. Dear God, what had gone wrong there? It'd need one of Janie's miracles to get the family back together. Meanwhile, should he go back to his office for one last check? Then he thought of Fran, curiously forlorn and vulnerable amidst all those boxes, and he headed straight back to his own car.

* * *

'Dear God! You call this a camper van?' Arms akimbo, Mark stared at the vehicle occupying — *parked in* was too feeble an expression — their parking area.

'Caffy's word, not mine.' Fran staggered from her car and joined him, almost collapsing into his arms, but more, he thought, with pain and exhaustion than any amorous intent.

But he kissed her all the same. 'I'm sure there's a proper literary term for understatement that Caffy would supply us with. How on earth did they get it down here?' He smacked his head. 'Of course, the traffic jam the other morning! It wasn't some farm vehicle, it was this!' Was it only yesterday? He blinked at their once gated entrance — now there were no gates and no stone supports. The stonework stood in neat stacks, against which the gates were propped. 'Oh dear.' He pointed at a couple of new additions to the site: an orange plastic boundary fence declaring that within was a hard-hat area, and listing all the site regulations, including boots, confronting familiar blue and white police tape indicating a crime scene. The fence and tape were millimetres apart, two frail armies squaring up to each other, knowing the big guns were in the rear and at the ready.

'Silly cows,' Fran declared, almost under her breath — rightly, since Paula and Caffy were no doubt lurking to watch their reaction. And to guard the huge Winnebago, the keys of which hung in the side door. She smiled at him. 'We have to put on a show, Mark — they'll be hoping you carry me across the threshold. Tell you what — you hold me and I'll jump.'

'So long as you keep your eyes shut — I want us to see the interior marvels at exactly the same time,' he said ironically. It would be pop-star vulgar, wouldn't it, a vehicular Elvis, all diamanté and fringes?

Obediently, she put her hands over her eyes, waiting just inside until he was beside her, closing the door.

* * *

'So we're very lucky with the caravan,' Fran, waiting for Mark to bring over their wine, told a coke-drinking Dave, glad to have someone to share it with. 'It's quite upmarket and pretty spacious.' She lied, of course. It was extremely upmarket and very spacious, with a well-appointed mini-kitchen and a bijou shower-room; they could live in it without any problems as long as it took. Everything was top of the range, from fluffy towels and fine bedlinen to bone china, lead crystal and the sort of cooking pots she favoured, still mysteriously in their cardboard box in the self-store.

Kindly, she attributed Dave's total lack of interest in anything she might say to the zombie-like state induced by long-haul flights. Since she wasn't far short of the same state herself, she could only manage chatter and banalities, but she remembered the way to a parent's heart was usually his or her children, and she detected a slight softening of his chill when he showed her picture after picture of two all-American youngsters, their grins broad despite the ironmongery in their mouths. She asked about their grades and interests and everything an ex-babysitter and potential step-grandmother needed to know, even if she doubted if she registered half of what he was saying, since his accent seemed to have thickened and her brain most certainly had disintegrated into cotton wool some time during the day.

In fact it must have done so pretty early on: she stopped herself clicking her fingers and tutting aloud when she recalled exactly what she should have been talking to the agreeable young man at the self-store about. He'd told her he'd be back on duty at eight next morning. Provided she ever woke from the slumbers she could rely on the superbly sprung double bed to provide, she'd arrive not long after.

CHAPTER ELEVEN

'Lost more boxes, have you, love?' the young man — Ed — asked as she rolled up the next morning.

'I'm searching for a bit more than a box,' she said, fishing out her ID and wishing the sight of it hadn't made him go visibly pale. 'How long has this place been open?'

'Years, miss. I mean, like, I've been here for three, but yonks before that. Why?' he asked, eyeing her with a mixture of fear and hostility.

'I'm looking for someone else's boxes,' she said, patting the ID and putting it back in her pocket.

'You'd better talk to the boss, miss. Shouldn't be long, now. Honest.'

'No problem. I'll go and have another look for my saucepans while I'm here.' Not that she needed them, of course, but there was no point in further rattling poor Ed unless she had to.

Tom, his boss, was so relaxed and expansive, pressing on her a plastic cup of truly evil coffee which reminded her why she was supposed to be sticking to green tea, that she immediately suspected him of something underhand. But he cooperated readily when she asked him about the firm's rental records, producing a dog-eared set of computer printouts dating from the days of daisy-wheel printers. Living history! Licking his index finger each time he turned a page, he worked his way through what appeared to be scores, if not hundreds, of entries.

'Thank God for proper computers,' he said, sweating as a result of his exertions. 'But even in them days we was thorough — see, we've got a record of everyone's name, address, phone, and driving licence or passport number, just in case. Here's the dates they dropped the stuff off, and here's the dates of each visit after that until the contract ended.' By now he was breathing stertorously. But, eventually, he had to confess he'd no record at all for a Dr or even a Miss Lovage some twelve to fifteen years ago. His face showed as much disappointment as she felt.

'We chose this place because it was nearest,' Fran mused. 'Do you have other branches?'

With a flourish, he produced a pile of flyers, listing locations in half a dozen towns in the south-east. Some he crossed out before she could even look at them as being too new for her requirements. But even as she thanked him for his help, she felt a frisson of disappointment that her own moment of detective work hadn't pulled even a rather grey rabbit out of a mouldy hat. Worse, trawling through the other depots' records was clearly going to be the task of the lowliest on Kim's team.

On the other hand, she had a meeting scheduled in Folkestone first thing, and her route could take her very close to Ashford and, on the way back, not all that far from Canterbury. Why not? Especially if she could phone ahead and bum a cup of tea from Janie.

* * *

Mark cut the call politely, but he could have thrown the phone across the desk. How on earth could he have agreed to have lunch with Dave, when he had to be on the thirteen eighteen from Maidstone East for a London meeting involving the election of police commissioners? Eventually, he'd suggested a sandwich at the station, not great family PR, but the best he could do. Would such unpromising surroundings make for a more meaningful conversation than the others? Fran had toiled last night to establish some — any — point of contact, but he had a terrible fear that the harder she'd worked, the more Dave had withdrawn into himself. And none of them had mentioned Sammie.

Would it make matters easier if he phoned Ms Rottweiler — damned if he could remember her real name! — and told her to back off? Or should he urge a speedy resolution, so that Dave would be there to pick up any pieces? But now wasn't the moment to do either: he was being summoned to the Wren's den again. No, it was the Wren's nest, wasn't it? For the first time in the day he laughed aloud.

* * *

If ever a woman deserved a treat, Fran sighed as she headed north up Stone Street, it was she. Despite Tom's assurances, the Ashford self-store, once she'd run it to earth, turned out to have come too recently on the scene to have been the place where Dr Lovage had left her belongings. But even such a short diversion had made her marginally late for the CID meeting in Folkestone, something she always found embarrassing. Her colleagues had heard plenty of rumours about Wren and were, unsurprisingly, either alarmed or surly. To try to reassure them that all would be well but that they should be prepared for difficulties required an ability to walk the tightrope of truth she wasn't sure she wanted to possess. At least she left her colleagues believing that in her and in the ACC (Crime) — so long as such a post existed, of course — they had officers who would fight dangerous cuts with every fibre of their corporate bodies.

Although she'd have loved to stride along the Leas for ten minutes to get a healing blast of sea air, she returned dutifully to her car, even if her destination was less than appropriate for someone of her rank. She should absolutely be above such routine enquiries — but after the meeting she felt that she was honour bound to cock a snook at management, even if no one would ever know of her gesture.

* * *

Janie laughed when she heard of Fran's one-woman mutiny, but became serious as soon as their conversation touched on her protégée.

'This Cynd business is really troubling me,' she said, pushing over a plate of leaden flapjack Fran knew from experience would test every filling in her head. Somewhere Janie had got hold of the idea that anything with oats in it must be healthy, managing to ignore the Golden Syrup and butter that held the oats together. 'You know more about street drugs than I do, but I'm wondering if she didn't imagine the whole thing while she was away with the fairies.'

Fran merely said, 'The forensic tests will tell us more.'

'Haven't you had them already? On TV—'

'On TV they don't have vice-tight budgets,' Fran said flatly. 'But a bit of corroborating evidence would be nice — from CCTV or whatever other source. Even someone turning up in A and E with a hole in his side might have been helpful.'

Janie's eyes narrowed. 'Take care what you wish for. Take me, now — I always wished I had smaller tits, and now I'm due a mastectomy. I might go for broke — have a double,' she added with what might just pass for a grin.

Fran cried out: Janie was supposed to be immortal! But this wasn't about her own needs. So, as if she herself was the strong one, she reached for Janie and hugged her until she could feel her friend relaxing in her arms. At last Fran asked, 'How long have you known?'

'Wednesday night. Not news you'd want me to break in front of Cynd, now, was it?'

Did Cynd know? But Fran wouldn't interrupt her.

'I go in first thing on Monday. As luck would have it, instead of popping into the Kent and Canterbury, I've got to pound across to the William Harvey. For seven, would you believe?'

'I'll take you.'

'With your schedule? We'll argue about that later.'

'No, we won't. I'll pick you up at six fifteen, which should get us into Ashford with time to spare. Should. OK?'

Raising work-worn hands in surrender, Janie smiled. 'OK. I can see how you got to be a chief superintendent.'

'Being a steamroller doesn't always work — not when it came to finding our temporary accommodation. But this is about you, Janie, not me.'

She rocked her head in reluctant acquiescence. 'Would you believe it, good is actually coming out of this? My wee sister and I have hardly done more than send Christmas cards for twenty years, but now she's coming down to nurse me, having had the same problem herself. The good news is they think it's not spread.' Fran didn't like the word *think*, but she held her tongue. 'So I shall be able to officiate at your wedding.'

Fran gaped. 'How did you know about that? Because I was going to tell you today, since it's another thing we could hardly discuss in front of Cynd.'

'Your old boss phoned.'

'Shit and double shit! I know he's an old dear, but just now he's an interfering old bastard.'

'He seemed a polite old gentleman to me. Full of Dickensian charm.'

'That says it all — he's only in his sixties! And he had no right—'

'Loving people gives you a lot of rights, and even if love's too strong a word in this instance, he's very fond of you and Mark. Anyway, he phoned to ask if I'd be able to officiate in the Cathedral. In your dreams, sonny, I told him. I mean, I would be able, if given permission — but you two probably wouldn't be eligible anyway. Sorry. But I take his point about

St Jude's. You want something a bit more photogenic, Fran, for your big day.'

However much this might have been music to her ears, she protested, truthfully, 'But we want you to take the service, to marry us. Because — because we love you, Janie, and as you've just said . . .'

Janie blushed. 'We'll find a way round it, never fear.' She looked at her watch. 'Now, I've got to push you out: I want to check on young Cynd, who's taken the news of the op far worse than I have — would you believe, I found her on her knees howling outside my bedroom door last night? Plus one of the lasses in the mothers' group is likely to be evicted, and I need to go and talk to her social worker. Fran,' she added, putting her hand on Fran's, 'I know you're not so sure about the power of prayer as I am, but I'd welcome your getting into God's ear for a bit: I trust the NHS, but a bit of extra insurance never came amiss.'

Personally, Fran would have liked to give God a good kicking for letting cancer exist, let alone descending on such a good woman.

'Now, a bit of a hug, and off you go,' Janie continued.

'I'll see you at six fifteen,' she managed, ready to howl, like Cynd, with rage and horror and fear. But she didn't. Not until she was safely in her car.

* * *

'I'm sorry to be in such a rush,' Mark said, arriving at the station café five minutes late, despite having an official driver this time. He plonked his mobile on the tiny table Dave was already perched at.

'You always were in a rush,' Dave responded unsmilingly, putting his mobile down cheek by jowl with his father's — same make, same model, same everything.

Mark blinked: hadn't Dave had something altogether sexier? 'New toy?' he ventured, touching it.

'Poor coverage over here,' Dave said dismissively, before continuing what sounded like a prepared tirade. 'You never had a moment for us. I can't recall a single birthday party, Sammie's or mine, which you didn't arrive late for or leave early.'

He didn't argue — hadn't he beaten himself up for the same thing?

'Mom was a saint to put up with you. In fact, I'm even beginning to feel a little sorry for this Fran of yours.'

'When we retire—' Mark began bracingly.

'*If* you retire. If you live long enough. Anyway. Sammie. I'm going to see her. I've not been before because I wanted to see how the land lay.'

'And?'

'I can't see how you got yourselves in this financial mess, to be honest. And it disgusts me that you have. And that you need to sell our home to sort yourselves out. You've behaved like crazy kids.'

Again, how could he argue? But he scrabbled on to safer ground. 'If you haven't seen Sammie yet, you may not know the provision I've offered to make for her until she and Lloyd have sorted themselves out. For all they're not living together, he's still got a job, and they're his children. Whatever the state of their marriage, he can't shirk that responsibility. Meanwhile, I'll make sure she has a roof over her head, clothes on her back and food in her and the kids' bellies. When the house is sold, I can make you a gift to the same value.'

'So we don't have to wait till you're dead?' He snorted. 'Why didn't you say this before? Only just thought of it?'

Why indeed? Because he'd had other matters to worry about?

'You always did try to bribe us.'

'This is nothing to do with bribery: it's to do with fairness. Fairness to you, to her and to Fran. And — somewhere along the line — to myself. And speaking of lines, that's my train. I'm sorry, Dave, but when you're meeting the Home Secretary you can't be late.' And he had a terrible feeling that the Home Secretary would be less hostile, less implacable, than his only son.

* * *

The young man's name badge might have said Fred, but Fran was sure that it should probably say Frydyryk, or whatever was the nearest equivalent to the Polish first name. He greeted her as if she was at least a duchess even before she flicked out her ID, at which his eyebrows shot up. Then he found her a chair, which he insisted on dusting before he presented it with a flourish. Together they pored over the relevant records — and this branch's were as meticulous as those in Maidstone.

As he ran his finger down the fifth or sixth page, Fred remarked idly, 'Lovage is a curious name, isn't it? For a person, not a herb. A very useful herb, too, with very high levels of quercetin.'

'Which is?'

'Something that is a natural antioxidant — it inhibits free radicals.'

Despite herself, she trotted out a joke she'd used before, her only excuse being that the young man probably hadn't heard it. 'I thought the Home Secretary had locked them all up.'

'I wouldn't have expected a police officer to make such a remark,' he said, not quite straight-faced.

'I wouldn't have expected a self-store security man to know about quercetin,' she countered, eyes a-twinkle.

'Then we are both surprised — I to find a police officer with a sense of irony, and you to find a man halfway through Med School doing a job like this. Money, Detective Chief Superintendent, money. Ah! Here is our useful herb. Dr Marion Lovage. Unit One-Seven-One B.'

She was ready to leap to her feet and punch the air. But she confined herself to an exultant: 'Really?'

'And the strangest thing is that she hasn't been back since, according to our records. Not in fourteen years and more.'

'You're sure?'

'See for yourself. I'm surprised my bosses have never checked — space is short, apart from anything else.' He looked at her shrewdly. 'Much as the police would like me to, I can't just unlock the unit for you.'

'I'll organize a search warrant. Thank you for your help.'

'You're welcome. But ma'am, may I ask when you plan to open the unit? Because if it's so important, I would dearly love to be the one on hand to supervise you.'

She grinned. 'Give me your mobile number. Oh, and your boss's, come to think of it.'

'Of course. I'm sure the Home Secretary worries about such procedures as much as about free radicals,' he declared.

Heavens, why couldn't Mark's son have been as charming and witty as this young man? Maybe she could conjure some sort of reward for him for Crimestoppers or some other crime-fighting charity.

'Meanwhile, can I have her passport number? And that of her driving licence?'

He looked puzzled. 'We seem to have a lacuna in her details. See — all we have is the word "Pending" in both columns. A real lapse in security there, Chief Superintendent. Possibly because she paid so very much cash up front. Enough for — say — five years. I can only apologize.'

'Come now, it's hardly your fault. You weren't even in infants' school then. But I'd like to meet the person who nodded her through, as it were.'

He stood to one side, pointing at a totally illegible signature, clumsy as if a child was practising a grown-up autograph. There was a small run of them, but it soon stopped. Then the usual signatures returned. 'Perhaps someone new to the firm. Or temporary. I'll ask my boss to check staff records for you. And ask about this.' He pointed. 'Another cash payment, only two months later. Very strange.' He picked up the card she gave him. 'And I will ask my boss to do everything urgently, ma'am. Any case meriting a detective chief superintendent asking the questions must be serious indeed.'

CHAPTER TWELVE

One day maybe she'd stop worrying when Mark was late. But not yet. And because she was so tired, Fran wasn't at her most logical. Some of her weariness was relaxing after a job well done: she'd set up everything for what she mentally called the Grand Opening of the storage unit. It was easier to hide hopes behind the irony that had appealed to young Frydyryk. A written explanation pinned to a packing case was not on the cards, she was sure of that — a woman wouldn't go to so much trouble to erase everything from her home only to blurt it out later. She didn't see Dr Lovage summoning a priestly ear to receive her deathbed confession, either. But there must be something . . .

Why on earth hadn't she set an earlier deadline for Kim to come up with Lovage's biog? She didn't want to wait till Monday. But she'd said from the outset that the budget was limited, and more speed meant more officers working, and possibly unnecessary overtime, too.

Maybe it was warm enough to take a G and T outside and enjoy the view, such as it currently was. But there was a nip in the air, and the only chairs, white plastic ones some of the workers had left out, were so thick with building dust it'd take five minutes to clean one. And a G and T wasn't a good option anyway, not with the prospect of going to collect Mark from the station when he eventually arrived. Why hadn't he at least phoned to say which train he was on? She felt the usual clang of fear in her gut when anything might go amiss with him.

At last her phone rang. 'Mark! Thank God. Where have you been?'

'It's David Turner here,' came a stranger's voice. Dave, of course, distancing himself from her deliberately.

'But you're on Mark's phone?' Image chased image — Mark ill, all the important phone numbers and highly sensitive contact details in someone else's hands. You needed a password to get into the memory, but for all she knew of him Dave might be the sort of geek to get round that sort of thing in the twinkling of digitally adept fingers.

'He left it at the station when he met with me. He must have mistaken it for mine.'

How had he made such an error? 'Could you give me the number of the mobile Mark's got? I need to know what time he'll be back so I can prepare his supper.' She had a vision of herself in a frilly apron wielding a wooden spoon, just like the mother in one of the old Ladybird Janet and John books. In fact, all she'd be doing was exercising her index finger pressing microwave buttons to heat one of the selection of ready meals she'd picked up from Sainsbury's on her way home.

He rattled through it too quickly for her to pick up a single digit — something to do with the Transatlantic blurring of his T's into D's, maybe.

'Maybe you'd be kind enough to hold on,' she said with a creaking formality. 'I don't have a pencil and paper handy.' Eventually, with several embarrassing requests for him to repeat a digit, she had the number. She was ready to cut the call — but, of course, he'd contacted her in the first place and might have wished to say something. 'Thank you. Now, how can I help you?' Wrong words, wrong tone — perhaps it was tiredness that had summoned her standard office enquiry.

There was a long enough pause to suggest that he was taken aback. 'I guess I just thought it might be profitable for us to talk.'

'What a nice idea,' she said with cheery duplicity, as if she'd not picked up any subtext at all. 'I don't think either of us is working tomorrow. Why don't we shout you lunch at Leeds Castle or somewhere equally picturesque?'

'I was thinking more of just you. My father being so busy,' he added with something horribly like contempt.

She strapped a smile on her face in the hope it might reach her voice. 'The trouble is, Dave, that your father and I see so little of each other that we try to make sure we share everything we can at weekends. And I'm sure he'd be mortified if he thought you and I were off on a jolly without him.' She waited. Nothing. So she breezed on: 'How are your family managing without you? How's Phoebe's tooth?'

She forced the conversation along family lines as long as she dared, feeling like poor Miss Bates exhausting that irritating girl Emma's patience. At last, she declared untruthfully that she had a call waiting and hoped audibly it might be Mark managing at last to recall her mobile number without any electronic assistance. Pause for girlish giggle and a silent reflection that she wouldn't, in similar circumstances, have a clue what Mark's might be.

'Incidentally, there's something wrong with his phone.' Dave sounded puzzled or aggrieved. 'I couldn't access the memory — it's a good job I'd kept that business card of yours.'

'It is indeed. Look, I'll tell Mark you called — or perhaps you could call him yourself? — but just for now I must go.' What the hell was going on? Why should Dave want to speak to her without Mark? More important, why had she failed to ask him why?

Meanwhile, there was something more urgent to deal with. There were people at HQ on duty round the clock just in case one of their colleagues lost or was robbed of his mobile or his computer. She speed-dialled the number. A few moments' conversation established that Dave would find his father's phone suddenly and inexplicably unusable, not just the memory. Which brought her to another imponderable

— how much of this should she tell Mark when he eventually got home? Correction, to the Winnebago.

* * *

Arms wrapped around each other, as if they were drunken kids, they staggered, almost dropping, to the car she'd insisted on driving over. An official police vehicle would have been available, and calling for one would have made a lot more sense, but it wouldn't have made his heart leap like the sight of Fran, waving as the train drew in.

'Just talk at me,' she said, starting the car. 'Or I shall fall asleep, and then where will we be?'

'I can tell you I still don't know how I picked up the wrong phone,' he said obligingly. 'First sign of senility or what?'

'Not if someone had one just like yours.'

'I thought he had a quite different one. But when we put our phones down . . . It's like marking territory, isn't it?' he reflected whimsically. 'Then there were definitely two identical ones on the table. Weird.' When she said nothing, perhaps because she was making an awkward right turn, or perhaps not, he asked, 'What did he say when he called?'

If she hoped he wouldn't notice her hesitation, plus a bit of a swallow, she was wrong.

'Forgotten already?' he asked drily. 'Or would you rather talk about it later, over a drink? But don't think we won't.'

'I think the rule about not talking shop at home applies in the Winnebago, doesn't it?'

'So do you want to talk now? Something's really bothering you. Perhaps if you switched your lights on?' he prompted.

'I don't know if my head's up to doing two things at once.'

'It was up to going into theft-of-phone mode earlier. As it happens, I think you were right, both as a cop and as a stepmother elect. I called in the loss myself as soon as I realized I had the wrong one, and they said you'd already alerted them. Well done.'

'I wasn't sure . . . If you've got dementia, I've got paranoia. I don't think he wanted the chief's home number or the car pool. I think he wanted my number, to talk to me without your being present. Just a feeling.'

He could tell she was lying; what had Dave said? 'Talk about what?'

'No idea. Truly, no idea. Maybe what you'd like for your next birthday.'

He pointed skywards. 'Look, there's a pig up there doing loop the loops. Or not. Come on, Fran, we've always been honest with each other.' *Unless it's really suited us to lie*, he added silently, touching her hand and the ring he'd never meant to be an engagement token.

'I've told you: I've not got a clue. And the birthday present idea's as good as any. No? Whoops — wasn't that our turning?'

He waited while she manoeuvred the car. 'Why don't you call him and agree to meet?'

'I've told him our weekends are sacrosanct. Oh, Mark, you haven't got to work tomorrow, not really?' Her question dwindled into something between a wail and a sob. Not Fran!

'I can work in the caravan on my laptop. Only for an hour. And maybe another hour on Sunday. Tomorrow we'll nip into Maidstone to get me a new cheapo phone to tide me over till Dave returns the other one. Then we'll see if the village cricket club is playing at home, and we'll eat in the pub in the evening. And go to church on Sunday.'

'St Jude's.' She explained about Janie. 'And we'll leave our phones at the end of the Winnebago that doesn't get a signal?' She sounded like a little girl begging permission to hang up her stocking for Santa.

'Indeed we will. And we'll only check for calls every six hours.'

'Probably five, knowing us.'

'Five then. Now tell me all about your day — because mine's covered by the Official Secrets Act . . .'

CHAPTER THIRTEEN

The cricket wasn't up to much, but sitting and, to their chagrin, sometimes dozing, in the late summer sun was just what they both needed. If they needed to justify time out, then they could point to the ordered chaos of the house and the garden, neither of which they dared invade, and the still-pristine state of the Winnebago, though Fran had insisted on a flap of a tiny fluffy duster and a whizz round with a mini-vac. Housekeeping heaven.

They weren't surprised that their presence at the match didn't cause any comment, but both had expected a little conversation from the people in the Three Tuns, whether welcoming, which would have been nice, or expressing disbelief that anyone could have been crazy enough to take on the rectory. Amusement or resentment at the arrival of the Winnebago. Anything.

Eventually, Mark held up a finger. 'Listen to the accents. Shit, everyone's a weekender. I doubt if there's a single local here.'

Fran pointed to the menu. 'Even the lamb's from Wales.'

'No matter, sweetheart — the idea was for us to get out and be coddled, not for you to ask questions about Marion Lovage.'

'I never! Well, just a few. Do you think, as a treat, we're entitled to some steak — although the beef's Scottish?'

* * *

Before he collapsed into bed — would there ever be a time when he wasn't tired to his very marrow? — Mark conceded under protest that Fran and he should continue to try to build bridges across the gulf separating him from Dave. He trudged, as if through deep snow, to the end of the Winnebago where he could get coverage and left a message on Dave's original mobile suggesting Sunday lunch together. Only as he cut the call did he realize that what he'd said was ambiguous — he hadn't mentioned Fran's presence, which he took, of course, as a given. Also at Fran's behest, he'd named a pub well away from Great Hogben: he couldn't see a problem himself, but if she did, he would indulge her. She still had what he, now desk-bound, was rapidly losing — a cop's nose for trouble and, better still, for preventing it.

They'd both slept like the dead, awaking to bright sunshine and the realization, alarming to people who never slept in, that it was almost ten thirty, and that they simply could not reach St Jude's in time for Janie's service. Mark would have stayed in bed another hour — for ever, if possible, his eyes were so heavy. But duty called. So All Saints at Great Hogben it was, to find the smallish church, probably old but certainly messed about by the Victorians, about two-thirds full. Most of the congregation were older than him and Fran; the dress code seemed to be slightly less than smart casual, with cords and body-warmers in evidence on some of the men. Predictably, the women had made more sartorial effort. The hymns rang out heartily, the sermon was brief, Communion reverent and the prayers to the point. What more could a worshipper want?

Any worshipper but Fran. She'd want to pick the vicar's brains, wouldn't she? So he hung back with her, gathering stray hymn-books as an excuse, and joined her to shake the vicar's hand at the end. She might have been giving a masterclass in tactful approaches, talking briefly about the sermon to show she'd actually been listening. Then she introduced him as her fiancé, saying they'd just moved to the village. That was it. No rapid-fire interrogation. Over to you, vicar. Or was it rector, and were they usurping his house, long lost to the parish?

This time her warmth and charm weren't working their magic. The vicar, old enough to have retired in any other profession, fiddled with his ear and cocked his head towards her. 'I'm terribly sorry — my hearing-aid battery's just died. Better now than during the service. But you're very welcome and I hope to see you again.'

A final handshake all round and that was it. And so — via the Winnebago, to change into genuinely casual gear — to lunch.

* * *

But not before Fran had a phone call. Since it was from Jill she took it.

'I just thought you'd like to know we've got a body. Woods, to the south of Canterbury. Nearest village, Bridge. A young man with a single stab wound just where Cynd said it would be. It's really Don Simpson's case, but since he knew about my possibly imaginary corpse he thought I might like to know it's real. And we thought you might want to come out to the crime scene,' she added ironically, as if Fran had any choice in the matter.

'Rather than sit and enjoy Sunday lunch? Yes, well . . . Tell me where.' She jotted the coordinates as Jill dictated them. 'You've organized everything?' She knew she would have done, from white suits to the press officer.

'Don did. You know, Fran, if you really are having Sunday lunch somewhere, I can always call you later — pretend this call never happened?'

'It's tempting.' On the other hand it was even more tempting not to have to eat with and talk to Dave. But what about Mark? How would he feel about his son's unadulterated company? 'I'll call you back in two minutes,' she promised. 'How much of that did you hear?' she asked Mark.

'Enough to make me know you ought to be somewhere near Bridge, not feeding your face near Sissinghurst. We'd best call Dave and tell him lunch is off.'

'Are you sure that's the best plan? If you want to build bridges, that is? We still don't know how long he'll be over here for, do we? We don't want to give the impression he's not important to us.' For *us* read *you*, of course. 'He might even have news of Sammie, of course.'

'Don't sound so damned enthusiastic! Look, I'll call him and the pub to say we'll be late, and I'll drop you at the crime scene. And then you can have a whale of a time inspecting cadavers and I'll politely consume roast beef. And I really will try to get to the bottom of this phone business. Promise. Though I think it would have been easier with you there.' He looked at her sideways. 'What are you not telling me? I can always tell, you know.'

'You know he called the night . . . I just wondered if he wanted to get hold of me and bend my ear without you. I've no more idea than you what he's up to — but I don't feel that enjoying a pleasant *tête-à-tête* with his stepmother elect is truly one of them.' Had that been too honest?

'I was a shockingly bad father, you know. Really, really bad. I left all the hard work to Tina — all the discipline, going to school functions, sitting with them when they were ill — everything.'

'Show me a policeman who didn't. Oh, things are better now, but in those days that was the role you accepted when you were a copper's wife. And at least you two stuck together, not like other police couples. Why not tell him how guilty you feel? How you'd want to do things differently if you had the chance?'

He shot her an amused glance, winding her up. 'Sounds a bit touchy-feely to me. You're right, of course. But Fran, tell me this: is my bad parenting wholly to blame for everything?

Sammie? Dave? They both seem like creatures from another planet to me. However angry I was with my dad — and I had due cause, believe me, growing up watching his casual unkindness to Mum — I'd never have nicked his phone, or the equivalent. Thank God you had the presence of mind to get mine closed down — though he'd probably already had time to worry away at my password.'

'On the principle of all those monkeys writing the works of Shakespeare? Come on, the security people said it was a grade-A password. Talk to them tomorrow, anyway — get them to check if there's been any untoward activity on lines he shouldn't even know about. But maybe you should ask Dave himself? Pull over here, sweetheart, and make your calls.'

* * *

Fran, the predictable white suit a little short in the leg for her, stood with Don Simpson, Jill and the forensic pathologist surveying the young man's body. It was already so decomposed that it was clear that unless there was anything in his pockets to help, ID would have to be by DNA — or by more searching questions, under caution, to Cynd than anyone had yet risked. Her early confession should do her a lot of favours if she ever came to trial.

'All this grass—' Fran pointed. 'Was it crushed by whoever found him? Or by us? Or was it already like this?'

'The couple who found him said they'd not got in close because of the smell. They also say they're sure it was all flattened down when they and their dog arrived.' Don, a decent cop in his early forties, added, 'I'd say he came along that path over there, wouldn't you?' It was already cordoned off. 'The SOCO team'll check for blood and so on.'

'Would the "so on" involve other people, carrying something heavy, like a young man? And then — dear God — laying him down there and abandoning him?'

'Going for help would be a better scenario, guv.'

Jill said, 'We've checked all emergency ambulance calls, remember — nothing at the right time on the right day. Assuming Cynd is telling the truth, of course. And assuming she may not have been, we checked a couple of days either way — nothing.'

'Don, Jill — this is in good hands. Keep me informed — I'd like to be at your briefings. Let me know if your budget needs expanding.'

'Expanding!' Don snorted. 'We'll be lucky to have a budget if the rumours are to be believed.'

'When was a rumour ever to be trusted?' Fran grinned. 'Come on, we have a murder here, and a rape. You have a young woman confessing: could you bear to bring her in yourself, Jill? Since she's a victim too? It'll be a difficult time for her, without any support. Remember Janie's off into hospital first thing.'

'Shit, so she is. I was hoping we could get Cynd bailed to her care.'

'If Janie gets so much as a whiff of that she'll call off the op,' Fran declared. 'And I'm not sure breast cancer will hang around for that. Shit and shit and shit.'

'Do you suppose she's sorted out a good solicitor for Cynd?'

'Only one way to find out. By the way, I'd rather Cynd didn't get landed with Whatsisname — that duty solicitor who might almost be batting for our side, not his client's.'

'Quite.'

Don, who'd backed off during what he no doubt feared was Women's Talk, approached again.

Fran shot him a smile. 'With luck, this should cost no more than a week's pocket money to tie up — but you never know, do you?'

The three old pros shook their heads and sucked their teeth in unison. One thing in policing was certain — you could never be certain.

Another thing was certain — Fran would have liked to spend the afternoon here, with her team. But in truth she'd be wasting her time — worse, theirs, since they all had roles that didn't require an old bat like her breathing down their necks. The forensic scientists didn't want extra people messing up their site. It was hot here and very smelly. Much as she'd have liked to go with Jill to arrest Cynd and reassure Janie, she didn't want to do anything that might damage Jill's confidence.

And Mark needed her. So she made her farewells, checked he was still over at Sissinghurst and bummed a lift from a disconcerted DC. 'Meanwhile, we need the full procedure, and bugger the expense. OK?' she concluded, knowing there'd be no dissent.

* * *

Mark was pleased with one part of his time with Dave: he'd remembered that his son had always liked photography and had suggested he might like to take his camera — did he still always carry one? Oh, he had the iPhone that'd do everything, didn't he! — round the grounds of Sissinghurst Castle. So lunch, in the absence of Fran, was a short and businesslike affair, simply devoted to the consumption of some indifferent salmon steaks. At some time he'd have to grill Dave on the matter of the mobile phones, but while half of him preferred the idea of having people around to stop Dave creating a scene (he used to have a terrifying capacity for tantrums — had he grown out of them?) the other half wondered if it might be better to have a little privacy to raise almost certainly embarrassing questions.

As they joined the straggling queue waiting to pay their entrance fee — goodness, were elasticated waistbands *de rigueur* for Sunday National Trust visits? — Mark made his first bold move. 'First up,' he said, 'let's sort out our phones.' He held out Dave's, expecting his son to produce his. Perhaps expecting was too strong a word.

'Sorry — I brought the other.' He flashed the expensive one. 'In case I wanted to take photos, of course. Yours doesn't seem to be working, by the way.'

'It wouldn't. We're required to notify security when we even mislay our phone.'

'So that woman grassed me up!'

'I did, Dave.' It wouldn't do any harm to fillet out a bit of the truth.

'You contacted the police!'

'I *am* the police, Dave. It's our policy. I had no choice. And as for making it personal, forget it — I just said I'd left it on a train. Mark's a silly old duffer, and so on.'

'Fucking hell! What about that woman? She sounded very suspicious too.'

'If you cut either of us, you'd find POLICE written inside. I followed procedure, son, no more and no less. But I'd rather you didn't refer to her as *that woman* again. She's Fran. My future wife. And a very good woman. Your mother was very fond of her. Now, the best place to start is up the tower — you can see all the grounds laid out at your feet.' How about that for fatherhood above and beyond the call of duty? There was an awkward step without a handhold at each point the circular stairs met a landing. He always made a point of offering his hand to older ladies here — but he admitted secretly it might be as much for his benefit as for theirs. As for the top of the tower itself, it actually had quite a decent parapet, but even so he preferred to let others jostle for the best view and lurk towards the middle.

'Did my mother know you were having an affair?' Dave demanded as they joined another queue to climb the dreaded stairs.

'Have you stopped beating your wife yet?' Mark laughed, as if there really might be some humour in the situation. 'There was no affair for her to know about, Dave, I promise you. In fact, when she'd come back from university — she did a course without any support from us, to our shame — Fran was seeing some badminton player. She's county standard, you know. Was. The only thing — only! — that kept me away from you kids and Tina was the job. Pure and simple. Climbing the promotional ladder. And if you ask me if it was worth it, I'd have to say it probably wasn't.' Remembering Fran's advice, he added: 'I'm sorry I was such a bad father. Very sorry. You don't even like me, and Sammie — well, I haven't been able to have a conversation with her for weeks. Ah! Up we go.'

Dave turned, and it seemed to Mark that he looked at him for the first time. 'Are you really coming? You always used to chicken out when we did anything like this. Scared of heights, aren't you?' It seemed he couldn't resist a jeer.

'Shit-scared, since you ask. But needs must.' He set off up the stairs. All the same, he was glad to stop at the first room and feign an interest in the contents.

Dave looked at him again. 'I'll catch you on the way down.'

As Mark opened his mouth to protest, Dave was up and away like a greyhound. But he wouldn't be written off. He'd do it if it killed him. And then he remembered Fran's face when he made jokes like that. What did he have to prove? That he cared enough about Dave to overcome his fear? Stolidly, he set off — one step at a time.

He'd just reached the quasi-safety of the top when his new phone rang. 'Fran?'

'I'm about ten minutes from Sissinghurst. Where are you?'

'Up the Castle tower with Dave.'

'Idiot. Brave idiot, but idiot all the same. I shall get our colleague Inderjit here to drive me up in state to the front gate. Actually, shall I see you in the White Garden? We can't miss each other there.'

He noticed Dave was staring as he put his phone away. 'What on earth are you doing up here?'

'I just wanted to spend time with you, son — and I'm buggered if vertigo is going to stop me.' But he waited till he'd got down safely before he asked, 'How come you got the wrong phone, Dave? Really? And why didn't you bring it today?'

Something in the garden claimed Dave's attention. He said, over his shoulder, 'Forgot — I just picked up this one.'

Why had he bothered with such a stupid detectable lie?

Mark said, trying to sound reasonable, 'Which is far classier than mine — and your new one. What's up, son?'

'Nothing's up, for Christ's sake! I bought a phone. You took it by mistake.'

Suddenly, Mark could see the little tea-stained table on the up platform at Maidstone East. It had only one phone on it, the one he naturally took, since it was identical to his. Why didn't he dare point this out? At least he asked another question: 'So why bring that sexy iPhone with you today and not mine? Sorry to go over it again, but none of this makes sense to me.'

'For God's sake, we'll go back to my hotel and pick it up — right? Before or after I take the photos you want me to take?'

God, he was a spiky teenager again. Surely there must be a way of breaking these patterns.

But now Dave was pointing, with a hand apparently shaking with rage. 'And now who's putting in an appearance? The fragrant Fran. God, you can't spend ten minutes apart. You're fucking pathetic, the pair of you!'

* * *

'Body. Decomposing nicely in this heat,' Fran greeted them, as if one of them had asked how she'd spent the last couple of hours. But it was clear from their faces that neither was interested; she got the strong impression that more problems had erupted, with the original ones still unresolved. 'Have you explored yet?' she asked, ambiguously, to her ears at least. 'Or could you fancy a cup of tea?'

'I'm finished here,' Dave said, so angrily that a couple of people leaning heavily on sticks looked at him in apprehension, as if he might suddenly kick their supports from under them.

'But I've not even started,' Fran said, heading for the more open ground of the orchard. She didn't look to see if the men were following; when she walked like this, they better had. At last, she turned, arms akimbo. 'Dave, I should imagine you're pretty angry about this phone business.' What on earth was Mark signalling? That it had been he who'd grassed up Dave? She'd best continue in neutral terms, then, though she'd much rather have told the whole truth. She kept her fingers crossed that she didn't slip up. 'I'm sure he's told you that anyone losing one has to follow policy he himself set in train.' She waited in vain for a response. She opened her mouth to find it was saying things she'd wanted to say for some time. Why now, though? But out the words came. 'When we first met, you thought I'd be some painted Jezebel — right? But now you can see I'm not, you still have a problem. I think it's to do with what Sammie's been telling you. And I also think you came here to see if you could help sort out a silly family mess.' This wasn't wholly true, but it gave him a chance not to lose face, didn't it? 'We should be allies in this, not a trio of grown-ups behaving like toddlers. Now, what's your take on the whole thing? What do you think Sammie's afraid of? And what problems does this cause you?'

'Why should I talk to you?' His lip jutted; if he'd been younger he'd have kicked the ground.

'Because life is far too short to waste time on inessentials.' She took a deep breath which threatened to become a sob. 'That young man whose body I saw today might have had a row with his girl and thought he'd sort it out later. And — phut! — he doesn't get a chance. I'm sorry . . . it's bad enough when the victim's old, but a young man in his prime . . .' She turned away, convinced for a few seconds by her own narrative. If what Cynd had said was even halfway true, the corpse was that of a raping scrote, but the truth would hardly appeal to this self-righteous prick of a man. But she still affected grief and brushed Mark away when he touched her arm, no doubt in sheer disbelief.

Suddenly, to her horror, the emotion became real. Her former protégé, Simon, was dead, wasn't he — a waste of a life if ever there was one. And they'd been too worried about investigations and Police Standards and even the damned cuts to reflect on it. He'd become an irritation, not a human driven to despair. While she was sure Human Resources had done all that was proper, neither she nor Mark had been able to offer words of comfort to his family lest their words be construed as an incriminating apology which would open the service up to compensation claims. In her own garden a man had once died, and she had seen his remains at best as a fascinating case, at worst as a damned nuisance. What had happened to her? What was happening now? All those tears, all this sobbing, in a public place? But she could no more have stopped than she could have flown to the top of that tower.

CHAPTER FOURTEEN

'At least you've got your phone back,' she said, getting in Mark's car after possibly the most embarrassing hour of her life.

They'd hustled her straight back to the car park, despite her utter longing for a quiet cup of tea, even one of those wonderful looking cakes in the Sissinghurst restaurant, and thence to Dave's hotel, where the phone, but still no tea, made an appearance. Hardly any words were exchanged. If she'd hoped, by showing she was human, to get Dave to open up, she had failed miserably. Clearly, the two men were equally embarrassed, though Mark might well have been as scared as she'd have been had the situations been reversed. Every time one surge of emotion subsided, another took its place: having no proper home, having a dear friend with a life-threatening disease, Mark's crazy lifestyle and the risks he kept taking . . .

'I'm sorry. I'm all right, really,' she managed at last.

'Like hell you are. Dr Stagg for you first thing tomorrow.'

'Can't. I'm taking Janie to hospital for her breast cancer op. And then it's all systems go at the self-store. And a briefing meeting later today, actually — but just this once I might let someone else take it. I'm so hungry I'm light-headed. I used to be able to do this meal-skipping-who-needs-sleep thing — but suddenly I'm bone tired and desperate to eat and drink. Age, maybe.'

'Even so . . .'

'If I'm like it again, march me off to the funny farm. Meanwhile, do you know anything about Simon's funeral?'

'No. Hey, where did that come from?'

'I knew him before he became a management flunkey, remember. When he was human. Have you been questioned, by the way, about Simon? I've hardly spoken to you this week, what with one thing and another.'

'Fortunately, I was on record as saying that even if Caffy was prepared to take risks with her safety to entrap him, I wasn't. It constituted too grave a risk. Mr Management, you see. I wanted his room checked and every movement watched on CCTV. Dear old Adam — it seems strange not being able to call him the chief, doesn't it? — said it violated the man's privacy. Look, there's a pub over there doing cream teas: do you fancy one?'

* * *

'I feel so much better now,' Fran said at last with a sigh. 'All this wonderful cholesterol and refined sugar and bad carbohydrates. Lifesavers. But I'm sorry we got no further forward with Dave. How was lunchtime?'

'OK — just — if we kept the conversation strictly neutral. Tell you what, I'll take you home for a nap and we'll eat out again tonight, provided the village pub serves grub in the evening. I have a strong yen for a few carbs and a dose of cholesterol myself. And enough alcohol to send me off the scale of any breathalyser.'

Fortunately, the landlord of the Three Tuns was on duty, and though officially there was no food, he managed to rustle up a ploughman's platter apiece. 'Since you're locals,' he added, with a grin. 'As from Thursday, was it? Have to take my hat off to you taking on that old place. Throwing a bit of money at it, aren't you? But that motorhome — brilliant idea. Ollie,' he said, shoving a hand across the bar.

'Mark and Fran.' They exchanged handshakes in turn.

Had they struck gold at last? 'Did you know the woman who owned it before?' Mark asked casually, pausing to draw on his Spitfire ale, as if it was nectar itself.

'Not me. Heavens, how old do you reckon I am? But my dad did. Why? Leave something behind, did she? Apart from a body, we hear? And aren't you police?'

'You hear right,' Fran said, deciding to skim over the second question. 'No idea whose, yet, of course. I don't suppose it was a local, or you'd all remember someone going missing.'

'Village of two hundred souls, you'd notice if you were one short,' the barman agreed, accepting a half himself. 'They say she was a fine woman, that Dr Lavender. No, some other herb. Not a medical woman, you understand, but a teacher.'

'So we hear. But we'd really like to know more about her — after all, not many people leave all their money to badgers. That's all the solicitor told us when we asked.'

'They say she used to go badger-watching down Stelling Minnis way. I'd have thought she'd prefer to find setts closer to home. It all started when she rescued one that had been run over, they say — she'd have liked to start a colony on her own land, but you can imagine what the farmers had to say about that.'

'Bovine TB,' Fran agreed, with a sad shake of her head. 'So she was a bit eccentric, was she? According to your dad,' she added quickly.

Ollie looked at her sideways. 'Now, are you asking as neighbours, like, or as police?'

Fran smiled apologetically. 'Technically, I'm in charge of the team working on the skeleton. But since you might say my loyalties are divided, I'm not actively involved. I just set the budget of those who are.'

'But you're still asking questions.'

'Because I'm a nosy old bat? Mostly, you get to meet the people who lived in the house before you — pick up their vibes. But with all the work we've had to have done, there's not much chance of that, is there?'

'Not a lot of her vibes left, either. Are you thinking Dr L — shall we say, she caused the skeleton?'

'Off the record, he was a pretty big bloke for a small woman to kill,' Fran said. 'I could probably manage it, if push came to shove. But she was tiny, wasn't she?'

'Are you suggesting one of us did it? Or helped her?'

'Absolutely not!' Fran was genuinely aghast. But as much at the realization that she'd never even considered a conspiracy of villagers as at the suggestion. 'If such a thing had even crossed my mind I'd have been in here waving my ID as soon as we found the skeleton.'

Mark nodded. 'I suppose we could dash back and pick them up now to flash, but it'd spoil a good pint. We're just incomers this evening, after a gossip.'

'Maybe you should pick another subject to gossip about. I'll see to those ploughman's platters, then.'

'Shit and corruption,' Fran breathed as they found a table. 'Messed up there good and proper, didn't I? We'll probably be drummed out of the village.'

'Could be. Is a village conspiracy a line you propose to follow?'

'You sound awfully like ACC (Crime), Mark. Rightly so. But I'd say we wait and see what tomorrow brings. In fact, I might just feed him a bit about opening her storage unit, to see if it pacifies him.'

'Don't bank on it. Hey, those look good,' he said truthfully to Ollie, who came up bringing their food. 'Above and beyond the call of duty too. Thanks. My fiancée needs a good feed: she was dealing with a week-old body when she should have been having her lunch.'

'Where might that be?' Clearly, he was interested despite himself.

'Just south of Canterbury. After all this nice warm weather.' She grimaced. 'Only a youngster, I'd say. It'll be on the local news at half ten tonight.'

'So are you investigating this one?'

'I told you: I'm a bean counter these days, as is Mark.' She added: 'But I can't ask other people to deal with things I wouldn't deal with myself if I had to. So I tend to turn up to give a bit of moral support. And because I'm nosy.' And because she had to be, because of her place in the hierarchy, but there was no need to shove that down his throat. 'I'm sorry about before. I really didn't mean to imply anything. In fact, it should all become a bit clearer tomorrow: we're opening the self-storage unit where we think Dr Lovage put her stuff. Canterbury,' she added.

'You get around, don't you? So do you reckon you'll still have jobs when they've made all these cuts?' He addressed himself to Mark, as the more easily forgiven.

'If getting rid of older, senior officers like us means we keep front-line officers, I'd retire tomorrow,' Mark said.

'Funny you should say that: we've started getting a police van in the village once a week. And there's a young lad going round telling farmers how to secure their tractors.'

'Yup. We thought it was more than time they had support. Seems the farm machinery manufacturers thought it'd make their lives easier if they had a standard ignition lock for every piece of plant they made. But of course it doesn't just make their lives easier, it makes thieves' lives easier too. Only last week we intercepted three at Dover all heading for Poland,' Mark said. 'As for your weekly visit, Fran wanted us to fund more, but the budgets . . .' He shrugged.

Ollie raised an eyebrow in Fran's direction. 'It was you who discovered we don't all live in towns, was it? Well, I'll take my hat off to you for that,' he said grudgingly. 'And to you for the lad talking about tractors, Mark. Look, if you're a bit more upfront about your interest, I'd say you should talk to my dad. Actually, I'd do it soon, if I were you. His memory comes and goes — though he'd more likely remember something in the past. Early Alzheimer's,' he said sadly. 'Crap way to go, isn't it? I'd rather have a bang on the head like your skeleton.'

Fran froze. How could he know that?

Ollie's laugh wasn't particularly amused. 'Ah, caught you there. You thought I must have done it 'cause I knew how he'd been done in. Truth is, a couple of your lads were in here and someone overheard one of them yelling down his mobile phone. So we all know.' He grinned. 'Tell you what, I could put up one of those posters — *careless talk costs lives.*'

'And I might have to put up another one at work,' Mark said grimly. '*Careless talk costs jobs.* Stupid bugger. And why do people always feel they have to shout when they have a mobile in their hands? *I'm on the train!* Heavens, we all know they're on the bloody train . . .'

CHAPTER FIFTEEN

They were up before six the following morning. Mark had a breakfast meeting to report on his session at the Home Office, and Fran had to sprint across to Canterbury to keep her promise to Janie, who, despite her protestations of complete trust in God and the surgeon, in whichever order, was mutely terrified, staring grimly ahead the entire drive despite the beauty of the morning. Fran, who thought that in Janie's situation she'd have been gazing around trying to absorb every last memory, insisted on accompanying her to her ward and staying with her in a waiting area. But, not knowing what to say, she ended up simply holding her friend's hand in silence, which at last became unbearable.

'My brother-in-law — he's a clergyman too — always reckoned to take away the worry of anaesthetics by saying the Lord's Prayer,' Fran ventured at last. 'He says he usually manages to get as far as *Hallowed be Thy Name* before he goes under.'

'I must try and get to *Thy Will be done*,' Janie said grimly. 'I don't want to have to be brave, Fran. If I've got to go, I'd like it to be while I don't know, if you see what I mean. And may God forgive me.'

Thank God a nurse came to take her away.

As she reached the door, Janie turned abruptly. 'Fran — that child Cynd. She slipped off somewhere yesterday afternoon, as that nice woman Jill probably told you.'

What the hell? Why hadn't Jill told her?

Janie added: 'Bless her, Jill came up to the door as casually as if she was offering the child a lift somewhere. She does you credit, Fran. Tell her that from me. But Cynd didn't come home last night. Don't let her do anything silly. Watch out for her.'

What the hell was up? Cynd was brave enough to turn herself in; now she'd damned well skipped.

'Of course I will,' she said with perfect truth.

And the moment she was out of the hospital, she jabbed a text to Jill, asking what was going on. She waited in vain for a response.

Thence it was back via a rush-hour-clogged Canterbury ring-road to the industrial estate and its hidden treasure. Heavens, she wasn't about to uncover Tutankhamen's tomb. She whiled away the time waiting for the others to arrive wondering why the last syllable of his name was commonly spelt with an *e*, but pronounced by the experts as if it contained a *u*.

At last the whole circus was gathered: Kim and a couple of officers Fran only knew by sight; photographers; SOCOs; Fred and Fred's boss. Bingo. Full house. Fred's boss produced a key he assured everyone was the duplicate Dr Lovage had been required to leave in his safe.

If it was, it didn't open the padlock. What the hell had the woman been up to? But Kim had apparently already thought of that eventuality, and soon the most diminutive person present, a veritable waif of a girl, was wielding bolt cutters.

At bloody last.

There was a collective groan. There was nothing to be seen except wrapping. Lovage must have bought bubble wrap by the acre. But was it to protect or conceal further? Although Fran knew she was being fanciful, she suspected the latter.

To her immense frustration the SOCOs demanded that everything be loaded into an as yet non-existent van to be taken to the lab for examination. She could have literally torn her hair at yet another delay while Kim summoned transport.

She turned to the equally frustrated storage centre employees. 'I'm so sorry! Look,' she added, turning to her colleagues, 'is there anything that isn't wrapped? We're like kids denied our Christmas stockings here.' Funny she should ally herself with the two men outside the team.

'Can't see anything, ma'am.'

She turned to the men: 'I promise you'll get photos of everything I can let you see. Believe me, I'm as fed up as you are. I wanted everything to spill out — ropes of pearls, boxes of sovereigns, like pictures of Aladdin's cave.' She spoke nothing less than the truth.

* * *

Mark stood in the corridor juggling his mobile phone — the one that had gone AWOL with Dave. For all they'd said about policy, he felt the strongest revulsion in handing it over to the geeks to see if had been interfered with. 'Only obeying orders' smacked of supine acquiescence to unreasonable demands — hadn't half the Nazi war criminals pleaded such an excuse? Which should you put first, your family or your country? Not that there was the slightest reason to think that Dave might harbour malice to anything other than his own father — not his fatherland. Hell, there he went with Nazi-speak again. E.M. Forster, in an essay he'd read when he was in the sixth form (was this the start of senility, remembering books you'd read so long ago?), had concluded that in a choice between your friend and your country, you should betray the latter. But as a seventeen-year-old, Mark had disagreed: if your friend was betraying his country, he was betraying you. Now he'd have liked to be so sure.

He stared at his phone: if only it was an upmarket one that displayed the most recent calls. That was all he wanted to know. On the other hand, he needed it to be unblocked, so he could use it again. Straightening his shoulders, but trying to look casual, he plunged into what was clearly electronic media heaven and handed it over.

* * *

'We ought to take this stuff apart,' Kim said, staring at what even Fran knew was priceless furniture, now safely locked in the evidence store. In particular, Kim had her eye on a cabinet which clearly had a lot of cupboards and drawers, but which, having no visible keyhole, simply refused to open.

'No. Absolutely not. These are works of art. We need to get an expert on them.'

'Budget?' Kim asked drily.

'Quite.' Fran was equally dry. 'Let's look at everything else in detail — from the outside, however — and see if we have any reason to proceed further. Meanwhile I'll bend my brain and see if I've got any favours I can call in. Me or Mark — he's more likely, come to think of it. What about that pretty kneehole desk — is there anything in there?'

One of the technical staff shook his head. 'Not so much as a bent paper clip.'

Fran gave a bark of laughter. 'Nothing in the house, nothing in the garden, nothing in her furniture — she seems to have been quite obsessive. Maybe we should call in a shrink.' She stopped. 'Hang on — she left that wheelbarrow, for all it was under six feet of muck. Has that thrown up anything useful yet?'

'In half an hour, with luck.' Kim flicked a glance at her watch. 'We've got a progress briefing in twenty minutes: will you be coming?'

'Cue jokes about bears or popes, Kim. I'll be there.' But not until she'd contacted Jill again; she liked instant replies to important questions.

* * *

'Let's start with the good news,' Kim said. 'We have an ID for our rectory garden victim. Francis, known as Frank, Grange. Before you feel too sorry for a man coming to such a violent end, pause to consider his CV.' The PowerPoint presentation produced its first page. 'As you can see, he was almost professionally brutal. First conviction: age thirteen, stabbing a teacher; next, age sixteen, aggravated stealing and taking away — left the victim of the theft for dead after running her over. That seems to have got him started on a long career of crimes against women.' She pointed. 'Sexual assault; rape; attempted murder; rape again. He got a good long sentence for that, largely because of the evidence given by the victim's sister, Mary Ann Minton. Now, as you can see, the pattern is clear. Offend; time in gaol; offend; time in gaol; offend. A clear cycle.'

An ironic voice from the back observed, 'Prison works.'

'Quite. But fourteen years ago, released from Parkhurst, this time, he stops offending. Cured! Either it's the sea air he's been exposed to or he's emigrated. Or he's been walloped on the head with a large shovel and popped into a trench to improve the quality of the runner beans. Fortunately, we've got plenty of mugshots of him so, although it's a long shot, I suggest we get on to the media, in particular *Crimewatch*, and see if anyone can place him round here, and with whom.'

'Do we need to go that far? Isn't it a fair supposition that he tried to rape Marion Lovage and she killed him?' the voice at the back asked.

Fran nodded enthusiastically. 'It'd help my budget if we could simply say that was that and move on to the next case. On the other hand, I think the coroner might like a bit more than an educated guess, don't you? At least a suggestion as to why, having killed him, she didn't just call the police.' She looked down to the document in front of her. 'The pathologist says he was killed by one blow — I'd have thought she'd have got away without a prison sentence for that. Unless, of course, she had a criminal record herself. Kim?'

Why should the younger woman look guilty, as if a dog had eaten her homework? She almost gasped with relief when one of her team passed a piece of paper. 'Could I just mention the wheelbarrow before we go through what we have of Lovage's CV? It's as clean as a whistle.'

'Surprise, surprise. And the CV?'

'Almost as clean. She suddenly emerges from nowhere at a school in Lincoln with a degree and a teaching qualification. If they're real, we don't know where she got them. Because no British uni seems to have had a Marion Lovage on roll, either as a degree student — Geography — or on a PGCE course, not ever. No health records, no pension records, no driving licence, anything.'

Fran frowned. 'But there was nothing about her record at the school or at this one to suggest she wasn't qualified? I mean, poor results, poor discipline, that sort of thing? After all, she was notably successful at improving Great Hogben Primary.'

'Especially the fabric, apparently. She got all sorts of grants no one had ever heard of, and it became the go-to school for all the middle-class parents. But essentially she kept it as a village school for local people. People still speak of her as an ideal head.'

'So what was her name before all this?' Fran asked sharply. 'Come now, you've had time, budget or no budget, to check that.' She got up, looking at her watch. 'A complete CV, including her birth weight, by this time tomorrow. Is that understood?' She swept out. It was ordinary, basic, probationer-level police work, and it hadn't been done.

Perhaps it was her anger that brought a name to mind. Bruce Farfrae, the husband of a woman she'd once played badminton with. He'd once been a cop, but now he was flying solo, in the lucrative world of antiques. She had an idea he lived out in Kent, despite working for the Met. But a quick check on the Internet showed a New York business address. Nonetheless, he might be worth asking for advice about the impenetrable cabinet. She dashed off an email.

And now to join members of Don's team for the Bridge corpse's PM. Happy days.

* * *

'Only one call made on this, sir — and that was to DCS Harman's number. I don't know how the thief got hold of that.' The geek handed back Mark's mobile, but he was clearly still anxious.

'She gave him her business card. I was overreacting, Stu — and possibly so was Fran. Someone picked up my phone by mistake, but she's always keen on a bit of belt and braces — that's why she contacted you and had all use stopped.'

'I'd say she was right, sir, though no harm was done. Not with your password.'

Mark felt the floor shift beneath his feet. Caffy would have forbidden the use of *literally*, but that was what it felt like — being in an earth tremor. They'd had one in Kent some five or six years back, which had done a lot of damage in Dover and Folkestone, and he'd not forgotten the weird experience.

'And did this person try to break it?' he asked, dry-mouthed.

'Only the most amateur attempt.' Stu's face relaxed. 'It's this mixture of letters — upper and lower case — and numerals that stopped him. Something like your birthday or wedding day anyone serious would have cracked, sure as God made little green apples.'

Mark was just going to reply he couldn't have done, since the wedding day wasn't set yet — but then he remembered with a pang that Stu meant his first wedding. To Tina, Dave's mother. And now Dave was trying to hack into his phone. No, he was just trying to get Fran's number. Surely. Nothing sinister.

Safe in his office again, he covered his face with his hands. Was it all his fault that he had a crazy daughter and an even crazier son? It was certainly his fault that he'd never learned to communicate with them. If only he could have his time again — if only he could somehow make amends by being a wonderful grandfather. But he suspected the latter was as impossible as the former.

CHAPTER SIXTEEN

In the shower — she always needed one, no matter how clinical the surroundings and indeed the whole business of a post-mortem — Fran pondered anew the frailty of life. All her tears might have been shed yesterday — and she still couldn't believe her lack of control — but she worried herself when she found herself speculating on what might have continued but for a well-placed knife. And then she told herself off, more comprehensively than if she'd been a rookie, throwing up over her first corpse. By Cynd's account this was a rapist. And Jill at least believed her; maybe she herself did too. So what would Cynd's story be now they had a body to check it against? Assuming they could find Cynd, of course.

She sailed into the briefing room to catch DCI Don Simpson in full rant: Cynd was still missing. Arms folded, she stood quietly by the door, letting him get on with it. Losing a self-confessed killer wasn't good policing, was it? And the press would love it.

Where on earth was Jill? There was no sign of her. No text, missing a vital meeting — that wasn't like Jill, since her illness the most efficient of officers. But she didn't like to ask publicly. After all, she herself had been a tad late — had she missed something Don might have said?

Meanwhile, there was other information to absorb, mostly about trying to ID the dead man. Given that the evidence on the ground suggested he'd been carried to where he was found, Don had decided to check on what vehicles might have driven him to the point in the woodland where the little procession must have started. There were recent tyre tracks from a large van. CCTV from Canterbury Ring Road had shown up several white vans — cue derisory cheers from the team — heading in the right direction at the right time. Several? Several hundred, more like. And it had fallen to the lot of two of the team to chase up each number plate and check ownership details. That was still ongoing.

Poor sods. Fran had carried out similar eye-watering tasks in her time, though by the time CCTV had become so universal she'd been promoted beyond having to carry out that particular menial but vital role.

Others in the team were going through all the mugshots of the drivers and front passengers, using all the magic of digital enhancement, which managed to produce usable material from the grainiest of shots. The clever computer then matched the faces to faces on file — how on earth had they managed without? But although the technology delighted and amazed Fran in equal measure, so far it had come up with little that was useful. Early days yet, however.

Some more of the team were interviewing members of known gangs. Everything was going smoothly, it seemed, except that there was no DNA match on record for the young man, which would have helped everyone a very great deal.

As for Cynd, Jill had at least acted on Fran's information that the girl had been to Maidstone. CCTV from a number of shops showed her drifting round, in the time-honoured manner of someone about to shoplift. Naturally, the cameras followed her. But she left, apparently clean, until she reached House of Fraser. Here several items disappeared into that ultra-large bag. But then, possibly to the chagrin of the store security staff, and certainly to the surprise of the officers and her colleagues, Cynd retired to a corner — presumably she thought she couldn't be seen there — and fished everything out that she'd taken, carrying bras and briefs as if she might be about to take them to a till. She didn't. Haphazardly, it seemed, she wandered back to the rails she had robbed, replacing every last thing. Janie would have been proud of her. The images, grainy and jerky though they were, showed a tenacity of purpose Fran would never have expected.

She wasn't quite so virtuous at the station, Maidstone East. Footage showed her rooting around in the scurf of dropped tickets and gleaning one that got her on to the platform. She disappeared finally on a Canterbury bound train. She was tracked back from Canterbury West to the vicarage, talking to various people en route — but there was no sign of any drug deal going down, not involving her at least.

There was other footage, but not much. Someone with a hoodie pulled down so far that it denied the cameras a chance of picking out any detectable feature turned up at the vicarage, but stayed only a minute or so. Whoever he spoke to was invisible. Several others of Janie's waif and stray brigade made similar visits, some staying longer, some less. Cynd didn't seem to leave the vicarage at all, until she walked briskly with Janie to yesterday's morning service — the one Fran and Mark had missed.

And she duly headed back. And that was the last they saw of her. There were some good shots of Jill approaching the vicarage, just as Janie had described. Nothing of Cynd. At all. From any angle. Anywhere.

Someone had to ask the obvious question, so Fran did. 'Has anyone checked the vicarage itself? Attic to cellar search?'

'According to Jill, with Janie's permission and help. She said she was as puzzled as Jill was. And very upset.'

'And Jill is—?'

'In court, ma'am. That Chartham Hatch domestic violence case.'

She clicked her fingers in irritation. 'Of course.' Before she could continue, her pager announced its malevolent presence. 'Looks as if I'm late for a meeting. Sorry. Don — let me know of any developments, won't you? And let me know if you need more resources. I'll find them somehow.' She hoped.

An interview with the team investigating Simon Gates' death was the last thing she wanted, partly because she was dreading letting herself down with another outburst of emotion. But the grey familiarity of the room kept her in check. The questions were routine to the point of prosaic. She was about to flare at them that they were talking about a human being, before it dawned on her that Simon would have conducted a similar enquiry in an identical way.

Somehow, although that silenced her, it failed to cheer her.

* * *

Mark, on the other hand, looked almost pleased with himself as, armed with a couple of carriers with plunder from Sainsbury's, they arrived back at the rectory, which was still festooned with two rival sets of plastic tape. He said nothing until they'd eaten Fran's new speciality, prawn risotto, featuring some fine organic courgettes.

'From our own vegetable patch next year,' she promised as they cleared their plates.

'So long as both teams have finished by then. Meanwhile, I've been busy in another way. I had to escort Wren round some of our outposts today, and, once I'd dropped him off, I took the chance of nipping into Loose.'

'You've been to see her? Sammie? Well done!' Fran leaned across the doll's house table to chink wine glasses with him.

'We shall see. But at least we managed to speak, not least because the kids ran up to me. I was carrying a bunch of balloons at the time,' he said, half-apologetically. 'She didn't invite me in, because she said the place was a mess — well, with two toddlers, I suppose it must be. And I think she's pregnant. Which means there's a man in the picture.'

'Wow! With powers of deduction like that you might be a policeman. Could we go one further and suspect that she's back with Lloyd?'

'Or that she's found another guy? How can we tell?'

He could have asked, she thought. But she stayed shtum.

'Would the bulge be somehow different?' His laugh was bitter. 'Whichever, it means throwing her out is more problematical. No?'

'Not when your solicitor is involved. Mark, where are you on this? The same planet as the rest of us? People can't just completely ignore a solicitor's letter. OK, I know she wrote back. But Ms Rottweiler said her letter wasn't worth the paper it was written on.'

'She's my own flesh and blood—' he began. 'Hang on, what are you doing?'

'Getting my coat. I'm going for a walk. I've tried to keep the lowest of profiles in any dealings with your children, but I'm about to lose my temper. I really am. So I'll go and walk till I'm calm. OK?' She grabbed her bag and fished out a torch. 'See you later.'

She half expected him to protest — even run after her. In her exasperation, she didn't want him to, lest she said things that shouldn't be said after one of the most frustrating days she'd had at work in years. Certainly, she wanted to shake some sense into him, but only when she was calm to start with and wouldn't lose her temper completely. My God, what if she burst into tears again?

To her surprise the pub was in darkness. Perhaps there wasn't enough trade on a Monday to justify opening. But lights were on in the village hall. She moved closer. She might have told herself that this was the country and solitary walks in the dark were safe, but the lack of streetlights in the village was unnerving. An outside light shone on a blackboard, with the information — hard to pick out even with her torch — that there was a Gardener's Club meeting tonight. Mentally, she corrected the apostrophe. Even as she did so, however, an idea formed. She opened the door and slid into the back of the room.

Someone wearing a caricature of a patched tweed jacket was packing away a venerable slide projector, the sort Moses might have used to show views of Mount Ararat. A woman who was as svelte as if she'd stepped out of her office at a bank was dispensing tea to a knot of people in their middle to later years. There were more of the latter, one couple very old indeed. At last a small but very erect man with the air of having been in one of the armed services noticed Fran and marched towards her, greeting her with a smile and a hearty pump of the hand. 'Bill Baker,' he said.

Her gaffe in the pub still hot in her mind, she produced her most disarming smile. 'I'm afraid this time I'm not hear to learn about slug control and hostas: I need to pick everyone's brains about a far more serious matter.'

'Ah, you'll be that policewoman then.' He spoke loudly enough to penetrate the rattle of cups and rumble of voices. The room fell unnaturally silent.

Fran stepped forward. 'Good evening, everyone. As a neighbour, I'm Fran Harman, soon to be Fran Turner. Tonight, I'm Detective Chief Superintendent Harman, in charge of the investigation into the death of a man called Francis or Frank Grange. Yes, we've identified the skeleton found in our bean row. I don't know if Dr Lovage ever won your produce competitions, but her runner beans must have been magnificent, with all that nitrogen.'

This time she seemed to have hit the right note: murmurs of amusement and interest seemed to be stronger than mutters of dissent. But she was sure someone whispered to someone else, 'We did tell her she needed a trench — fill it with newspaper and such.'

'Not that sort of "such" though,' Fran observed. 'To be honest with you, some of my colleagues would rather wrap up the case by saying it's clear that Dr Lovage killed Grange in cold blood and buried him. That may be the case, but — let's say anyone living in that beautiful house, amongst the lovely furniture we've found in store, isn't necessarily my first image of a cold-blooded murderer. Aerial views provide evidence of wonderful gardens too. Was she a member here? And if so, did any of you know her? I want to build up a full picture of a woman whose interest in badgers makes her sound a bit of an eccentric, to be honest. But eccentrics don't make wonderful head-teachers.' She'd dropped her voice so that she sounded almost confiding, a tactic that always worked well in brainstorming meetings. 'And wonderful head-teachers don't usually kill people.'

Bill pushed forward a chair. 'Why don't we all take the weight off our feet and see if we can help?'

The chic woman spoke up. 'Someone was saying you suspected us of engaging in some conspiracy to kill this man Grainger or whatever.'

'I would like to say quite categorically that nothing could be further from my mind at the moment. I don't expect anyone to incriminate him or herself — though if anyone steps forward to confess, then obviously I'll be interested. But all I really want is a mental picture of Dr Lovage. At this stage, I don't have a notebook with me, let alone a warrant card,' she added, needing now to be scrupulously honest. She sat down.

One or two others did the same, but it was clear there wasn't universal trust. She fished her mobile out of her pocket. 'Actually, there's a matter here I should deal with,' she said. 'Where's your best coverage?'

There was some laughter. 'Ladies' loo,' came a voice. Male.

What she wanted to do in fact was text Mark, so he'd know she was safe. Being angry with him was one thing; making him worry unnecessarily about her safety was another. As a bonus, her time away from the others would give them time to make a collective decision, which she thought, with Bill's leadership, would be to stay and help her.

'Since you don't have anything to write on,' Bill said when she returned, 'we thought our secretary might minute what we say. If that's acceptable to you? She says she should have the notes written up by Thursday.'

And today was Monday. But Fran nodded. After all, the secretary would almost certainly want to show what she'd written to the other members, so they were happy with her record. The session began. 'Let's start with my phone number, in case any of you recall anything after this meeting . . .'

* * *

'When I had my mini-breakdown,' Fran said carefully as she poured Mark another small tot, 'the shrink said to write down my decisions and seal them in an envelope so I didn't waste energy going over and over the alternatives. That was the only way I could get any sleep and the only way to get things done. I know you're not having a breakdown, but you've got so much on your plate I wonder if that technique would work with you.'

Mark nodded miserably. Fran had never walked out on him before, and he was still trembling with a mixture of fury and anxiety. However much he might want to yell at her that since she'd never had children she couldn't understand his dilemmas, he had to admit that recently he'd become Mr Indecisive — hell, even their present accommodation came courtesy of Caffy's good offices and the kindness of some superannuated pop star he'd barely heard of. He managed a thin smile. 'I've half a mind to go on a decision-making course.'

'Quite.' Her voice was dry, almost unsympathetic.

He should have said something else, something more important. He hoped it wasn't too late. 'I didn't know you'd had a breakdown. You never mentioned it.'

'I didn't sing it from the rooftops. It probably went down on my record as compassionate leave to look after sick parents. Cosmo Dix always was imaginative in such matters, and he didn't think mental health problems were popular in the service. I took a few pills, but better still had psychotherapy. So I gave up the pills and was back to work within four weeks. If I'd had any sense I'd have said one of my parents had had a stroke and then taken a few more weeks off, but I never was like that.'

Humbly, he asked, 'Was that when you were doing half of my job, as well as yours?'

'When Tina was ill? No. Earlier. You remember that badminton player? Anyway, I'm better now. But I'm worried about you. At the risk of starting yet another hare, have you thought about family counselling? The three of you together?'

'More talk? We studied a play at A-level, and one of the characters said something like, "*You don't get money back on a broken bottle.*" And I think that's what I should be saying about Sammie and Dave. I've left a message on Ms Rottweiler's phone by the way, telling her to send another letter saying that if Sammie isn't out of the house within seven days she'll send in the bailiffs. As for Dave, I don't want to make a song and dance about it. He might just have been trying to phone you. Let's see what transpires and only worry about it then. Hey, what are you doing?'

'Looking for a bit of paper for you. I don't think this place runs to envelopes, but I've got the back of a shopping list somewhere.'

He laughed, but took the slip of paper and ballpoint she dug out of her bag. As he wrote, he said, 'And since we've thoroughly broken our *no shop talk* rule, you can tell me what you got up to at the village hall.'

She pulled a face. 'For a start, I put all my cards on the table this time, and it was a good job I did, because there's a rumour going round that I'm out to nail the whole village for the killing. And they insisted on minuting everything that was said. A plump little woman with the most amazing shorthand speeds took down everything verbatim, as far as I could see. No, no whisky for me, thanks. There's a drop of white wine in the fridge needs finishing off.'

He still had difficulty working out which immaculate cupboard door concealed what, but eventually he ran the New Zealand Sauvignon Blanc to earth and even found one of Todd Dawes' elegant wine glasses before taking his place beside her. They'd agonized about using them, until Caffy had blithely assured them that Todd's wife had bought six dozen of everything when they'd fitted out the Winnebago, on the grounds that things would get broken and need to be replaced without messing up a set. They weren't even into their second dozen yet, Caffy said.

'Marion didn't like talking about the past. They all agreed on that. In fact, someone said she'd been in a serious accident that had affected her memory. They all agreed she'd been to uni as a mature student on the back of a successful career in something quite different. They said she'd got plenty of money — well, to buy this place outright she'd need it.'

'Outright? Wow. Some success!'

'Some of them also reckoned that although she said she'd found charities to fund improvements at the school, she'd actually dug in her own pocket. She went to church, helped at the fête, declined to run the Sunday School on the grounds she saw enough of the kids every day, and toyed with singing in the choir, but decided her voice wasn't up to it — apparently, she found that particularly upsetting. On the other hand, someone else said he thought Marion had found the *singing* upsetting, so made the lack of voice an excuse for not going to any other choir practices.'

'Interesting, that. Any family, any bloke?'

She squeezed his hand. 'You old romantic, you. One of the old guys — he still has a gleam in his eye if you ask me — said she was very, very attractive but not sexy. For all her good looks, she never had that spark. Whatever that is.'

'Look in the mirror. Anything else?' He inspected the bottom of his whisky glass but decided against any more.

'Apparently, she once mentioned a sister, but there were no photos anywhere in the house. Some good paintings, but the sort you buy, not inherit, someone said. I think I get that. Possibly. No one knows what happened to them when she left.'

'Do they know where she went? Was she in a hurry?'

'Measured, someone said. Purposeful. As if she'd made her mind up. No one could get any sort of reason from her, except possibly she might be going to stay with her sister, and she promised to send a forwarding address but she never did. That upset a lot of them. They thought she was a friend, and friends don't behave like that. They didn't even know she was dead until the sign went up outside the rectory and they asked at the estate agents.'

'Perhaps she knew she was ill and didn't want to dwindle in front of them.'

'Maybe. I don't think Kim and her team have even got hold of her death certificate yet. I'm seriously worried about that woman — Kim, I mean. She's letting the team slack. Probably my fault for overriding her a couple of times.'

'Or maybe she's just not got the hang of leadership yet. Not everything's your fault, Fran, though I know you like to take the blame. Look — I'm sorry, but I'm so weary I can't stay awake any longer.' Nor did he want to. He just wanted to put a full stop to the whole vile day.

CHAPTER SEVENTEEN

Fran and Mark had just finished breakfast — which in their borrowed palace involved stowing of used items in what they presumed was a state-of-the-art mini-dishwasher, more economical with water than conventional washing up, according to Caffy, who strolled by with a friendly wave that brought them to their front door.

The stable half open, the bottom half to lean on, they felt like Toad's friends, ready for the open road.

'Much hope of that, I suppose,' Caffy said, when Fran confided their fantasy. 'But the good news is that our Sparks has got hold of some more cable and should be starting soon. He's been doing emergency work down in Ashford after that huge robbery. Tell me, why didn't the criminals fry themselves alive? I'd have thought stealing from a substation was a fairly risky enterprise. And why don't they get squashed like so many flies when they nick stuff from railways?'

'Good questions,' Fran said cautiously. It was, after all, one of the many points that had been made by the joint police-transport police team — that inside knowledge was involved. You couldn't nick fifty million pounds' worth from Railtrack alone without knowing more than Joe Average. But she had other investigations in hand. 'Caffy, between you and

Paula you must know everyone in the restoration business. Do you know any antiques restorers? People who'd know how to take pieces apart as well as gluing them together? Work,' she added, as if Caffy wouldn't know. 'We've got a cabinet we can't get into, and I don't want it smashed as we try to persuade it to give up its secrets.'

'Old?'

'Older than the house I'd say. Much fancier, at least.'

'Did you say "smashed"?'

'Pretty well had to stop one of my officers taking a hatchet to it.'

'Hell.' At last Caffy's frown cleared into a hesitant smile. 'Do you do unconventional? In the police, I mean? Oh, I suppose you used that detectorist instead of giving what they call on TV a fingertip examination. That's quite left-field.'

'Ask the ACC (Crime),' Fran said with a grin and a jerk of the thumb.

'The ACC (Crime),' Mark said, 'says cheap and cheerful — but an expert. Actually, possibly not an accredited safe-breaker.'

'Fee?'

'Professional expenses,' he temporized.

'Whatever those might be when they're at home. I do know of someone — really an antiques dealer. Tripp and Townend. But also a bit of a "divvy". Like a water diviner.' She mimed a fork-shaped stick.

They exchanged a sceptical glance. 'Have you got their details handy?' Fran asked, aware that, no matter how pleasant the conversation, she ought to be heading into Maidstone. She also knew she'd do it with a lighter heart — there was something about Caffy that made you smile after any time in her company.

'Nope. But I'll email you as and when.'

'The sooner the better,' Fran said. 'I don't know how long I'll be able to keep the people with hatchets away.'

Caffy narrowed her eyes. 'Don't tell me it's DI Thomas who's the potential vandal. Now why aren't I surprised?'

Mark smiled uneasily. 'Maybe if you just keep it to yourself, Caffy — we don't want to escalate the tension between her and Paula.' He nodded at the plastic tape. 'In fact, now you've made your point, I don't suppose that stuff of yours could come down?'

'Actually no, however much it might lead to a welcome détente. The dear old Elf and Safety folk . . . And I'm sure your blue and white tape's a legal requirement too? Even if it's ugly and looks petty, Mark, think on the bright side — it designates the boundaries of the warring factions.' Turning, she blew them a kiss and headed for the rectory. Fran could have sworn it opened its arms to her in welcome.

Today, since both had meetings scheduled — in theory — to end at the same time, they could share a car: now official money-saving policy, and an economy they'd always practised anyway. Fran drove; for once, Mark, stowing the paperwork he usually perused while he was being driven, allowed himself to sit back and stare at the countryside. 'If I could find some occupation,' he mused, 'to keep me sane, the R option doesn't seem so bad on a morning like this. I know, I know: on a cold, wet, dreary day, when the sun never appears and the cold eats into your joints, I might long for a desk in a centrally heated office. But think of that lump sum. Think of that pension.'

'Think of the drop in your blood pressure; think of the long walks to shift your cholesterol. Or do they fix your blood pressure? Whatever. The trouble is, after more than thirty continuous years in one institution, it's so hard to think of a non-institutional life. I'm terrified, you know. Even if it's a life shared with you,' she admitted in a whisper.

He reached for her hand and squeezed it briefly. 'Two scaredy-cats together. But let's give it some thought, some positive thought, once this crisis is over.' His mobile told him he had a text. 'Just think, no more being summoned by bells before seven thirty . . . Tell me,' he added, fishing the mobile out of his pocket, 'is it usual for people like Caffy to start work so early?'

'I can't think of a single thing that's usual about Caffy. Paula says she always arrives early — takes on the role of site manager to check in the day's first deliveries, and so on. She brews her coffee and reads in the quiet periods.'

'I wonder if she can read text-speak. This one's gibberish . . .'

* * *

Fran was girding herself to do battle with Kim Thomas and her team when Alice popped her head round her door.

'I'm not sure you want to hear this, Fran, but Kim's stuck on the M20. A lorry's hit the bridge where the M26 splits off. She was in the middle lane when the accident happened and hasn't been able to move for an hour. She wants to know if the briefing can be delayed till she returns.'

Kim was useful, of course, but hardly indispensable, surely. Even though they still lacked a DCI, surely the rest of the team could manage to give Fran an account of their activities to date without her?

'It's not just her, Fran,' Alice continued. 'It's DS Harding, DC Rains and DC Bowden as well. Car-sharing, in line with the new diktat.'

Fran managed not to raise her eyebrows at Alice's tone. What had annoyed such a gentle soul?

'Unless she's set up a video link in her car, I suppose it'll have to be. Thanks, Alice. Hey, I wonder why she called you, not me.'

'She did call your landline, Fran — I just fielded the call. I called Traffic, by the way. It's bad. Dead driver, probably Eastern European. His cab's wedged into solid concrete. They need engineers to assess any possible damage to the bridge. And they think it'll be up to five hours before the tailback can be cleared.'

'Shit and double shit. Very well, Alice, let's work on my in-tray, shall we? See how much we can bin and how much we should file. But maybe a cup of tea apiece while we do it . . .'

'. . . Amazing,' said Fran, an hour later, 'how much paper this so-called paper-free communication generates. Do we really need to download all these emails? I really think another memo is due. No?' She shot Alice a sideways glance.

'I think the secretariat are memoed out, to be honest, Fran. And it'd mean yet more paper.'

'So it would. In that case I'll have a word with the IT people — they could just add a line to every single incoming and outgoing email saying, "*Please don't print me*," or words to that effect. Better still, why not have a word with Sally and get her to help the new chief to have the idea? It'd suit his ideas of economy and benefit the environment.'

'Which were you thinking of — your office environment or the big wide world out there?'

'Many a mickle makes a muckle, as someone used to say. Let's play another game, Alice. Let's imagine I'm a detective and I have some detecting to do. But it has to be this side of the motorway — and as far away from all the A-road chaos the diversions will have caused.'

'Can I come too?'

'You know, I really don't see why not. How can you do your job without knowing what people the other side of the desk do? I'll clear it with the secretariat, and we'll have a trip to the country.'

* * *

'You have to stop harassing her. She'll get an injunction, she says.' Dave's voice was more than loud enough for other people in the reception area to hear every word.

Mark stared. It was bad enough for Dave to turn up again and summon him from a meeting, but now he was talking nonsense. Quickly, he ushered him into an interview room.

'Has Sammie said I'm harassing her? In what way?'

'Turning up unannounced and uninvited.'

'And carrying a bunch of balloons for my grandchildren. That's harassment, is it? Dave, does this make sense to you?' Mark sat heavily on a chair, conscious that while he really did not want to conduct family business in a room so small it hardly merited the description, he was even less keen on having Dave in his office. 'I'd really welcome your input, son. Especially as whatever I do is wrong,' he added ruefully. As Dave drew breath, he continued, 'If I tell her to have the whole house and be damned, what happens to all my personal stuff? And Fran's? And, of course, yours. We always kept your bedroom for you, you know, with all your treasures just where you wanted them. Your swimming cups, the football trophies.'

Dave looked embarrassed, but managed to ask, 'The model railway layout?'

'Do you really expect we'd touch that? After all the hours we spent organizing it?' Or was it fewer than he thought? 'All the engines are still safe and sound in the round house your auntie Meg gave you that snowy Christmas. Hell, do you remember how cold it was in that loft?'

Dave smiled slowly. 'It was freezing up there, wasn't it, but we still drove all the locos in, one by one. You must have cursed me.'

'Only because you'd had measles or something and your mum was worried about you catching your death. Didn't I tie a hot-water bottle on your back?'

'Don't remember that. I just remember being cold. My hands were so cold it was hard to fit the locos on the track.'

Mark risked one more push. 'You see, it's not just half of *my* life that's in that house. It's half of yours. Have you been in there yet?' he asked at last.

Dave drew breath again, but exhaled slowly. At last he said slowly, 'I almost believe you. I'm this far from it.' He held thumb and finger a millimetre apart. 'But then, I believed what Sammie was saying. I'll go see her again, I guess. This time I'll insist we meet at the house, whatever she says. I'll try to talk to Lloyd, too.'

Mark could hardly believe his ears. 'You will? Dave, what can I say?'

But Dave was on his feet. 'I guess you'll have plenty of time to work that out.'

* * *

Fran thought that breaking pretty well every rule in the book was worth it just to see the expression on Alice's face as they left the building. Their first port of call was the vicarage that had replaced their rectory as the incumbent's abode. It was a smallish, detached sixties house, with a flat-roofed garage alongside. The big windows probably made it hell to heat. The garden seemed to be given over to vegetables — presumably, he encouraged his runner beans in a different way from Marion Lovage.

'The Reverend Peter Bulleid,' Fran said, deciphering the tiny scrap of paper crumpled into the slot in the electric bell-push. 'How do I address him, Alice?'

'Plain Mister, I think. Is he related to the railway engineer?'

'Railway engineer?'

'He designed locomotives. My brother's a railway buff,' she explained, almost apologetically, pressing the doorbell again. 'You know, I don't think there's anyone at home.'

'He's deaf,' Fran said, inclined to be dismissive of such frailty, but remembering with a pang that Mark's hearing was no longer as acute as it should be. Lesson one for those contemplating retirement, she told herself: don't sneer at age-related problems. Reaching for a business card to pop through the letters flap, she printed a request to contact her about Marion Lovage on the back. No one could say she wasn't being upfront this time.

Or when she called at the back door of the Three Tuns. She greeted Ollie with a flash of her ID and a clear introduction to Alice, specifying that she wasn't an officer but was a colleague with experience in dealing with the elderly. Alice turned not so much as a hair at Fran's lie — perhaps she considered her job gave her the requisite skills and patience. 'How would you feel about us talking to your father?' Fran asked. 'There's no reason why you shouldn't be present. We just want his memories of Dr Lovage, that's all.'

'I'll phone my mum,' Ollie said, digging in his pocket for his phone and walking towards a stack of logs. 'Signal's best here,' he said over his shoulder.

Alice turned to face the sun, as if warmth on her face was a new experience. 'This is such a treat, Fran. Takes your mind off redundancy, at least.'

'Redundancy? You? Over my dead body, Alice.'

'It's just a general warning as yet. But — you know what — if I had a halfway decent deal offered I might take it. A lot of us would. I know you officers deal with dreadful stuff face to face, but we get the fallout, if you see what I mean. And maybe I'm young enough to retrain.'

'As?'

'God knows, to be frank. What can women do these days? Go to uni? End up with a debt like a millstone and a job in a bar instead of at the Bar?'

'Quite.' And there she had the luxury of making a choice. At the moment, at least.

Ollie sauntered back, but he was shaking his head. 'According to Mum, he doesn't know his arse from his elbow today. But if you like I can give her your number so she can call you when he's a bit more with us.'

Fran handed over her card. 'We'll be there if we can. Thanks. We don't want to distress him, you know, or your mother. Actually, wouldn't your mother have known Dr Lovage as well as, if not better than, your father? WI and church flowers and so on?'

Ollie blinked. 'Good point. Never thought of that.' Without being asked, he returned to the log-stack. He was back almost immediately. 'He's just shat himself. Don't worry, I'll give her your number when it's a better time.'

They walked back to Fran's car in silence.

'Is police work always like this? A series of no-shows?' Alice asked.

‘All too often. That’s why we usually send a PC — cheaper. But to be honest, I was bored out of my skull and I thought you were looking a bit peaky . . . Is it just the threat of redundancy or—?’

‘I’m fine, Fran. Just the usual things. Money; food; school uniforms. We didn’t manage a holiday, that was a problem — and I suppose on a day like this you want to skive. So this has been great. Even if we didn’t achieve anything.’

Fran looked at her watch. ‘Ollie doesn’t do midday food, but I bet we can find a place that does. My treat. Come on.’

CHAPTER EIGHTEEN

A flurry of texts and emails, ably assisted by the wasps that bombarded their rickety table, drew their lunch to an end. So much for their rural idyll.

The most interesting message was from Kim, who'd used her M20 imprisonment to good effect and organized a slot on the evening's local TV news to appeal for information about Frank Grange's last known activities. The programme, she added, probably wouldn't allow them enough time to ask about Dr Lovage, but she'd do her best to talk them into it. Did Fran have any preferences for an officer to front the piece?

Which was a tactful way of asking if Fran wanted to do it herself, of course.

Y not U? Fran texted back. *Go 4 it.* Then she added a stream of instructions about setting up a team to answer what she hoped would be a deluge of responses, though she suspected at best there'd be no more than a thin trickle. But she did worry that the dead case should take precedence over one that was very much alive, and so, using the hands-free phone, she called Don to ask how things were moving.

'Still no ID on our victim; still no sighting of the alleged killer, Cynd.'

'Do you think it's time to find some funds for facial reconstruction people? So we can get the public at large involved? Someone must know his face, for goodness' sake.'

'Ma'am, has anyone ever told you you're an angel?'

'You'd better wait to see how much I can find before you ask that.'

She'd barely sat down at her much tidier desk than there was a call from reception. Someone described doubtfully as a young person was asking for her by name. Cynd! It must be Cynd! Should she call for backup to make sure Cynd didn't get away? But she didn't want her scared by a sudden inrush of officers, intent — rightly — on arresting her. So she hurtled down the corridors, bouncing down the stairs in case the delay would so put Cynd off that she stomped away.

It wasn't Cynd, however. It was another young woman, dressed in a retro summer's dress, which looked as if it was genuine fifties, not this season's *homage*. She greeted Fran with confidence, shaking hands firmly and with the sort of smile that suggested that she could help Fran, and not vice versa.

'Lina Townend, of Tripp and Townend, Antiques,' she said, producing a business card. 'I'm the divvy — the diviner — that Caffy said you wanted,' she added.

'Well I'm blowed,' Fran declared. 'I was expecting—' And perhaps should have waited for Bruce Farfrae to contact her.

'A tweedy old man with a shock of white hair and an overused twig? Sorry. Even my partner, Griff Tripp, doesn't look like that. Now,' she continued with the air of someone for whom time was money, 'I understand you have some furniture you can't open and that someone wants to force.'

'It's in our evidence store. There's a procedure to ID you and put you through security. I can't pretend it's anything other than tedious, but I'm sure you understand.'

'Of course. I've got a couple of friends who are police officers — DCI Webb, whom you probably know. I'm sure Freya'll vouch for me, though she's on maternity leave. And then there's DCI Morris, once of the Met but currently on secondment to Interpol,' she added with a slight change of voice that made Fran wonder about the backstory. 'And I believe that you know Bruce Farfrae, though he's left the police and is busily coining money in the US. He emailed me last night to ask if I could help you; he sends his apologies for not getting back to you earlier, but he was on his way back from Afghanistan — antiquities thefts.'

Fran was horribly aware that she was letting the conversation run away from her. She grasped at part of it as she led the girl out of reception into the body of the building. 'Tell me how Freya is,' she said. 'And then I must find a photographer and someone from the team investigating the case this is relevant to.' She paused, embarrassed. 'Do you need special equipment or anything? A darkened room?'

The girl threw her head back and laughed. 'It's not witchcraft, Ms Harman. Sometimes it's easier if I sit quietly on my own, but I'm not into what my partner calls jiggery-pokery.'

'Come and sit in the office the secretaries use: they can organize a cup of tea while I deal with the formalities.'

* * *

Wren sat — dared Mark allow himself to use the word *perched*? — behind a vast new desk, which suggested a permanence about his appointment that made Mark suddenly and quite deeply resentful, as if he'd been usurped, and hadn't flatly declined the offer of temporary upgrading for himself. As for a chair for Mark himself, there was no sign of one.

Wren was tapping something — a small sheaf of papers — on his desk. Mark had an idea that the finger doing the tapping had been manicured. Fran would have asked reasonably why it shouldn't have been; Mark merely found it something else to loathe.

But not as much as being kept standing like a naughty schoolboy. He looked round for a chair and dragged it forward, sitting and ostentatiously crossing his legs and then, as Wren raised an eyebrow in his direction, his arms. 'You sent for me, sir?' he asked, not quite insolently.

The finger moved to the TV remote. 'This is not a good situation, Turner. Deal with it.' Wren seemed to signal that the interview was over by leaning forward and moving his mouse, eyes now fixed to the new computer screen.

'To what situation do you refer, sir?' But even as he framed the question as pedantically as he could, he knew — with an absolute certainty — that it must be something to do with Sammie, Dave and the house in Loose.

Wren pressed the zapper, clicking the mouse with the other hand. 'As I said, deal with it.' Not quite yawning with boredom, Wren picked up his mobile, not even bothering to look at the images he'd summoned up.

* * *

Kim was all bustle and stir, finding forms and documents Fran didn't know even existed — not bad for a woman who'd just arrived in the force. Ten out of ten for homework. She even wanted the Townend girl's prints and DNA, but received such a hostile look from the girl that she dropped the suggestion, coming up with protective clothing and gloves. 'Everything in here is covered by surveillance cameras,' she said. 'Do you want to come to the loo to change?'

Lina Townend flickered an ironic glance at Fran: this wasn't sitting quietly on her own, was it? At last she said, but with an amused edge to her voice, 'Just now I need peace and quiet. Could you clear the room? Ms Harman may stay.'

Kim huffed and puffed her way out.

'Such busyness.' Townend sighed. 'OK, let the dog see the rabbit. What do you want me to check first?'

Fran shrugged. 'You're in charge. But I'm most interested in that lovely desk and the very complicated cabinet. In particular, accessing the cabinet's compartments. And of course, we've no key.'

'Sometimes it's a matter of knowing where to look,' Townend said quietly. 'Sometimes,' she added more ominously, 'it's a matter of waiting for the piece to tell you what it wants you to know.'

Fran managed not to scream. Possibly because the young woman had been reassuringly professional so far, this sudden attack of feyness seemed all the worse. As quietly as she could she slipped out of the store and returned with two stacking chairs. They might not be Hepplewhite, but at least both she and Townend could listen to the other furniture in comfort. To assist even further, she switched off her mobile.

But Townend, now changed, despite the cameras, into her paper suit with her pretty little dress slung on one of Lovage's chairs, was already absorbed in conversation with the writing desk. Fran was about to point out they'd already had the main drawer out and found nothing at all, as if it had been thoroughly valeted, when as if from nowhere, Townend was flourishing a tiny key. From somewhere came the image of Alice in Wonderland. Had the Tenniel illustration had Alice on one knee? It certainly wouldn't have had her lying on her stomach and then on her back inspecting a desk.

'It's a very fine piece,' she declared. 'As I told you, I'm no expert when it comes to furniture, but I'd have thought you were looking at three or four thousand for this.' She came up to sitting position with an ease Fran envied. 'But I'm damned if I can find anywhere to fit this key.'

'But — didn't you bring the key with you?'

Townend laughed. 'Why would I do that? No, it was in the desk. In the drawer.'

'But my forensic colleagues . . .' Fran stopped. She didn't think this young woman would relish the words *practically took it to pieces* any more than Caffy would have done.

'Just didn't know where to look, that's all. I don't like to sound like some children's author talking about secret drawers, but often furniture has a drawer or cupboard within another in which to conceal especially precious items. Look, I'll show you.' Standing, she leant inside the drawer, putting her hand right to the back. 'Put your hand where mine was, reach up and press. There.' She beamed at Fran's startled face.

'Well, I'm blowed. Amazing. Thank you very much.'

'Don't thank me till I've done the rest of the job — and found what this little chap belongs to.' She waggled the key.

'I shall certainly thank you then.' As they started to strip the bubble wrap from Lovage's other pieces, she asked, 'Do you get asked to do this sort of thing very often?'

'This is the first time. Sometimes I get asked to tell an owner if a piece is genuine. Mostly I'm just a common or garden antiques dealer.'

Fran shook her head: there was nothing either common or garden about her. 'How can you tell if a piece is genuine?'

'How good's your hearing? Can you tell if someone's off-pitch? Because that's what it's like for me. First of all I know, then I look for reasons why I know. Does that make sense?'

'Possibly. I think coppers have an equivalent nose.'

'Good coppers,' Townend agreed darkly. 'Now, how about this chiffonier?'

'Why that?' Fran wanted to get on to the cabinet.

'Because if I'm right, we're part of a game of hide and seek. One piece will lead to another. And the chiffonier's got drawers and cupboards for concealing the next clue. Now, will our little key work on that lock?'

'Isn't that a bit of a long shot?'

'Not really, because at that period there weren't too many variants in keys — not so many Burglar Bills around, plus maybe the servants were afraid lightning would strike them if they nicked anything. Here you go.'

Fran took the tiny key and tried it in the drawer. It turned easily. 'Heavens, it might have been made for the lock.' Her face fell. The drawer was empty, even to Townend's experienced search. Likewise the cupboard underneath. 'But clearly it wasn't.' She waggled it in despair.

'But she wouldn't have concealed this key for nothing, would she?' Clearly, Townend was entering into the spirit of things. She flicked a smile at Fran. 'Deduction, of course — nothing to do with intuition or dowsing. Let's see if there's anything here — yes!' She turned the drawer over to reveal another key taped to the underside. 'Someone was enjoying this. Even misleading us, maybe.' She pointed to the key Fran was fingering resentfully. 'What was the name Bruce gave me? Dr Lovelace?'

'Not Lovelace. Lovage.'

'Right. Dr Lovage. Did he make a living setting crosswords or something?'

'She. She was a teacher when she lived round here. Caffy's probably told you we bought her old house.'

Townend shook her head. 'Caffy just told me that there was a job and that I should contact you. She's not one for gossip. Professional to her fingertips, as I'm sure you know.' Her sudden frown was almost forbidding. 'Anyway, let's move on to the next part of the puzzle. What does this little beauty fit?' She flourished the latest key.

* * *

In his situation, Mark would probably have been as annoyed as Wren had been: a TV news item putting your immediate second-in-command in a very poor light was the last thing you wanted when you were trying to feel your way into your post. With every journalistic cliché played for all it was worth, Mark was depicted as an arch villain, intent on evicting an innocent young woman, pregnant with his own grandchild, from her own home, while he basked at his ease in a sprawling Kentish mansion with a woman described as a live-in lover.

Unable to reach Fran — where the hell was she, with her phone switched off? — he called Ms Rottweiler, but could only leave a message. He was on the verge of calling Dave to demand to know his part in this travesty of the truth, when there was a knock on his door. His summons was peremptory, at very least, but Cosmo Dix, the strangest head of

Human Resources he'd ever met, but no less admired and held in affection for that, came in as if assured of a welcome.

'Darling Mark, I know, I know. And I know I'm not really PR, but the poor loves over there are all at sixes and sevens. Redundancies . . . Anyway, worry not: we can deal with this. Fire with fire, dear boy.'

Mark managed a laugh. 'I don't have so much as a box of matches.'

'Oh. Yes. You. Do. Heavens, I sound more like a pantomime dame with every breath I take.' He flapped a wrist, camply, drew up a chair, and became every inch a hard-boiled professional. 'I have press contacts, Mark, but so do you — and especially Fran. That reporter who was being stalked a while back — Dilly Pound, she of *TVInvicta News*. She owes Fran big time — it's not everyone who saves your life. Get her to do a counter piece, presenting you as the victim. Heavens, you're reduced to living in a caravan, for God's sake.'

'I'm not some hapless East European fruit-picker, though, Cosmo. I'm not living in a virtual shack. It's a veritable Blenheim Palace of a caravan.'

'Get it off site. Move a few things into a tiny corner of your rectory. Look thin and haggard, not a hint of uniform anywhere. Talk movingly of needing to pay the starving workers toiling away to restore a delightful example of bijou domestic architecture. Stress the retirement angle — tilling your fields. Oh, and there's your skeleton — but it might be better not to dwell on that. Or even mention it. Let me think about that. Come on, Mark, what are you waiting for? Get on that phone now. One, shift the caravan. Two, call la Pound. I'll be back anon.'

* * *

Fran knew she should have been doing a million other things, but she couldn't bear to tear herself away from the evidence store. All the main items of Lovage's furniture had now been unwrapped and the next key found. All but the cabinet.

There wasn't a visible keyhole, of course, as Kim and her colleagues had discovered.

'Don't say we've got to take it apart after all,' Fran breathed as Townend circled it, like a tiger kept from its goat by a strong fence.

'Absolutely not. Never. Not in the way your colleague would like.' Townend stood still, head slightly cocked, as if literally listening. For what?

At last Fran said, 'A friend of mine had a new car, big, sleek thing. He mastered the heating system, the music system, all those symbols and figures on the display that tell you you're about to land on Mars. But he couldn't work out how to fill the thing with petrol. There wasn't a lever inside, not that he could see, nor was there a keyhole on the flap covering the filler cap. One day — he was down to his last litre or two — he literally slapped the flap with frustration. And it opened, sweet as a nut.' Where had that come from? Nothing to do with Lovage though.

Townend beamed. 'I wonder if that's what we've got to do here. Go on, slap it. Very gently, mind you — you don't wallop sixteenth-century Italian cabinets as if they're dodgy drinks dispensers.'

'You mean I can help?'

'Why not? If you don't mind any of your colleagues thinking you're off your head.'

'They do already.' She waved to the surveillance cameras.

And started patting.

CHAPTER NINETEEN

'Where the fuck have you been?' Mark demanded as she practically skipped along the corridor. 'Doesn't matter! Turn round and keep walking.'

It was a long time since he'd spoken to her like that, and though he had every right to bollock her if she'd done wrong, these days rebukes felt personal, a threat to all she held precious. And for him to swear at her — she could only put that down to his hellish stress levels.

Once outside the building, she began, 'What's the problem? I've been—'

'I needed to find you urgently, and you'd disappeared from the face of the earth. Sammie's got us on the news. No time to swear. This is what Cosmo told me to do . . .'

She tried to take everything in. 'So you've got the Winnebago moved?'

'I even had to ask Sally to organize thank-you flowers and a bottle of fizz for Todd Dawes. Think of that. I've never had to ask her to do anything so menial before.'

'Where are we living, then?' she asked stupidly.

'I'm trying to explain. You know we talked about camping at the rectory — that's exactly what we're officially, and for tonight at least, doing. Caffy, who is next best thing to a white witch, has conjured from nowhere air beds and sleeping bags. We use the Pact team's cooking things and their loo. Caffy's also removed from the Winnebago all the clothes and toiletries — everything she thinks we'll need — and stowed them in the rectory. And we have to be on the road now, because Dilly's meeting us there — wants to go live on the six thirty local news. She's pulling all the strings she can, and meanwhile you're messing around somewhere or other with your sodding phone and pager off.'

Fortunately, he was walking so fast she didn't have breath to point out he could have asked Kim where she was. Or more likely Alice. Except she hadn't told Alice where she'd be . . . If he was angry, she was just as angry with herself. For someone at her level to be incommunicado was outrageous. For all she'd made progress this afternoon, she'd spent far longer with Lina Townend than she'd intended — or could truly justify.

Without asking, he threw the car keys at her. 'Put your foot down — but remember, being booked for speeding at this stage would not look good at all.'

'How did all this come about?' she asked coolly once they'd eased out of Maidstone — well below the speed limit, as it happened, given the volume of traffic — and hit the open road. Her absence was her fault, but at least it hadn't triggered a TV programme.

'Dave — I phoned him the moment I knew — insists it's nothing to do with him, although he admits he went to see Sammie. God, Fran, did I say "admits"? I make it sound like a breach of probation, not a young man going to see his sister. I rather think he may have told Sammie she was out of order behaving as she was, which seems to have pushed her further.'

'You've spoken to Ms Rottweiler?'

'Eventually. It took forever to get hold of her, but she's contacted Sammie and told her of the legal consequences of slandering me. Let's hope Sammie understands what that means.' He added, 'She offered to get a super injunction, but

I told her no — I know how you feel about hiding behind such things.'

'Absolutely.' She didn't ask how much all this would cost, and not just in terms of money, either.

'She's also emailed me a statement to read to Dilly — only, I have to make it sound spontaneous, unprepared. We're into damage limitation, but with luck it'll be a five-day wonder and die. Until then, I reckon we've got no option but to live the intolerable life I'm telling the great British public we already live.'

'No problem.' It was. Something deep inside her was revolted by the whole business, but now wasn't the moment for moral probing, either of herself or of Mark, who was so tense she was scared he might have a heart attack there and then. She thought it was best to stay shtum, concentrating instead on recalling all her pursuit driving skills, while equally trying to remember where the hidden speed cameras lurked.

At last slotting the car into the space left by the Winnebago — it was presumably Caffy who had done a bit of window dressing and organized a haphazard heap of pallets to cover one set of tyre marks — Fran followed Mark to the house.

Paula, arms crossed, greeted them with a slow smile. 'Welcome to your new abode. You're supposed to carry her across the threshold, Mark,' she began, but was swift to pick up the vibes that suggested Mark was more likely to sling her across it. 'We've not tidied up for the cameras; at least, not out here. One room looks as if it might be a bedroom — it's the one you said would be your dining room, eventually. Take a look.' She didn't offer to lead the way — obviously, her smile said, this is your place, not mine. But with a deep, ironic bow, she passed them hard hats. 'To be worn even in bed. Obviously.'

In silence they picked their way down the hall, which, while having a central pathway, had enough detritus along the margins to convince anyone that work was well and truly in progress. It wasn't until they were inside their new room, however, that Mark spoke — laughed, in fact. 'Why do I think Caffy had a hand in this?' He pointed to the row of books on the wonderful broad window-sill, which would one day be covered in cushions and become one of her favourite perches, with its view down the potential garden and actual crime scene. 'And those,' he added, pointing to the white plastic patio chairs that had once been outside near the Winnebago, but had now been wiped clean and placed one either side of a couple of packing cases with a door on top doing duty as a table. Sleeping bags lay on air beds in the far corner. 'You don't think she's over-egged the pudding? Get changed while you think about it — Cosmo wants us in total mufti for this. Humans, not police officers, if you get his drift.'

'Sure.' She stripped off the smart trouser suit she favoured on duty, grabbing jeans and a T-shirt. Presumably, it was Caffy who'd rigged up a scaffolding rail loaded with clothes on hangers — obviously, she'd just done a wholesale raid on the Winnebago. Even as she zipped the jeans she wondered what would have happened to Caffy if Paula hadn't recognized potential talent in the ex-prostitute and taken her into the original team of painters and decorators. She tucked her suit at the far end of the rail, easing Mark's fleece over the uniform he'd discarded for an outfit like hers, before she responded to his original question. 'Does the place look like us or a stage set for us?' she asked aloud. Now her mouth took over. 'How about some mugs on the table? I can't imagine you doing anything without your green tea to hand. And something else on the table? A lamp? Paperwork that suggests we slave till all hours?' To her ears, her voice sounded brittle, forced.

'Far too much egg.' But he managed a laugh as he looked at his watch. 'Five minutes to spare, I reckon.'

'A damned close-run thing.'

'It's not over yet. I've got to act my socks off, and acting's not my best suit.'

'Don't do yourself down. You deserve an Oscar for the way you play a doting and respectful acolyte to our acting chief. How did he take it, by the way, when you told him?'

'The trouble is, Fran, he told me. Showed me the clip, in fact. And you can imagine that he was not amused. Hell, I wouldn't be, if I was in his position.'

'Which you could have been,' she reminded him soberly.

'Quite. And I think I'd have had no option but to resign. As it is, it's touch and go, Fran, touch and go. But we'll talk about it later — let me just read through what Ms Rottweiler wants me to say. What's the matter?'

She turned from him, her voice now cracking. 'I can't do it. You can't do it. All our lives we've told the truth — think of all the times we've sworn to do that in court — and this is living, if not telling, a lie.'

'You're serious. Aren't you?'

'Yes. I know it's your interview, and I know it's your family, but — I'm sorry.'

He strode to the window, turning at last on his heel and staring at the room and at her in exasperation. She could hear the blood in her ears and throat.

Then she could hear his indrawn breath. 'Sod it all, you're right. Absolutely right. OK. Business as usual?'

'Not if you mean scrapping the interview. Get her to do it outside. Just as true. More honest.' It would have been more honest still if they'd left the Winnebago, but she could do nothing about that now.

* * *

'I'd love Sammie to have the house, if she needs it,' Mark declared, against the backdrop of their peeling front door. He clutched his hard hat like a talisman. 'But that means my son would miss out. When you're a parent, you want to be fair to everyone. So I'm thinking about not just my English grandchildren, but my US ones too. At the moment, the house is crammed with personal possessions — my son's are locked inside, too, and some of my fiancée's. I never wanted our dispute to come to this. Sammie, if you're watching — just pick up the phone and let us sort out the whole mess so you can get on with your life.'

'Mr Turner, thank you very much. And now it's back to the studio, Debbie.' Dilly Pound finished her smile to the camera, listened to something in her earpiece, and relaxed. 'Thanks, Martin,' she said to the cameraman. 'Hell's bells, she sounds an absolute cow. Not that we're allowed to say things like that anymore. And she *is* your daughter, Mark — sorry. So when's the wedding, Fran? And where?'

Fran would rather have asked about Dilly's life since they'd last met, which had been at her rather grand wedding to a man Fran really did not like. She was inclined to worry about Dilly's determined brightness, as if she were afraid of switching off even for a moment. But it was truly none of her business, and Dilly had asked a question and was awaiting a response. 'The vicar we wanted to marry us is in hospital just now — cancer. So everything's on hold till she gets her prognosis. But it wouldn't be anything big, Dilly. Not at our age.' She forbore to point out that the guest list might be a little tricky, as far as family was concerned.

But Dilly understood. 'And in the present circumstances, of course . . . All the same, you want a bit of a do.'

'And we want a bit of a house and garden to hold the do and live in, with luck, happily ever after.'

'Fingers crossed.' Dilly smiled. 'It'll be nice for you to sort out that skeleton of yours, won't it? Actually, we're doing a piece on that tonight. I recorded an interview with DI Kim Thomas earlier.'

'You're not tying the two pieces together?' Mark gasped.

'Only with a bit of continuity. All she said was that the police had found the skeleton of Frank Grange and wanted to know his last movements. We put up a pic and gave the hotline number she supplied. We didn't want to make people think they knew stuff, but wanted to nudge them a bit in case they needed it. So we just mentioned Great Hogben and several other villages round here — nothing to connect it with you personally, Mark.'

'That's terrific. Thanks.'

'No problem.' Dilly pulled a face, gesturing at the house. 'Where do you cook and eat?'

'There's still a canteen at work,' Mark said, 'and an excellent village pub. I'd offer to take you both,' he added, with a smile at the cameraman, who'd passed the entire conversation texting and had just resurfaced, 'but it's closed on Mondays.'

Dilly looked unaccountably disappointed. 'Well, another time, maybe.'

'Definitely. I'd love to invite you in to show you what the Pact team have done so far,' Fran said, 'because they've achieved miracles, but as you can see,' she continued, pointing at Paula's official notices, 'they're very keen on Elf and Safety so it'd be a hard hat and heavy boot affair. But you and Daniel must be some of our very first dinner guests.' *Possibly*, she added, under her breath.

'That'd be lovely,' Dilly declared, with a smile that didn't look very happy. Fran opened her mouth, but shut it again: this wasn't the time or place to probe Dilly's feelings, and they were none of her business anyway. But then she heard herself saying, 'We must do lunch sometime, Dilly — have a girly natter.'

Mistake.

'Oh, Fran, that'd be lovely — I'd really like that. I can see you're up to here at the moment, but next week, maybe? Can you call me?'

At last, standing hand in hand by their demolished gateposts, they waved her and the taciturn Martin off.

Mark hung his head. 'I never mentioned the Winnebago.'

'So you didn't. And I think Nemesis was watching you. The Winnebago is no longer with us, sweetheart. Tonight we sleep on those air beds . . .'

CHAPTER TWENTY

Penance, Fran decided, was right to come in the form of sackcloth and ashes. It ought probably to have come in the form of beds so short that your feet stuck over the edge and so narrow that you rolled on to the floor if you risked turning over. Mark's obligatory trek to the loo in the small hours, lit by only a torch, was probably part of the deal too, though possibly earlier penitents had been allowed a chamber pot.

And confession must have come into it.

It wasn't, of course, so much ash as plaster dust that was her penance: it was in her hair, her mouth, her nose. There was a fine collection under her eyelids. And her clothes, for all Caffy's efforts to provide a rail for them, were dust-covered — dust-filled! — too.

It wasn't Caffy but Paula who greeted them as they emerged, fully-dressed but blinking and scratching, into the fine morning.

'So you've proved your point,' she said coolly, stirring her coffee but not offering to make them one. 'Shall I tell Caffy to reinstate the Winnebago? Or do you want to wait and see if the TV piece generates any more press interest?'

Mark, looking like a schoolboy caught scrumping apples, shook his head slowly. There was probably dust in his brain cells too. 'Best hang fire with the Winnebago, I suppose.' Then he produced the smile that had made Fran realize she had to share her life with him. 'You were right all along, Paula — all our wishy-washy plans about living here while you were still working. Getting in your way, too, and wasting your time, of course.'

Paula nodded. 'For which you are paying, Mark — so that's OK with us.'

Fran had an idea she wasn't joking. 'You're not usually here this early, are you?'

'The birds were clog-dancing on my roof. No point in wasting a fine day like this, not with the long-term forecast telling us to build arks. Which reminds me, how much longer will you be treating the garden as a crime scene?'

'As long as it takes, Paula,' Fran said. 'We're dealing with a really odd case. I'd like to say what Caffy's friend Lina found yesterday would speed things up, but I can't promise.'

Paula switched on the kettle and reached for two more mugs: presumably, this was her way of asking for details.

'We found a collection of good quality furniture in a self-store unit,' Fran said, as if Paula wouldn't know. 'But it took this Lina Townend to get into any of the cupboards and drawers. And a big Italian cabinet looked as if it was about to defeat even her.'

Paula nodded, reaching into a hessian carrier bag for a plastic box. Peeling off the lid, the sort that always broke Fran's fingernails, she offered thick sandwiches of dense wholemeal bread. 'Home-made marmalade,' she said.

'Like Paddington's,' Mark quipped, taking one. 'Thanks.'

She ignored him, prompting Fran: 'I take it the cabinet *didn't* defeat her?'

'Until she slapped it in frustration it did. And then a panel shifted, and she found a lock. And then she managed to remove section after section. Like a three-D maze, as it were. She's still not sure if she's got every last one. There may still be drawers within drawers, cupboards with false bottoms. It's a work of art.'

'And did you find anything useful?' Paula prompted, making their coffee.

'Not yet. But Lina's gone off to do some research — to find the ultimate hidden drawer.'

'And are you expecting a signed confession?'

'God knows it would make our task easier.'

'And cost the taxpayer less. On the other hand,' Paula continued, offering her a sandwich, 'I can understand why you want to cross all the T's and dot all the I's. I would myself. My grandfather used to say that if a job was worth doing it was worth doing well. Now, I'm expecting a delivery — it would be much easier if you could move your car. And no Winnebago — right?' She smiled darkly. 'Though you're permitted to change your minds.'

* * *

Dismissed like errant children, and still munching their doorstep sandwiches, Mark and Fran scuttled off to the car, already a few minutes behind their schedule, which had to include time for showers at work.

Fran's hair was still damp when she went into the latest briefing meeting about what she mentally termed Cynd's murder. Don Simpson looked as if he'd been working ever since she'd last seen him — which he probably had. There was good news and bad news. The bad — very bad — was that there was still no sign of Cynd. The good was that the pathologist had established that the victim's fillings weren't done by a British dentist. Apparently, there were different fashions according to where in the world they were put in. 'They have these down as Eastern European, ma'am.'

Fran had a sudden pang: she'd never let the self-store team in general and young Fred in particular know their progress so far. And it mattered, in her book at least. If you wanted the public to help you, the least you could do was update them on the way a case was going. She made a note to call them later. 'Any particular part?'

'Bulgaria, possibly. Or maybe Albania.'

Fran was going to ask how on earth such information could be contained in a small dab of amalgam, but Don's scarcely suppressed yawns became so emphatic that she feared for the safety of his jaw.

'Don — go home to bed. That's an order. The rest of you, be sensible with your time. You need breaks, however macho you think it is to keep going as long as you can. Another order — right? We want this case sorted but not at the expense of you and your families.' She spread her fingers in a checklist. 'Get on to Interpol — see what they can come up with. Borders Agency. SOCA. They're supposed to be there to fight crime, and so are we. No point in reinventing the wheel, however much we'd like to. Meanwhile, I want Cynd. Still no sightings? Come on, think outside the box. Surely there's CCTV coverage of all the places she might have been working, or where she might have got her fix?'

'Absolutely. And there's no sign of her.' Don yawned. 'Nor any signs — heavens, Fran, we've checked everywhere. Forensics doesn't show a struggle at the vicarage or the church — we were trying to rule out abduction,' he added.

She pointed. 'Don — go. I don't like giving orders twice.' But she smiled with some kindness. They'd both come up through the ranks when fatigue was regarded as a weakness to ignore, and in his situation she was sure she'd have insisted on swilling endless caffeine and trying to carry on. Meanwhile, before she headed to the next briefing, she put in a quick call to the self-store, even though she could report nothing concrete.

As she left, Alice said, 'Someone called Lina Townend called: she's still researching possible locations for secret drawers, but hasn't come up with anything yet.'

'Hardly surprising — you're not going to put instructions out on the Internet, or the seventeenth-century equivalent, are you?'

'You look as if you could do with a cuppa. Sit yourself down and I'll dunk a tea bag for you. Green?'

'You're an angel.' She checked her watch. 'But I'll have to drink it on the hoof. Next briefing's five minutes ago.'

* * *

'Good news, ma'am,' Kim declared the moment Fran stepped into the smaller briefing room. 'We've had a couple of calls about last night's piece on Grange. Both callers said they'd seen him years ago — and not so far from here. You're a local: you probably remember that the National Trust took over some run-down stately property called Verities for some reason and kept it exactly as it was until they could catalogue everything? It was so cluttered that you had to have a timed ticket if you wanted to go round.'

'And?' Fran prompted her, loath to admit that she hadn't a clue what Kim was talking about. If Don was a workaholic, so had she been, and her overflowing working life had been complicated by the need to take regular, exhausting trips to Devon to help her ageing parents. It would have taken the murder of Thomas à Becket himself to stick in her mind. Someone's abandoned home wouldn't have registered then — though it certainly would now.

'Two women say they remember issuing the man with a ticket — he was very insistent, jumped the queue to get it. But he never turned up at the proper time to do the tour. One was inclined to be a bit ditzy, but the other one was very clear.'

Fran put down her mug. 'I'd like someone to talk to them both. And to talk round their experiences there. It might take time and resources we don't really have, but they might reveal something. And I can't understand for the life of me why someone like Grange should suddenly show an interest in social history. Can you?' She took a swig. 'Tell me, did either of them mention our Dr Lovage having worked there?'

Kim shook her head. 'No. They were both adamant. But we'll get them interviewed again as soon as may be. And any other National Trust volunteers who might have been around Verities at the time. Mind you, fifteen years . . . A lot of Trust guides are retired when they start volunteering, which makes sense, so some of them . . .' She shrugged — the implication was clear.

Fran reported what she'd been up to, and her general lack of progress, and sent them on their way. To her shame she'd still not phoned the hospital to see how Janie was getting on. Nor could she now. She had a meeting with Ashford CID, to brief them on the latest management developments, and didn't fancy battling with a hospital switchboard while she was driving. And making that sort of call certainly wasn't a job she could delegate, to Alice or anyone else.

* * *

However, she reasoned as she left the meeting, there was no reason why she couldn't nip into the William Harvey and ask in person — she could even grab a sandwich there. Once she could park, of course. Cursing the fact she wasn't on official business and entitled to park in a reserved slot, she joined the queue of equally frustrated drivers. Until she got bored. Very bored. An official slot it would have to be. Tucking her card on the dashboard as she always did, she parked and stomped into the building.

CHAPTER TWENTY-ONE

'Guess all I did was make it worse.' Dave stared into his coffee cup. He and Mark sat at a table placed on the pavement, perhaps in the hope of making Maidstone look like the home of bohemian café culture.

Mark didn't care overmuch if it failed to. He couldn't remember when Dave had last suggested lunch together without a challenge in his voice: this time there had been a conciliatory, even apologetic note.

'I don't think so,' he said almost truthfully. 'Sometimes it's best to bring things out into the open. Not necessarily via the media, I admit.'

'Will you have to resign?'

'Not necessarily. Yes, probably,' he conceded. 'My boss isn't best pleased, but neither in his place would I have been, seeing my second in command's dirty linen being washed on the midday news. Since we've already lost the two most senior officers in the force, casting aside a third might look a bit profligate. But — and don't tell Fran yet — I can see it happening.'

Perhaps it was the implied shared secret that brought a faint smile to Dave's face. 'I can't imagine you not being a policeman.' He shook his head.

'I'm not a policeman now, Dave. I'm Meetings Man, a Manager. Not what I signed up for at all. Fran's still making a difference. Investigating crime; putting bad guys away. I'm allocating diminishing resources, and I can see I must soon allocate myself my P45 and head off into the sunset.'

'You'll miss it. Miss everything.'

'Might get to see more of you and Sammie. Not to mention the grandchildren.'

Dave shook his head. 'Distance apart, there's no reason why you shouldn't see more of my two. But Sammie — don't hold your breath, Dad.' He looked round, but dropped his voice anyway. 'There's something really wrong there. I got as far as the front hall. There was no way I could get further, though believe me I tried. After all, as you said, a lot of the stuff in there is mine, and it would be nice to ship some of it back for the kids.' He took one last swig of the coffee.

'The train set,' Mark agreed.

Dave responded with a smile. 'Who's paying all the bills, by the way?'

'Me. Everything's on direct debit. For God's sake, I couldn't leave her without light and heating, couldn't have the water cut off.' Despite what both Fran and Ms Rottweiler had suggested.

'It was always Mum that did the tough love, wasn't it?' Dave stared at memories Mark could never share. But then he turned. 'You were such a soft touch, you know. Sammie — she'd swear black was white, and you always believed her. And me, half the time. And you a cop, too,' he added with a jeer, which was, to Mark's ears, somewhat less hostile than his usual jeers.

'And a very poor father.' Maybe his constant reiteration of *mea culpa* had helped improve things, and it would do no harm to continue. 'Why did you ask about the bills?'

'See, you *are* still a cop. And maybe a bit's rubbed off on me. The place was just too much on the warm side for such a chilly house. Even in the hall. Sorry, Dad, but it'd be just like Sammie to turn the heat on full blast even though she didn't need it on at all simply because the money's coming out of your account.' He stood, picking up the cups. 'Another?'

'Not for me, thanks. Tell you what, though: I could do with one of those sandwiches. It's been a long time since breakfast.' Heat full on? In August? On a day like this, even?

When Dave got back, he brought a rather grubby wooden spoon with a number on it. 'Seems it's waitress service for food. Dad, did Sammie say anything about Lloyd?'

'He was the reason she moved back home in the first place. She said he'd hit her.' Mark gripped the table. 'He's not — not again?'

'Or still. She'd got some nasty bruises.'

'But he's an educated man — got a good job. Neither of which,' Mark said with a groan, 'precludes him from being a violent bastard. Maybe they'd make him a clever, more cunning bastard. The nastiest piece of knitting I ever got sent down for domestic violence wasn't your drunken navvy but a prosecution barrister we could pretty well rely on to get us a conviction . . . But why would she let Lloyd into the house? She even changed the locks, remember.'

'But that was to keep you out, Dad. And she's pregnant, remember.'

'What about the kids? What are they having to witness? Dear God.'

'You know what I'd say? And I'll admit I've gone pretty well into reverse on this. I'd say, get her evicted and make sure Social Services are involved. They might check on you and make you out to be Mr Bad Dad, but they might just check on the father of that unborn child.' He picked up the wooden spoon and waved it. A waitress approached with two overfull plates. 'I said hold the fries. No fries?'

The girl — she looked a young, possibly illegal, fourteen — stared blankly. 'You want fries? More fries?'

'We'll have the fries,' Mark said. 'So long as Fran doesn't know.'

'She seems to be looking after you pretty well.' The comment sounded humorous, not grudging. Dave pushed his own portion firmly to one side and peered inside the baguette, which was supposed to have been the healthy option.

'She is. Dave — you never talk about your own family, except to Fran, when you're both being polite. Is everything OK? I mean—'

'Everything's fine. Truth is, I've sold my business. Made a good profit. Things were going way bad over here — so I thought I'd stick my nose in.' His hand strayed chip-wards. 'Actually, I really came to punch your nose, old-timer — but now I'm not so sure. God, these fries are awful.'

'They are, aren't they? So I can tell Fran I left them, with complete honesty, and bask in her praise for being virtuous. So how long can you stay?' *Please let it be long enough for us to get to know each other properly*, he added under his breath.

'I guess until we've sorted out this Sammie business — as you pointed out, I'm involved too, far more than I knew.'

Not by his father's plight, Mark thought — but ultimately by the thought of his beloved train set. Absently, he took a chip. With extra salt you didn't notice how bad they were.

* * *

'They say they'll let me out, drains and all if necessary, the moment my sister can get down — which will probably be tomorrow afternoon.'

'So soon?' Fran gasped. 'That's amazing!'

'Och, aye. You'd expect a couple of weeks' bed rest. Not anymore.' Janie patted the arm of her chair. 'Rest is bad and exercise good. And hospitals — for all the good they do — are bad.' She smiled. 'Talk about *Nineteen Eighty-Four*. Anyway, I'm fine. I even did the crosswords this morning, and such a luxury it is to be able to sit and work them out without having to worry about what I really ought to be doing.' She patted the *Times* and the *Guardian*. Then she shot Fran an unreadable look. 'I was worried about my brain, after the anaesthetic, you know. And after last night.'

'Last night?'

'Indeed. I suppose it was all the drugs they popped into me, but I hallucinated, Fran. I thought there was an angel sitting by my bed. Not a big, shiny angel with a halo and wings — I was quite disappointed to be honest — but a wee waif of a thing. I was afraid to look at its face — but then, it was in shadow, so I wouldn't have seen much anyway. I was minded for a moment to ring the emergency bell, just to see what happened. But it took my hand and held it until I fell asleep.'

Fran asked carefully, 'Was the angel comforting you, or were you comforting the angel?'

Another opaque glance. 'That's a very interesting question. All I can do is think of that line from the poet — *who can justify the ways of God to men?* And the bugger of it is, I can't be sure if I've got the words right. Anyway, next time I woke, I was on my own. Which was better than the poor dear opposite, who found someone else getting in beside her. Seems the old soul in the next bed had peed herself and didn't like wet sheets, so she did the obvious thing — hopped into the next bed and told the occupant to hitch up. We had a lot of screeching, I can tell you. No wonder the angel hopped it. I might have done so myself, if I'd been able.'

Fran, no angel, took the nearest hand herself. 'I'm not very good at praying,' she said at last. 'Without wishing to talk shop, of course, Janie, but—'

'Go on.'

'I suppose it's my background — my parents were a cussed pair of Baptists, given to telling God what he should be doing.'

'That's Baptists for you.'

'I always suspected a humble prayer might work better than a barked command, but now I command all those people, I find I'm treating God like a recalcitrant constable.'

Janie cackled. 'Come on, Fran: didn't Christ once heal a Roman soldier's daughter in pretty hierarchical circumstances? Now, I'll mutter the words, and you can just tack an

Amen on at the end. We'll have some proper praying lessons when I'm better.'

'Tell you what,' Fran ventured, 'I wouldn't mind praying for that angel of yours.'

The other woman squeezed her hand. 'I'm glad we understand each other.'

* * *

It didn't take Fran long to realize that there were far too many places in a hospital for her to continue searching alone for what she was sure was a very corporeal angel. On the other hand, since there was just the remotest chance that Janie had indeed been hallucinating, she didn't want to make a complete fool of herself by calling for reinforcements. There was no reason, however, why she shouldn't stroll down to speak to the head of security and ask for a look at the CCTV footage in Janie's ward area for the last twenty-four hours.

'Good heavens! It's Roy Winstanley!' she declared, once she'd got herself past his suspicious minions. 'How are you?'

'Nearly as well as you look,' he said, clearly not sure whether to salute her. 'Fran,' he managed — she was no longer *ma'am*, at least.

She didn't think he was on her hug and double air-kiss list, so she compromised by laying her left hand on his right when they shook hands. He'd been a perpetual constable who'd turned down every chance of promotion because he liked what he was doing too much to want to step on the paperwork ladder. On the other hand, he'd opted for retirement the moment he could. And here he was in uniform again. Would this be the future for her and Mark? Still pretending to be what they once proudly were?

'Know where I'd look for this kid first?' he asked. 'Down the canteen. A good place to scavenge, see. All those half-eaten sarnies and cakes. People buying coffees they don't drink.'

'Really? Drinking from the same cup? My God, I can't imagine it.'

'If you're still imagining your nice china cup, of course you can't. But all you have to do is take the plastic lid from a paper cup and you're fine. And you don't eat the half-chewed sarnie, you eat the one they've not touched. Come and see. No, you're all right: I'll shout you a fresh bite, not a second-hand one.'

As they walked, he told her about his second incarnation: this time he'd actively sought promotion, he said, because he'd become bored and wanted a challenge. And he'd started to use the gym: all the cardiac cases around him had made him aware that he wore his belt below his belly, not around it. And — would she believe it? — he and his wife had taken up ballroom dancing. They were going on a ballroom-dancing cruise over Christmas.

'With all due respect, Fran, isn't it time you hung up your handcuffs? And not just on the bedhead, either — didn't I hear you and the ACC were tying the knot at last? Good for you. Spend some time together while you can. You don't want to be like Ian French — get your pension paperwork on Friday, drop dead Saturday. Yes, without a word of a lie. Grab the day — there's some fancy phrase, but that's what it means. Now, I always opt for salad on wholemeal . . .'

As they sat, healthy food before them, she said, almost tentatively, 'About retirement — I can't make up my mind, Roy. The force — except we shouldn't call it that! — has been my whole life, except when I went off to university.'

'Do you still wake up in the morning wanting to go to work? Think you can make a difference? Yes? Well, you're not ready yet. Besides, it'd be dead funny for you, both retiring at once.'

She froze, sandwich halfway to her lips. 'Is there something I should know?' She hoped she sounded mocking. But if she wasn't, was it something to do with Simon's suicide or with Sammie's media revelations? And, more to the point, why hadn't Mark mentioned it? Then she remembered that the jungle drums sometimes added an extra beat, and she took a bite, trying to smile casually as she chewed.

'Only what my mates down the pub are saying. That this new bloke, Sparrow or Starling or whatever, wants a clean sweep. No one over fifty in the senior echelons, and that's for starters. People your level will be replaced by new, telly-friendly high-flyers. Only rumour, of course. But would the guv'nor mind?'

She swallowed before she replied. 'We'd all rather jump than wait to be pushed, wouldn't we?'

'And, of course,' Roy continued, 'it'd be really bad for morale if all the top brass nipped off at once. Over there,' he continued, in exactly the same tone, 'no, don't turn, just swivel your eyes — over by the drinks machine. Is that her? She's been grazing at a couple of tables.'

Apparently preoccupied with the sandwich wrapper, she checked the girl. She was thin and waif-like enough, but too tall for Cynd. 'No.'

'OK, when we've finished, we'll have a stroll through the waiting areas and the shop, but we've both got *copper* written all over us, so I doubt if we'll have any luck. And then we check every single screen from every single camera at every single angle.'

* * *

Mark glanced at his watch. He'd probably just got time, and if one of the four parking slots outside the Royal Mail depot was open, he'd take it as an omen. He hadn't picked up his mail — kept back by Royal Mail since they didn't have a proper address yet — since he'd moved. He hadn't felt the need, since most of his communication was electronic these days, and his financial transactions were done, as he'd told Dave, by direct debit or standing order. But as he drove hopefully along Sandling Road, someone pipped him to the post — and he found himself grinning broadly at his silly mental pun. All because he and Dave were on speaking terms again. Or was it for the first time? Whatever it was, his heart sang with joy that he hadn't slung away what he thought was a broken bottle. Arthur Miller — that was the author he'd been trying to recall when he was talking to Fran the other night, and *Death of a Salesman* the A-level text. Was that what getting older meant? That things came back to you when you didn't need them?

Laughing no longer, he headed back to work.

CHAPTER TWENTY-TWO

'Go ahead — it's OK to use mobiles in here,' Roy declared, plonking a mug of coffee in front of Fran.

Glad to escape, if only for a few minutes, the confusion of images on the screens before her, she nodded, responding to the text.

It was from Lina Townend. *Eureka.*

End of message. So what on earth had the young woman found? And why the unnecessarily enigmatic message? She texted back a much blunter one: *What?*

Back to the screens and the over-strong coffee. Roy seemed to be tracking someone, shifting the camera to get a better image.

'No,' he said at last, sighing. 'It's the lass we saw earlier. Here — you have a go. Sit here — it makes the screens clearer. Amazing — no matter how much you pay for your glasses, they never let you focus on exactly the place you want. You don't wear them?'

'Should do. I've got an appointment next week. So long as I don't forget.'

'Or get summoned to a meeting at the last minute. According to my mates, life's one long meeting for you people.'

'Absolutely. I'm probably missing one right now. Hang on. There! Can you see her?' Cynd was, as Roy had predicted, scavenging. Thank goodness she was doing something as innocent as that, not trying to break into the pharmacy or ward drugs trolleys.

'How do you want to play this? I can track her as long as you need. Probably,' he added with a grin. 'I can get some of my people to pick her up, if you like. Though I'm not sure on what grounds.'

'I think it's my job, actually, Roy. I want to talk to her about a possible manslaughter charge — but that's between you and me. But I want to do it with the minimum of fuss.'

'Come on, you don't usually pussyfoot round killers!'

'Most of my killers don't spend a night holding the hand of a woman recovering from cancer surgery. And she's grabbing sarnies, not drugs. Tell you what, though, keep tracking her. She may not take kindly to talking to me, after all.' With very little reluctance, she abandoned the coffee and got to her feet. Before she could leave Roy's den, however, another text came through. *Postcards*, it said.

Which left her much wiser — or not.

As she retraced her steps, she worked out her plan of campaign. An arrest and chase through corridors cluttered with vulnerable people and equally precious equipment was not on, especially since she was sure Cynd would soon elude her — if not the cameras. And she was in no doubt that if Roy saw a hint of a chase he'd bring his heavies in — rightly, of course. She was also sure the story would get straight back to her colleagues, to their immense amusement. So she would try a casual approach — one which would give Janie pleasure, too, with luck.

'Hi, Cynd. Come to see Janie? I'm just on my way myself,' she said, as if PACE had never come into her life. 'Let's go along together, shall we? I can never work out how to get anywhere in a hospital this size.' Setting them in motion, she wittered on in a similar vein all the way to Janie's ward. If Cynd had wanted to speak, Fran hardly gave her a chance.

Still no caution, however — she'd have to work that in soon. But not until Cynd had exchanged a healing hug with Janie — assuming the poor woman was in any position to give or receive embraces.

If Janie was surprised by their joint appearance, she didn't show it — just beamed with delight.

'Two of my favourite people!' she crowed, grasping a hand of each. 'I've been so worried about you, young Cynd, having to manage without me. I even dreamt about you last night, just as if you were safe here beside me. Give me a cuddle, lass — no, not that side, that's the one that's been carved about.' Cynd's head firmly down, she mouthed over the sobbing girl's hair, 'What on earth?'

Fran mouthed back, 'I have to arrest her. Give us your blessing, will you?'

Janie's eyes rolled. But Fran thought she'd do it anyway.

At last, Fran eased Cynd to her feet. 'I'd like you to come with me now, Cynd — we need to talk again about your rape and what you told Janie first time you saw her. But first I'd like us both to close our eyes and let her pray for us.' Eye-closing wasn't an option for Fran, of course, but she lowered them reverently and sincerely. Cynd would need all the help she could get now, from whatever direction. And so, as arresting officer, would she.

The omens looked good. Cynd held Janie's hand while the older women kissed it as if all was normal. Pray God she wouldn't bolt the minute she could.

'OK, Janie — we have to go now,' Fran said, still trying to sound as if they were normal visitors. She kept the social, calm tone to continue, 'And Cyndi Lewis — you know I have to say these words because of what you said about the man you knifed — I arrest you . . .'

* * *

Roy appeared beside her as she stood outside the curtained cubicle in A and E. 'No drama, then!'

'How did I know she'd faint on the spot? A genuine faint? And that I'd get all the medics in the Western world shoving their stethoscopes in?'

'Better than her scarpering. At least you know where she is now.'

'And I know I'll have to waste valuable funds having her guarded here until they say she's ready to be released into custody. Shit and double shit.'

'Could have been worse — she could have collapsed in a cell, and think of all the forms you'd have had to fill in then.'

* * *

It was only after Jill had turned up at A and E, not best pleased, Fran suspected, by Fran's interference — though that would be nothing to Don Simpson's private reaction — that Fran could leave. She took in the quickest possible visit to Janie, to assure her that Cynd had recovered consciousness and was receiving medical care. Then she could turn her attention to Lina Townend and her gnomic texts. Apparently, she'd turned up at HQ asking to speak to her, and Kim had sailed in — rightly, of course, but no less irritatingly, since Fran regarded anything to do with the cabinet as her baby. And she would have given anything to be present when Townend had eased aside the bottom of a drawer to reveal a drawer within.

'Postcards. That's all,' Kim declared, patting a heap of individual evidence bags. 'I told her to invoice us for her time.'

'She's gone, then? But who'll put the cabinet back together?'

'Oh, she's already done that. Quicker than my brother can do a Rubik's cube. What's the problem?'

'Nothing,' Fran lied, resisting a strong urge to kick the desk and scream. 'OK, these cards — what do they tell us?'

'Sod all. Pretty seasides, nice stately homes. Very strange mix.'

'Is there one of Verities?'

'That National Trust place? First place I thought of. But there isn't. Just these.' She picked up a pile and let them slither back on to her desk.

Fran thought she showed great forbearance when she said quietly, 'They just demand a bit of old-fashioned detective work, don't they?' But she couldn't resist adding, like an overkeen rookie, 'Give me a list of the places they show and I'll see if they ring any bells with me. Actually, give them to me in order — the order they were placed in the drawer,' she added as Kim blinked at her. 'You have kept them in order, haven't you?' She took a deep breath so that she could explain without swearing or shouting. 'You see, if someone went to this trouble to conceal them, I regard anything — everything — about them as significant.'

Everything about Kim said she hadn't bothered. But she declared, 'Of course. No problem. Though maybe Ms Townend could remember any particular arrangement I've missed.' After a breath, which Fran could count in seconds, she continued, 'I'll give her a bell.' Grabbing her phone, she headed off, shutting the door behind her so Fran couldn't hear the ensuing conversation.

Not unless she put her ear to the crack. She got enough to prove her suspicions horribly right. However, never one to cry over spilt milk, and taking care not to change the order herself, she leafed through them. The first thing she noticed was that not all were commercial cards, though all were much the same size.

It looked as though Dr Lovage, assuming it was she who'd concealed the cards, had been a National Trust buff, even if they hadn't so far been able to connect her with Verities: her travels had taken her to Felbrigg and Blickling; Lanhydrock and Cotehele; Little Moreton Hall and Erddig. So far, all very pretty and no use at all. Still nothing from Verities to connect her with Grange. Dunstanburgh — looking particularly bleak. London's Docklands — but this was a photo, not a card. So was a view of Carcassonne. A chic place in what looked like the Cotswolds. Then there was another: a weathered gravestone.

Sacred to the memory of Thomas Parkinson, JP
Born 1815
Taken to the bosom of our Lord, 1877
And to his dearly beloved wife,
Anna, 1820–1840,
And his second wife,
Elizabeth Jane,
Mother of Herbert,
both taken to a better place in 1842
IN THEE WE TRUST

Could they be some of Lovage's ancestors? But she'd have had others, and there were no similar photos. She had an idea that from wherever she was currently based, Dr Lovage was having a sardonic laugh.

Before she could summon Kim back and give her the bollocking of her young life — not on record, not the sort of rebuke that would stick with official glue throughout the rest of her career — her phone rang.

'Fran? Fran Harman?' The voice was slightly overloud, as if the speaker was a little deaf, or simply didn't rely on his tiny mobile to carry the volume he wanted. 'Bill Baker here.'

'Bill — oh, Gardening Society Bill.'

'We were hoping you'd come along to last night's meeting, only my wife tells me you and your fiancé were tied up with the telly.'

'We were indeed. I'm really sorry, Bill — the meeting went clean out of my mind. Not being a great gardener,' she added.

'Yet,' he corrected her quickly. 'When you've mastered that patch of yours you will be. Anyway, I've got the comments we made all signed as true, and I could drop them over to your place tonight if you like.'

'I don't like to put you to any trouble,' she said truthfully.

'No trouble. I like a bit of a walk, and to be honest I'd love a nose round.'

'You'd be more than welcome. Make sure you wear heavy boots, if you've got any. I'll ask them to leave a spare hard hat. Very keen on the regs, my builders,' she added, almost apologetically.

'As they should be,' he said sharply. 'About seven suit you?'

It would give her a very good excuse to tear Mark from his desk — and herself, of course, from hers, or at least these photos. Meanwhile, she must have an apologetic word with Don and Jill, and see if Cynd had been released from hospital. But first, before all else, she needed a cup of tea and the loo — in whichever order.

The latter was a good choice, because that was where she ran into Jill. 'I'm sorry. Should have been your collar. Stuck my nose in.'

Jill responded with a laugh. 'Fran, the day you stop sticking your nose in, I shall consider retiring myself. Cynd will be discharged late this evening, or early tomorrow, with the proviso she's properly fed and watered at regular intervals.'

'Who's collecting her?'

Jill put her hands up in mock surrender. 'OK, OK — I'll do it myself.'

'Can you go via Janie's ward?' She waited while Jill tapped the details into her phone. 'She's too ill to have to worry about anyone else's well-being. Be sure to tell her about the feeding and watering. The poor kid won't have to graze on others' leavings while she's here, at least.'

'Nor in prison,' Jill agreed soberly.

* * *

With Mark grumbling that he'd meant to stay later and work through his personal emails in peace, but pacified by the promise of pub grub after Bill Baker's conducted tour, they arrived home — home! — with minutes to spare, pulling aside the inimical furls of plastic tape to improve his welcome.

Not that Bill seemed in any way fazed by the mess. Having handed over the notes he'd promised, he peered around the site with something like a nostalgic smile. 'I used to scrump here when I was a kid. Never got caught, thank God. Later on, when Dr Lovage took over, I did a few odd jobs. It was like painting the Forth Bridge, mind — though we can't say that anymore, now they've got that special long-life paint. At the start I mostly worked in the garden — heavy digging and cutting back trees.'

'Not the bean patch!' Fran said.

'Oh, she let me go long before she started on her kitchen garden. She was a slight little thing, but she didn't half muscle up — not in a bad way, mind, don't think of her as some Russian shot-putter. Toned, that's what she was — all because of her gardening. She'd be up and down ladders, too — like those girls working on the place now. Self-taught, she said.'

'So she'd be capable of digging that trench?'

'That's what I'm saying. She even borrowed — and I'm sorry, it's been clean out of my mind till I look at the place now — she even borrowed a pickaxe of mine to tackle some of the hardest ground. And a big axe so she could chop her own logs. A mighty independent woman, so it was strange she should be beholden for something like that.'

'You don't remember when?'

Baker shook his head. 'What I do recall is her breaking one of them. And replacing it with a brand-new one — top of the range, as you'd expect from her, for all it was one of my grandfather's she'd broken.' His bright eyes scanned their faces. 'I'm digging her grave, saying this, aren't I?'

Mark ushered him inside. 'I don't think telling the truth can ever do any harm, especially when someone's dead and gone. We're not going to scoop her ashes from the wilds of Dartmoor and cram them back in an urn and bury it at a crossroads with a stake through the middle. But — I'm right here, aren't I Fran? — I don't think they've found a possible murder weapon yet, and it would help Fran's team if you could remember what it was you lent and when.'

Fran nodded. 'I'll be honest with you, Bill — I do think she killed him. We've got enough to satisfy the coroner. But I want to know why. I like justice — even if it's only to someone's memory. Now,' she added, 'try this hard hat for size, and come and see what the Pact women and their sub-contractors have been up to.'

'I'll talk you through those notes as well. I'd forgotten she'd been on telly. Yes, some minister visited the school to sing her praises — but really to make them sound as if they were all the government's idea. Just about the time she borrowed my axe . . .'

* * *

'Hot? Your house is hot? Hot enough to worry Dave? It's good you've got him on side, by the way — well done.'

Mark returned her smile, lifting his half-pint glass to toast her gin and tonic. They'd walked back to the village with Bill, who'd accepted a quick half but then nipped back to watch some TV cricket. They'd stayed on to eat. But before Mark could tell her about his day, Ollie appeared, carrying bowls of local chicken and pea risotto.

'Sorry about Dad before,' Ollie said. 'You're about a month too late, I reckon, maybe two. I'll have a go at him myself if you want — but I don't want him rattled by new faces.'

'Talk to him if you can, Ollie — but we're not in the business of upsetting people for no reason,' Mark said, taking the lead with Ollie as they'd tacitly agreed.

He seemed inclined to stay and gossip, but soon a group of youngsters came in, and he wandered off to serve and incidentally control them. 'I'll bring you your wine as soon as I can,' he added, over his shoulder, to Fran.

She smiled: no problem.

'A house she won't let you into. Dave can only get into the hall — no further. What are you thinking, Mark?'

'I'm hoping it's malice, as Dave suggested. That's the father in me. The cop — soon to be ex-cop, if my suspicions are correct — says get the house under surveillance and alert the drugs teams.'

'Ex-cop? You slid that in neatly!'

He smiled apologetically, hoping she'd never find out he'd told Dave first. 'I can't stay if my own home's being used to grow cannabis. Can I? She's made me a laughing stock over the eviction and then with her TV moment. Wren's as furious as such a cold fish can be. Shit. Can a little bird be a cold fish? Even if I wanted to stay, if he were appointed permanently, he'd be reminding me of my inadequacies every moment of every damned meeting. So I'm sorry to break it to you like this, Fran, but I think — I know — it's time for me to go. I can simply retire. Lump sum useful, pension generous. And the exercise of bringing the garden back from the dead will do me good.' When to his terror she said nothing, he added, 'Will you mind very much? Do you mind? My leaving?'

'Mind? I think it calls for champagne,' she declared. 'If it's a decision, not just a possible decision?' She took his upturned hand. It was shaking as much as hers.

'Conflict of interest. How can I enquire into my own property? It'll look like a devious way of getting Sammie out without having to recourse to civil law. Actually, I'm going to talk to Adam tomorrow morning. See what he thinks about the timing. But — and this sounds really selfish of me — I wonder if you should stay put a bit longer? Or it might look as if we're throwing our toys out of the pram.'

She grinned. There was no other word for it. 'One at a time it shall be, Mark. To be honest, I'm so wrapped up in these two murders, I wouldn't have time to write a resignation letter. But I'll support you in anything — in everything — you do. You know that.'

'Even if it means heading back into work with me so I can check my emails? And my bank accounts? Just in case the electricity people have removed a huge sum by direct debit, as they're entitled to do.'

'Of course. And tell Ollie to hold the wine, too. I've an idea we may be about to need very sober heads.'

CHAPTER TWENTY-THREE

'You want me to force my way in?' Dave demanded, his voice squeaky over the phone, which Mark had switched to conference.

Mark leaned back from his desk and took Fran's hand. 'No. Absolutely not. But it'd save some, if not all, of my face if you could ask Sammie what she's up to. I'm going to have to resign — retire, whatever — after this debacle. I can see that now. But it'd be better for me if I had something more than an astronomical electricity bill to go on. And I mean astronomical, Dave. The direct debit payment they took emptied my bank account, though this month's salary had just gone in, and even tipped me into the red. I've managed to talk my way into an overdraft.'

'An overdraft? And your finances in their current state? Jesus.'

'The question is, Dave, what is she heating?'

'You're the policeman, old-timer, not me. Tell you what, I'll ride shotgun for you — only joking! — if you like. I go to the door, gain admittance, and then you barge in after — I'll even unlock the door for you. It's late, but I don't see why we shouldn't do it now. Having the kids in bed might make things easier.'

'I'll meet you there.' Fran was gesticulating like a dervish: the gist seemed to be to cut the call. 'Just park up and wait for me. Don't do anything till I arrive. Anything at all. OK?' He hung up. 'What's up?' he asked her, tetchily.

'I didn't want you to cut the call. I wanted you to abort the project. I don't like it,' Fran said. 'I just don't. I just think a police operation should be conducted by police officers, not by — well, you and Dave. Too dangerous, in terms of the operation and the possible publicity outcomes. I'm dead against it.'

'I gathered that. But I'm committed now.' He got to his feet and opened the officer door. 'I'm going. Are you?'

'I'm bloody driving. And talking while I drive. And you're going to listen. Think about it.' The pace he was setting along the corridors, she'd have to talk while she had breath. 'You've been to the pub. OK, not much drink, but if it goes pear-shaped, how will it look? Drunken officer burgles own home. Great. Just great. I do not, repeat not, want you to do this.'

He paused by the door to the car park. 'Do you think I *want* to do it? Do I have an option? I'm more than broke. And if I allow her to go on growing pot — as I have reasonable grounds to believe she is — I'm culpable. Right? On the other hand, if she's just pumping fan heaters out of open windows, to make me look a fool, how would that go down with everyone? I'd be a laughing stock. And someone would leak it to the press, you mark my words.'

'Just leave it to Dave to go in and check, then.'

'That's not you speaking, Fran — neither of us has ever led from the back.'

'I do know you can't just go charging in — not after everything Ms Rottweiler's been doing. Look, pull back Dave and get another old-stager, someone like Don, to go in. You could trust him with your life.'

'Fran: just drive. And I'll make a call or two. OK? Drive. Please,' he added belatedly.

* * *

Dave's hire car was outside Mark's house, every room of which was brightly lit.

Mark groaned. 'That's where my electricity's going — to light up the place like Blackpool illuminations. It's just her getting at me.'

Dave was striding up and down outside the house, from time to time banging with all his might on the windows.

'You need a Plan B, Mark,' Fran said. 'You daren't go along with this forced entry idea — and I must stop you. Tell Dave, for God's sake. We'll get our colleagues on to it when we've all had a night's sleep.'

'You may be—' He stopped abruptly. 'Now what?'

Dave came hurtling over. 'Quick. I just called triple nine. I heard a scream. I heard a woman scream. I tell you he's attacking her again, the bastard! The door's locked — I tried it, don't think I didn't. Shall we rush it again together? Have you got one of those ram things?'

'Nope. And if I had I couldn't let you use it. Fran and me — it's our job. Fran — the old Ways and Means Act, eh?' He stripped his jacket, ready to charge the door as he'd done so often years back. But he stopped short. Where the hell was Fran?

She was back at the car, talking rapidly into her radio, alternating it with her phone. 'Thanks to Dave, the cavalry's already on its way,' she announced, cutting both calls. 'Yes!'

The street came alive with noise and light, and suddenly he had to act with authority, either that or let Fran take the lead. His arms and voice worked of their own accord as he directed half the team round the back and reminded everyone that children would be in the house, if not in bed asleep. And that the woman whose scream Dave thought he'd heard was pregnant.

Only one of the team recognized him — even as he told them he was the house owner, he took that as an indictment — but most knew Fran by sight. After all, she'd been the one to go round as many nicks as she could, making sure they knew about policy first hand. She'd trained up the sergeant who was taking the lead with the raid. He felt like an outsider; just a taste of what it would be like when he retired, of course.

Worse, he realized he'd seen more raids like this on TV than in the flesh, certainly in the last three years.

Yelling like film cliché Apaches, the team streamed into the house. Suddenly, a couple of paramedics erupted from their ambulance and hurtled after them.

He was following when a gentle hand touched his arm. 'Goodness,' said Cosmo quietly. 'What fun they're all having. Have they got those clever little tasers? Will they use them?'

'What in hell are you doing here?' He tried to shake free, but the hand was now gripping with surprising force.

'Fran thought conceivably we might need some spin on this. And for spinning, I'm your man. I know — I know: it should be the PR folk. But can you imagine them stirring at this hour, when they're mourning their departed comrades? And I'm very fond of you — and especially of Fran, as it happens. I was so peeved when old Adam got in first with his bid to lead her up the aisle. Ah, who's that?' The paramedics were stretchering someone out.

This time Mark did run forward. 'Sammie — my darling Sammie — what's the matter? It's Dad here — Dad.' He took her hand. She shook it off.

A paramedic elbowed him off. 'Issues with the pregnancy. So if you wouldn't mind, sir—'

'*Mind*? I'll come with you, sweetheart.' He looked around for Fran, but there was no sign of her and he didn't want to hold up the ambulance.

'If you don't mind, sir—' Inexorably, they eased their way past him and stowed her inside.

'But—' Like a kid he tried to batter on the door — only to find Cosmo beside him, linking arms with him with such campness that Cosmo must have been into self-parody.

'My, oh my,' he cooed, his grip on Mark fierce, for all its casualness. With his spare hand he pointed at someone being forcibly led to the police van. 'Why did I never turn to crime?

Two lovely big blokes like that, one either side — heaven.' He added in his normal voice, 'Did you recognize him?'

'Never seen him before. Not my son-in-law.'

'Not that tedious Lloyd, no.' To Mark's knowledge, Cosmo and Lloyd had only met once — at Tina's funeral. That was Cosmo for you, the Cosmo who knew the name of every officer he met, whatever his rank, and all about their families and friends. 'But could he be the father?' He mimed Sammie's bump. 'No, of course, you wouldn't know. Thank God you've got all your doings with your daughter fully documented, Mark, and with a legal eagle like Ms Rossiter too.'

For a moment Mark couldn't think who he was talking about — then he remembered the other reason why they called her Ms Rottweiler.

'I'm resigning anyway, Cosmo. My God, what's up with Dave?' He ran faster than he knew how, faster with each of Dave's sobs. The man baying his grief to the moon morphed into his little boy with a cut knee. His arms were round him before he remembered otherwise. 'Let me look.' The words came out unbidden.

Because — just like a little boy — he was holding out something that was broken. Comprehensively. 'They smashed my train set,' he wept. 'When they were growing that damned cannabis,' he added.

'We'll get you another,' Mark said. 'Come on, son, we've got to let these guys get on with their work. It's all right, son, it's all right . . .' Where the hell was Fran? She'd have known what to do. Never, everyone swirling purposefully round him dealing for real with matters that these days he only dealt with on paper, had he felt so redundant. Part of his brain told him he'd made a bleak pun.

* * *

Fran had never been one for children, especially young, terrified ones. If they'd cried, she might have known what to do; their total petrified silence as they clung to each other in the lower level of a bunk bed worried her far more. At least they'd have dimly recognized Mark, if not as their grandfather then as a man who'd brought along, just a few days back, a lot of balloons. Where on earth was he, when he must have known he'd be needed?

She squatted down in front of them on the filthy floor, crisp packets and Lego bricks mixed with used nappies and who knew what else. Now what? She didn't have time to spring-clean, and there might, God forbid, even be evidence in here somewhere. Meanwhile, she had to help the kids. At last, she picked up a teddy bear at random from a heap on the floor. It was dirty enough to suggest it had been on the receiving end of a lot of attention, though why being loved precluded its being clean she didn't know.

'Who's this?' she asked. 'And this?' Another grubby bear.

Silence.

She wasn't up to a spot of instant ventriloquism, so she made the bears whisper in each other's ears, and then in hers. She told their round eyes and embroidered smiles, 'I'm not much good at cuddling. But I bet I know someone who is. I bet Frazer's good at hugging. And I'm pretty sure Lucilla is.' Where the poor kids' fanciful names had erupted from, she had no idea. Neither, to her knowledge, did Mark.

She made the bears nod at her, and then at each other. Then they looked enquiringly at the children. Frazer gradually accepted one of them but Lucilla shook her head and removed her thumb from her mouth long enough to mutter what sounded like Blubber.

Fran made a show of digging out all the pile of animals, one by one. At last she found another seedy looking specimen, this one with once turquoise fur, which smelt vaguely of vomit. Blubber? Blue Bear? Lucilla snatched it.

Fran eased herself into a more comfortable position. The chaos of the police raid still raged all around them, so there was no leaving the kids until she could pass them over to more expert hands. At least her colleagues knew where she was, should Mark ask — and she'd threatened them with instant evisceration should they barge into this particular room, which had the helpful notice '*Frazers room*' hand coloured in nursery-type scribble, Blu-tacked to the door.

At last a gentle tap on the door was followed by a woman in her later thirties. She had the nous to drop beside her on the vile carpet.

'Pat Clarke, Social Services. I've come to take care of the little ones.'

'Good. Is it usual to keep kids in conditions like this?'

Clarke rocked her head. 'Post-natal depression? Alcohol? Drugs?'

'I know. But not in a comfortable middle-class home, for God's sake!'

'Doesn't some fat-cat policeman own it? It's quite a nice place under the filth, pardon my pun. Not that he'll be able to move back anytime soon, what with the forensics people everywhere and the decorators he'll need. Still, on his salary . . .'

'Where are you taking the kids?'

'Emergency foster care.'

That sounded bleak, and her response inadequate. 'Their uncle's around somewhere, as is their grandfather, but I don't know if they'd be able to manage. Neither knows the kids at all well, and me even less.'

'Specialist care, for tonight at least. We'll talk to family members in due course, don't worry.'

Family members — she hated that term. Always had. Somehow it took away warmth and loving-kindness, though her own family had abounded in neither. However, in the absence of any positive alternatives Fran didn't argue. Heaving herself to her feet, she looked around for spare clothes — clean might be asking too much — but found nothing. 'I'll carry Lucilla,' she said, 'and that teddy — he's called Blubber. No idea what Frazer's is called. But he's not going to let it go, is he? Shall I lead the way?'

CHAPTER TWENTY-FOUR

With Mark, egg positively dripping from his face, closeted with Wren and Cosmo Dix, Fran got stuck into work, always the best cure for anxiety, not to mention lack of sleep: neither of them had returned to the rectory, just catnapping, when all the paperwork was done, in their respective offices. Perhaps it was good that they were apart: Fran was still more than equivocal over the way things had gone, and Mark was inclined to grumble at what he considered was her colleagues' overreaction as they broke in. She thought they'd been entirely reasonable given the circumstances — domestic violence and drug-dealing. And they'd caught a particularly low form of life, by the name of Stephen Minns, red-handed. His DNA would be scattered like confetti about the place. That called for one cheer at least. He'd been charged and had bail denied by a sensible magistrates' court. It wasn't up to Sammie to press charges or otherwise — the police could now initiate proceedings themselves. Not just for GBH, of course — but for running a minor cannabis farm. To Fran's eyes, as she'd checked the crime scene with her colleagues, the damage to Dave's precious train set had seemed wilful, a positive act of destruction. No wonder he was so devastated. She had an idea that Mark would while away his new-found leisure by building a huge layout in the rectory loft. But if it built bridges with Dave too, it would be worth the effort — even if the young man would rarely play with it.

Meanwhile, with Sammie likely to be hospitalized for some time, the children were now being cared for by foster parents. Mark was inclined to beat himself up for not being able to take them in; Fran had managed not to grind her teeth at the thought of kids getting anywhere near the death trap of the rectory. In any case, she strongly suspected that if such a thing had been possible, it would have been she, not he, taking compassionate leave to look after them. And she'd have been worse than useless, far worse; apart from odd stints of babysitting for colleagues — including Mark, of course, in an earlier existence — she'd had next to nothing to do with children. Her doze in her chair had clearly proved to her back and neck that her own childhood was long years ago. At least they'd managed to get hold of Lloyd, who was as bemused by the events as all of them, but very much wanted, he said, to have his children restored to him. But what if it was true that he had beaten Sammie in front of them?

All the emotion — and perhaps the amount of coffee she'd had to sink — had left her dizzy, but much as she wanted to huddle in a corner wailing for Mark, she had a meeting to go to and, moreover, to chair. Metal theft. After all, metal theft had now become personal, a point she was swift to make as she offered to vacate the chair.

There was, however, good news. The officer injured in the train incident was well on the way to recovery. There was a universal there-but-for-the-Grace-of-God sigh. And then there was something else: the torrent of metal crime had suddenly dropped to a mere trickle, for no particular reason. With a start like that, even chairing a meeting was a pleasure. She left the room smiling.

But not for long. It was time for the latest update with Kim's team, to find out how they were getting on with the Lovage enquiry.

Which was not far.

At least this time they'd done their best. They'd contacted their opposite numbers in all the locations depicted on the postcards to see if she might have been implicated in crimes there — nil returns, so far. But since Fran had never thought she might have a middle-aged schoolteacher serial killer on her hands, she was hardly surprised. Someone was still checking the gravestone to identify the occupant, as it were, to see if it might have been one of Lovage's ancestors. It was only when she was ready to scream with frustration that the youngest DC — the one who'd wielded the bolt cutters at the self-store, as it happened — dashed into the room waving a piece of paper, skidding to an all-too-embarrassed halt as she saw Fran.

'Deed poll, ma'am,' she managed. 'I've managed to track Lovage's previous names. A whole chain of them.'

Fran's smile returned. 'Well done. Very well done. And what have you found?'

'I started on the basis that if she came into teaching late, but with no records about her qualifications, she might have got her qualifications overseas — but I drew a blank there. So I reasoned she might have changed her name — but she'd have had to tell the interview panel that, wouldn't she? In case — like us — they looked her up and couldn't find her?'

'Quite.' Fran smiled with pleasure.

The DC ventured a smile back. 'So I found she'd once been Megan Woodruff. Before that Maureen Rose. Myrtle Wild.' She paused for them to drop in and for her colleagues to laugh. 'I don't think we were the only ones she's been mocking — you know, like with those cards. Anyway, that got me to the places she lived.'

'And they're linked to the cards?'

'Most of them. Not all. I couldn't find any reason for the Cotswolds one, or Carcassonne.' She risked an impish smile. 'I could go and check in person, ma'am.'

Fran responded. She had an idea this kid would go far. 'Travelling First on Eurostar, of course . . .'

'But I could do it via the Internet and the French police?' She shot a look at Kim, as if this idea had already gone down in flames. From Kim's thunderous expression, this might be an act of insurrection too far.

Time for tact, which was never Fran's strong suit. She couldn't back the kid over Kim, but she wanted the job done, and done yesterday. She also wanted the kid, if it was really her idea, to get any plaudits going. 'Sounds good to me, but DI Thomas may have someone else lined up to do that.'

* * *

It was all right when the adrenaline was flowing, but as soon as she stopped, Fran could hardly keep her eyes open. A quick phone call to Sally told her that Mark was still closeted with Wren and mysteriously unnamed others, and that this time she really dared not crash the meeting to find out how things were going. The moment Mark emerged, she'd get him to call Fran — or do it herself if he was still in the company of top brass. Untarnished top brass, Fran corrected her silently. What in heaven's name was going on? What were they doing to him? She'd half a mind to storm the bastion herself, but Mark would hate that. So there was time to fill. Lunch time, to be precise, as if such a thing had ever really operated in her career. But she needed food, and so would Jill, who was also, of course, a past mistress at missing meals.

'They're getting nowhere fast,' Jill confided, tucking into canteen soup. 'She's too frail to hammer away at for long. She's got the tail end of her cold turkey to deal with, and she's desperately undernourished. So even if we couldn't see it for ourselves, the FME says they can only question her for half an hour at a time.'

Fran frowned. 'You've stepped right back from the case?'

'It's hard to chase with the dogs and run with the hare. In my book, she's a victim. It's just this slight inconvenience of another victim that's the problem.'

Fran put down her sandwich. 'But Don Simpson's take is?'

'That she's admitted to stabbing someone and all the other stuff she's fed us is pie in the sky. The forensic evidence is indecisive — we know she had sex, but she'd had sex with a lot of people and the place is heaving with DNA.'

'The dead guy's as well as everyone else's?'

'That proves he was there, not raping her. They're found her DNA on his clothes too. No surprise there, of course.'

'Quite.' She applied herself to the sandwich. When Mark was a house husband, would he go into role and get into housework and home-made bread? She hoped he'd produce better filled sandwiches than this, at all events. 'Jill, what's the take on this business with Mark?'

Jill didn't drop her eyes as a less honest friend would have done. 'That he's been a fool, from start to finish. But I don't think it's tarnished his reputation as a career policeman, and I don't think you'll be damaged.'

'He'll resign.'

'So I should hope. He's messed up. Pressure of work isn't an excuse, not at his level — people don't expect ACCs to do silly things. Why didn't you smack his head for him?'

'Because — oh, a whole lot of becauses. For a start, Sammie didn't want him to have another woman in his life and behaved extremely badly to me. So in the hopes of future bridge-building, I tried to stay out of anything to do with his family or his house. In fact, when she asked to move in to his house — she said Lloyd was battering her — I was almost grateful, because it meant he moved in with me, a good sign of the commitment I hoped for. That's for your ears only, Jill. And then when the current crisis started, whatever he wanted to do, it was impossible he'd come out of what was originally a generous impulse, to let her have the house rent-free, with any credit. Anything he'd have done, from breaking into the house to sending in the bailiffs, would have given the press a field day. And now they've got one in spades.' She couldn't keep the bitterness out of her voice.

'How's it affecting the two of you?'

'I've hardly seen him since last night's raid. The risk was that the bloody woman was just wasting heat to get at him — and a mighty good job she did of it too. Except it wasn't exactly wasting heat, was it? Bloody cannabis, under his own roof. Literally. My God! But I'm delighted he's going to retire He's been so stressed I've been scared.'

'So the wedding will go ahead?'

'Why ever not? And I'm still counting on your coming with me to pick out a dress.'

Jill shook her head. 'I'd leave it a bit, Fran — unless you want the media at the church door.'

Fran felt the blood draining from her face.

'Even six months down the line they'll be pointing lenses at you if you do anything newsworthy — you must see that. And I tell you straight, a wedding in the Cathedral will be newsworthy.'

'You know, I'd do it to spite them,' Fran declared. But she added quickly, 'I won't, of course. It wasn't ever in our plans. You know that. That was the old chief's idea, remember. Never ours.'

'I know that. The people busily gabbing to the media don't. I bet you my pension your rectory's surrounded, and all the pics they take will make it look like a sodding mansion.'

'With scaffolding, at least,' Fran said. 'It's the only place we've got to live at the moment, Jill, media or not. We won't be moving back into the Loose house any time soon, after all.' She managed a bleak smile. 'The lane to the rectory's so narrow that maybe they won't find it.'

'And how will you reach it if they have? Helicopter?'

* * *

Alice looked up as Fran sloped back to what she hoped would be the sanctuary of her office. 'Mark's still in with the boss, according to Sally. But his son's in reception: could you face seeing him? I'll fix a room for you.'

'I better had, hadn't I? Let him come up here — see what luxury we work in. After all, it'll give everyone a bit more to gossip about if we have a stand-up row. I'll go and get him now.'

'I could—'

'To spare me all the whispers and nudges? The pitying looks? Quite. But I'll go anyway, thanks, Alice — because that's the way I do things.' Head held high, she sailed out.

To her amazement, a number of people made it their business to stop and speak warmly to her, which had the disastrous effect of making her eyes hot, as sympathy always did. So she was far from at her best when she reached the reception area, which was occupied by several people as well as Dave. Excellent, she told herself ironically — now the world and his wife will know how Dave blames me for everything.

But then he turned, and she saw what he was holding. However hard she fought it, she told herself she was strong and had dealt with the worst humans could do to each other without losing sleep, she burst into a pounding pulse of tears.

CHAPTER TWENTY-FIVE

Mark felt almost light-headed with relief. Between them, Alison Brewer, the press officer, Wren and Cosmo Dix — not to mention a guy representing ACPO and thus him — had finally hammered out a press release; Wren would front the press conference, as the coldest, most inimical to criticism, in the team. Somehow Mark's folly in helping the raid on his own home had been turned into an act of heroism, a decent, old-style cop reacting to the sound of a woman's scream — and not just any woman, of course, but his own flesh and blood. Cosmo, to the great disgust of Brewer, had fine-tuned every cliché, management and other.

'Poor George Orwell,' he sighed at last. 'How I love and revere that man and his pellucid prose; how I loathe this scrap of banality.' He lifted the final draft and dropped it as if it were an offending burger-wrapper.

As Cosmo and the others left, Wren turned and signalled Mark to a seat. 'I think we deserve a coffee.' He buzzed through to Sally. 'I won't be asking her to do things like this much longer — I shall buy a coffee-maker. Any recommendations? No?' He sat back in the depths of the new executive chair. 'Well, I have to tell you that I don't know what I'd have done in your place. Apart from a super-injunction, of course. Are you going to press charges against your daughter? Theft? She and that man of hers stole a lot of your electricity, Mark. How many thousands' worth? Criminal damage? One gathers the roof and rafters'll never be the same, and I don't know what your insurance company would make of a claim.'

It was a good job Mark had to wait for Sally to come with the coffee and then leave. 'I think Sammie might be the victim here, with all due respect. My take is that she was indeed assaulted by her then partner, Lloyd, and that her new partner, the father of her unborn child, took advantage of her frailty to move in and take over my home. At least we've nailed him.' Was that a ghost of a smile that his face made almost of its own accord?

'We'll see what the CPS have to say when all our enquiries are complete,' Wren said flatly. 'It goes without saying you're a witness, not part of any investigatory team. Very well, Mark, I suggest you take a few days' gardening leave and—'

'I thought I was retiring, sir, with immediate effect.'

'You must do as you and ACPO think fit. In my view, that could be an admission of culpability. Even if you went on grounds of ill health, which looking at you today would not be impossible. And in any case,' he added, less supportively, 'we need you to be available to help us with our enquiries.'

'In the clichéd or the literal sense?' Mark shot back.

'Good God, man, you've broken the odd rule here and there, but we won't hang you out to dry — you have my word on that.' As if sensing Mark's scepticism, he added with an almost quizzical smile, 'You're one of us, Mark — we'll look after you. Starting with an appointment with the FME. No argument. Our duty of care. You look sick enough,' he added, without noticeable compassion. He picked up his phone, demanding — and presumably getting — an immediate appointment for Mark. 'He'll be free in half an hour. Just get down there. Do exactly what he says about taking leave — and that's an order. Don't worry about clearing your desk or anything so banal, as that idiot Cosmo would say. That can wait till all this blows over. Go home.' He peered again at Mark. 'Except, of course, you don't have one to go to, do you?'

* * *

'He's about to be my stepson,' Fran said, gathering her authority about her, as if she had never disgraced herself by breaking down, 'and I think I can assure you that a bunch of roses does not constitute a security threat.' She tried to stare the reception staff down, but remembered, not too late, she hoped, the ever-present security cameras, recording her every move. So she aimed for a smile. 'But rules is rules, so we'll take these out to my car, Dave. No, we can't do that either. Because I'd need to get you through security to reach the car park. Let's go outside. I could do with some fresh air. No?'

'Whole lot of pressmen out there, Fran. Baying for blood, I'd say. In the absence of Dad's I guess they'd take yours instead.' He produced a rueful smile. 'Say I take these offending items back to my car and then I come back here?'

'Or say we go together, chatting like old friends. That'd give them something to chew on. As for ignoring the press, we were taught that on day one. Ready? And I'll carry the roses and tuck my hand into your arm, if that's OK? Right!'

'God, you've got balls. Except you might want to fix your mascara first. What's that?'

'Shit! My pager! Or, in this case, *deus ex machina.* I'm needed elsewhere, much as I'd rather be making a silent public statement with you, Dave.'

He nodded. 'Thanks. I think. What about Dad — any chance of seeing him?'

'I can't think of anyone in the world he'd rather see at the moment,' she said, with painful truth. 'Give me a second and I'll phone his secretary — see if he's managed to escape from the chief yet.' No response. She tried Sally. 'Apparently, he's been dispatched to see a medic — chief's orders. So you won't be able to yet.'

'I'll come back in an hour or so?'

'They'll find some way to make you talk if you hang around here. Retire to a safe distance and I'll call you the moment I know anything. I promise. When you can see him, see if you can persuade him to go back to your hotel with you. You'll be able to slide out of the back entrance together. Catch you — and the roses — later.'

'Sure.' He dabbed a kiss on her amazed cheek.

* * *

'I simply don't know what to do,' Mark said, realizing too late that he should have taken Fran, breathless for some reason, as if she'd been running, into his arms, to reassure her that all would be well. But he was still seated behind the expanse of his desk. He buried his head in his hands. Looking up, he managed, 'I'm sorry.'

She looked as hamstrung as he by his formality. But she took a step round the desk, arms ready to hug him. Eventually, she stooped to pull his head to her chest. 'Rest, for a start. You look done in, and why not?'

'As soon as I've seen Dr Brodie, I've got to make myself scarce.' Brodie was the least touchy-feely FME he'd ever met, but perhaps his astringency would help.

Fran pulled a face as if she had her doubts about the man too. 'When are you seeing him?'

He looked at his watch. 'In about half an hour.'

'Do you want me to come with you?'

'Why?'

'Not into the consulting room — just to wait with you. And then take you straight off.'

'Where? As Wren pointed out, we don't have a home to go to.' He grabbed her hands. 'Fran, they won't section me, will they?' Despite himself, his voice cracked.

Why on earth should he think that? Perhaps the very fear was a symptom of his illness. 'Jesus, no!' she declared, as if she believed it. She added: 'I'm sure the first thing they'll do is refer you to our GP — thank goodness we're still registered with Dr

Carlisle. A few pills, a bit of counselling, a lot of rest — and we'll find somewhere to call home temporarily at least.'

'The rectory. That's home. I know it's crap, but it's ours. I don't want to go to a hotel. Understand?' She must. She would. Whatever else had driven him to this state, money was part of it — and Sammie had deprived him not just of his home and source of income, but a whole lot of cash on top.

She squeezed his hand. 'Of course. I'll get on to Caffy and warn her.'

'That's something I can do.' With the palest smile he reached for his phone. 'After all, she's going to be my best woman. Isn't she?' It was more than a rhetorical question. Would Fran still want him, after this? 'We are . . . You will . . . ?'

She kissed him hard on the mouth. 'Tomorrow, if Caffy were free. You daft bugger, of course we'll still need her. Unless Dave wants to fight her for the job.'

'I'd forgotten Dave. He was a mess last night too, wasn't he? It must run in the family. Look at me, mad as a hatter.'

She grabbed his shoulders and shook him hard. 'You are not mad,' she said very clearly. 'You are overworked to the point of exhaustion; Dave was upset for a variety of reasons; Sammie has — probably — post-natal depression plus a bit more depression brought on by being pregnant by a violent shit of a drug-dealer.'

He almost nodded. Almost managed a bleak half-grin.

'OK. If you're sure you don't mind, I'll leave you for a bit. Don Simpson and Jill Tanner are at war over their murderer-stroke-victim — someone has to bang their heads together, and it seems as if it's me. Tell you what,' she said, with an almost enigmatic smile, 'put your feet up here for a bit and I'll be back as soon as I can.' She kissed him again.

Perhaps it would be all right.

* * *

'The long and short of it is, Fran, that we'd like you to talk to this Cynd of Jill's,' Don grunted, solid as if carved from the old-fashioned desk he'd hated sacrificing to new corporate designer office furniture.

Despite his gruffness, Fran detected a note of untoward kindness. Was he feeling sorry for her, hoping to take her mind off things with a spell in the interview room? She didn't do being pitied. 'I'm not up to date with the latest techniques,' she countered. 'And it isn't exactly a meeting of true minds, you know. Get some of the kids to do it. They've been on all these courses: it'll do them good to put what they've learned into practice.'

Jill shook her head. 'She trusts you because you're a friend of the Reverend Falkirk's. Oh, and she wants to know how the reverend is before she talks. Won't budge on that. And we don't want her fainting again, not on our watch.'

'And how is Janie?'

'The hospital people don't want to tell us — not related,' Jill said.

'Oh, for crying out loud! Lie your socks off. Tell them she's a vital witness in a murder case and you want to interview her. Actually—' Fran glanced at her watch — 'it might be worth phoning the vicarage itself. There was talk of her going home this afternoon.'

Jill got to her feet, with a venomous look at Don, and left his office.

'And you'll talk to the Lewis woman?' Don put in.

She looked at him squarely. 'As our suspect or as a rape victim?'

'Just get the fucking truth — ma'am,' he added belatedly.

'Gather together every last scrap of evidence, both of the rape and the murder, put it into some sort of order and prepare me some briefing notes. When you've got the latest on Janie — it wouldn't hurt to let Cynd talk to Janie if she's well enough — then if a couple of youngsters really can't talk to the kid — they know her language, for goodness' sake! — I'll talk to her tomorrow. Make sure she's treated kindly, Don. Very kindly. She came forward of her own accord and made the confession, after all. And she *is* a victim. I really, truly don't like the idea of her being locked up a second more than necessary. If only you could get her bailed to a place of safety.'

'She'd scarper again.'

'She didn't scarper the first time, Don. She went to be with Janie. Held her hand when she needed it. There but for the grace of God, remember.' Nodding home the point, she headed back to her own office.

To find Kim arguing loudly with Alice.

'I told you she wasn't in her office,' Alice said pointedly.

'We both will be for a few minutes,' declared Fran, opening the door and waiting for Kim to go in. She caught Alice's eye and shook her head before following Kim.

'Not that it's any of your business, but I was discussing another murder case,' Fran said. 'And you will never, ever speak to our support staff like that. They're paid a pittance, they have very little job security, and believe me, we could not function without them. So the moment you go out you apologize. Properly. Understand? Now, what was it you wanted?'

'That weirdo antiques dealer—'

For once Fran's brain produced a name almost without effort. 'You mean Ms Townend? What about her?'

'She's phoned saying she's got more ideas about hidden documents. I know you'd rather be the one to supervise her, ma'am.' Even though Kim was in the doghouse, she evidently couldn't help a sneer in her voice.

'One of my pleasing eccentricities, Kim, is to enjoy watching a job well done.' She waited for her to absorb that. 'So thank you for coming to tell me in person. Have you fixed a time yet?'

'I said later today, that we really needed to bring the case to a conclusion.'

Fran cursed silently but fluently. Of course, Kim was right, but if ever she needed to free up time this was it. 'And she said?'

'She had to wait for some pot to dry, or something. But she offered nine o'clock tomorrow.'

'Nine tomorrow it is.' When Kim looked mulish, she continued, 'I don't know what weird things happen in that head of hers, but we don't want to upset them, do we?' She smiled sweetly and nodded in the clear direction of the door as she reached for her phone.

CHAPTER TWENTY-SIX

As she negotiated Maidstone's late rush-hour traffic, Fran knew she was an accident waiting to happen. When had she lost the ability to function a hundred and one per cent with no more than a moment's shut-eye to rely on? It had certainly gone, along with her capacity to disengage herself from her cases, however horrible, and with being able to put a full stop to the day with a hot bath and a stiff whisky.

Perhaps it was knowing that another life depended on her. She'd known Mark wasn't coping as well as she — but his descent into irresolution and now something like dependency was terrifying. Their GP, to whom Brodie had referred Mark, had warned her that for the next few days, maybe weeks or even months, she might be dealing with the miserable, petulant, listless shadow of her fiancé. Living with someone depressed was often as bad as being depressed, he'd said.

She'd seen that when her father, previously a strong-willed dominant man, had slipped into senility. Now her mother was free of what Fran only now realized was an almost intolerable burden, she had returned to spry activity — still vile-tempered, still implacably hostile to Fran herself, but at least a human being.

But Mark was no more than middle-aged, fit and with so much to look forward to — in particular what seemed to be a reconciliation with his son. Ah, but there was the downside of his daughter. Fran had a nasty professional feeling that there was still more to come out. And how she'd ever want to speak to a stepdaughter-elect capable of treating her father like this, she didn't know.

'I think you'll find you're still supposed to keep to thirty,' Mark murmured.

She dropped speed promptly. But at least his rebuke showed he was less torpid than she'd feared. And, of course, he'd phoned ahead to Caffy. The fact he was capable of doing something was surely a good sign — wasn't it?

'Did I tell you Dave brought me some flowers and security wouldn't let them through?' she asked. 'Or did he manage to call you himself and tell you all about it?'

A bleak smile. 'I've been a bit elusive today. And I just couldn't face going through all my missed calls.'

'We'll do it together, later, shall we?' That was how she'd jollied her father along.

'Or I could say, "Sod the lot of them"?'

'I know a lot will be crap. But you never know with phone calls . . . And I'd have thought Social Services might want to discuss Frazer and Lucilla's future with you and Dave.' Wrong. She shouldn't have mentioned or even referred to bloody Sammie, should she?

He snorted with something like his old vehemence. Perhaps their doctor had been unduly pessimistic: God knew she hoped so. As soon as Janie was fit — and, without any reference to Cynd, she'd called the vicarage and spoken to Janie's sister, a woman with an accent so impenetrable it demanded subtitles, and found that Janie was home but was catching up on sleep missed in the hospital — as soon as she was up to praying again, she'd get Janie on Mark's case.

'If I know social services, I'll be the last one they consult. And actually, since Sammie has point-blank refused to see me, I'd have to say that in professional terms they'd be right. For all they know I might be a rampant paedophile who's already tried to abuse them. Or maybe I abused her. Allegedly. Fran, I never touched her, I swear. Or Dave. Or the kids.' He covered his face. And then a little of the old Mark gleamed out. 'Or anyone else either, for the record.'

She pulled over and parked. 'Listen to me: I love you and trust you with my life. You are a good man. You've devoted every day since I first knew you to making life better for people. Making a difference. That's what you do.'

'How can I do that if I'm retired?'

'You'll find ways, I promise you. Now, it looks as if the rain's coming on more heavily, and I think we should tackle that lane before it becomes a river. Don't you? Won't be much fun paddling out to the loo in the night, will it?'

'His and hers chamber pots,' he murmured. And then he fell asleep.

* * *

Why should the sight of the Winnebago reduce him to tears? All he'd done was warn Caffy that they'd be staying in their dining room again. And she'd gone to the trouble of getting that pop star of hers — the one Fran used to swoon over and might once more, if they ever came face to face — to lend complete strangers his property all over again. As if he was an invalid, Fran came round to ease him out of the car. Tetchily — far too tetchily — he pushed her aside.

'Christ, woman, I'm not in my dotage.'

'Sorry. All I wanted to do was hold your hand. I'm afraid all this kindness is going to blow me away.' Her voice was shaking, but whether at others' kindness or his unkindness he couldn't tell. She'd always been so strong. But now she'd got weepy — first at Sissinghurst and now here. Was she menopausal or something? No, she was over that. So — and he told himself off for being sexist and ageist and any other -ist — was she just as bone weary as he, with just as much cause?

* * *

Fran had to keep going. She had to put one foot in front of the next, and then repeat the process. Stagger she would not. Weep at the thought of walking through the drenching rain she would not. But she didn't want to drive. She'd scared herself, if not Mark, on the way here. Perhaps she'd be all right after a nap. But naps had to be on hold as long as Mark needed her — even if it was just to find the best mobile reception.

At last she could manage to put on the kettle. This time the sainted Caffy, or whoever, hadn't had time to stock the fridge, but at least no one had got round to throwing out the supplies they'd left when they'd asked for the precipitate removal of the motorhome from the rectory site. So they could have green tea and a digestive biscuit.

'I should have picked up the post,' Mark declared.

'When? When did you — when did either of us — have the luxury of nipping into town and leading our own lives? Just tell me.' Her voice had risen. 'Sorry. Look, you make the tea; I'll nip across into the rectory and bring across our clothes and so on.'

'But it's raining.'

She waited. Of course it was bloody raining, but he could scarcely spend the evening in his now redundant ACC uniform. And she needed a breather. 'Just our jeans and stuff.' She left without waiting for a response.

* * *

Was this how prisoners starting a life sentence felt? Penned in? Desperate for space? He couldn't stay in here. Couldn't face it. But where else could he go? No money, remember. In the morning he must talk to his insurance company, but he had an idea that things wouldn't be at all straightforward.

Of course, Fran was right. They couldn't go up to the pub in their working gear. His former working gear. What the hell had he done? Why on earth had he insisted on retiring then and there? He could have gone on sick leave, while they sorted it all out — Wren had even implied that that was what he wanted him to do. He'd meant to talk to Adam before he made any rash decisions. Adam had gone, of course — but he'd allowed a fellow officer to jump to his death. All Mark had done was let his daughter set up a cannabis farm and steal thousands of pounds. How did that compare on the great moral scheme of things?

Where the hell was Fran? It didn't take that long to pick up a few clothes, for God's sake.

He took the nearest mug of tea and sat down to wait. But by now he wasn't sure what he was waiting for.

* * *

Paula and Caffy were still in the rectory, ostensibly finishing some task but, from their glances, waiting for Fran.

Caffy, wiping her hands on a turps-smelling rag, though as far as Fran could see they were perfectly clean, spoke first. 'You may find that that TV in the Winnebago doesn't work for a couple of days.'

'No?'

'We adjusted the aerial so he couldn't pick up the news. And I'd venture to suggest that you find another resting place for the Winnebago. We brought it down because we thought you'd be private enough here, but we were wrong. We could hardly move for the bloody media. Some nice man called Bill Baker dropped by to see you, and he ended up driving a tractor up and down the lane most of the day, just to stop them parking.'

Fran shook her head, stupidly. 'But I'm not insured.'

Paula looked her in the eye. 'You're in no fit state to drive a strange vehicle anyway. And Mark can't be either.' She produced a sudden smile. 'But we could get the person who brought it over here to drive you. Are you OK to follow? It's not as if you're tailing a Mini, is it?'

She held her head. 'But—'

'Pick out enough clothes to last for about four days. I'm sure the media will be interested in something else by then. After that — well, your rectory awaits you. A good half should be habitable by then. Can Mark paint? Well, a bit of emulsion therapy might be good for him. Unpaid, I have to say,' Paula added, as if she really needed to make that clear.

'And then there's Dave — Mark's son. He needs to see his dad. He might even be on his way.'

'We can give him map coordinates. The post code won't help much.' She looked at her watch and raised an eyebrow.

Since she'd used pretty much the same technique on Kim earlier in the day, Fran knew she'd met her match.

* * *

With surprising tenderness, Dave moved his father's plate as Mark's head fell forward on to the table.

'I guess chicken bhuna might be the new cure for baldness, but I'd rather my father wasn't a guinea pig in the trials,' he said.

'This takeaway was pure genius,' Fran said, refraining from pointing out that the Winnebago would smell of it for days. On the other hand, Paula would no doubt be able to suggest an effective air-freshener, so what the hell?

'Glad you enjoyed it. Shall I help you clear? It was always my job at home.'

What should she say? Her first thought was that Mark was best left to sleep in silence. But if Dave was happy to do something he'd once done for his mother, surely she should accept?

'How are you on dishwashers? It's Mark's job, because he reckons I don't have the spatial awareness to get the maximum in.' She rinsed the worst residues; he took the dishes from her. 'Thanks.' Checking that Mark was still asleep, she ventured, 'Any news of Sammie? He's worried sick she may come out with weird allegations against him. Like child molestation or something.'

'You knew my mom, didn't you? Can you imagine she'd not have noticed if anything was wrong? And if Dad had been — harming — Sammie, she'd have grassed him up, sure as eggs. He wasn't a bad man, he was just a bad father, in that he was never there. We did have some good times. That train set.' He looked past her. 'That was the best. You know what he said when he realized Sammie had wrecked it? "I'll get you another one, son." See — he knew. He remembered.'

Wet though it was, she stretched a hand and squeezed his arm. 'Of course he did. And wasn't there something with Sammie and balloons?'

He managed a smile. 'You're right. Every birthday — so many balloons you couldn't count them. Balloons everywhere.'

'You've inherited his gift for giving.' She nodded at the roses, now in one of Todd's vases. 'He was so proud of you both. Pictures of you on his desk — and your mum. He used to touch them goodbye every time he went out on a risky shout. As if he was saying goodbye to you in the flesh. However much you might hate the thought of us getting married, he's never thought of me as he thought of Tina, I'm sure of that.'

'Uh, uh. Don't put yourself down.' He made a business of checking everything in the dishwasher was straight, looked for and found the detergent and set the load off. 'Hey — that's cool. It's almost silent. He told me he couldn't live without you, you know. Don't suppose he's ever told you that.'

'Don't suppose he ever will. I think he only proposed because he was scared of heights. But I'm glad he did. Will you come back over for the wedding — even if you can't be his best man? Caffy's bagged that job, and I think it'd break her heart if he changed his mind and asked you instead. Which I know he'd want to do, otherwise.'

'And I can't even lead you up the aisle!' he wailed. Then he produced a younger version of his father's smile. 'You just try to keep me away. Hey, you want a bridesmaid wearing the worst tooth braces you ever saw? 'Cause Phoebe'd be tickled pink.'

It seemed the wedding at least would flourish, even when everything else was collapsing about their ears.

CHAPTER TWENTY-SEVEN

It took her ten minutes and a phone call to Paula to run Bill Baker's notes to earth. Why on earth had she dropped them on one of the sleeping bags? Whatever the reason, at least they were in safe hands, and she dispatched one of Kim's team to collect them. Only then did she do what she'd wanted to and hurtle down to reception, where Lina Townend was waiting, unexceptionably dressed in jeans and a T-shirt.

'Sorry I'm late, Ms Townend,' Fran greeted her. 'I rather underestimated the journey time.' She signed her through security.

'Yes, Caffy said you would. She's a one off, isn't she? She and the rest of the team, of course. They're the only ones my partner will allow to touch our cottage.' She slowed to a halt and stopped, looking embarrassed. 'Look, would you mind very much if I worked without DI Thomas breathing down my neck this morning? It's hard to concentrate with such waves of hostility coming at you. Sorry. I shouldn't have said that — it was very unprofessional.'

'No problem,' Fran said easily. 'Someone will have to be present, but it doesn't have to be Kim.' She was quite glad to have a companion as she walked through what felt quite endless corridors, still filled with colleagues awash with gossip. If she was engaged in animated conversation, then she wouldn't have to make eye contact with any of them, whether they were giving pitying glances or encouraging smiles.

'She reminds me of the officers who used to run me in when I was a kid, that's the problem,' Townend continued. 'So it's probably my fault, rather than hers. All the same . . .'

'I thought I might bring my breakfast and watch you, if that's OK.'

'But you're one of the bigger cheeses, aren't you? Won't it be a waste of your time?'

Of course it would, but this time she'd at least let Alice know where she was. And she'd leave her pager on. 'Would you prefer a lowly constable? You shall have one if I can find one. Male or female?'

Townend giggled. 'You're having me on, aren't you? If I said, "Bring me Prince Charming on a white horse . . . ?"'

'I'd say you'd got your myths mixed up, and that health and safety didn't permit the riding of dumb animals on police property — except if they're on duty, of course.'

'So I could have a working horse or a Prince Charming.'

'Or me with a mug of coffee and a round of toast.' What a pity she couldn't conjure up that nice lad Fred from the self-store units. He'd have made a good prince.

* * *

Fullers. According to the stonework over the door, that was what their hosts' house was called. It was a beautiful building, a little larger and definitely older than the rectory. No doubt Caffy could have filled him in, but she'd left the house to go to work before he was even awake. Fran had gone too. However, Caffy'd left him the key to her flat, which had a separate door round the back, with an invitation to help himself to breakfast, have a deep, long soak (he could sing as loudly as he wanted because Todd and Jan were abroad) and a browse through her books. Acres of them, all glowing in their sense of being read and valued. No TV. Not even a trannie radio, unless one lurked in one of the immaculate kitchen units: the kitchen and bathroom were both state of the art — courtesy of Todd's money, not Caffy's, no doubt. How did she keep in touch with the real world? Perhaps reception out here on the Isle of Oxney was poor — he'd noticed the Winnebago TV was on strike this morning. She'd also left him a book of local walks, with a couple asterisked. She'd even got rid of yesterday's rain. There was a Post-it note attached.

If you're not used to walking, you might want to have your long soak after your long walk. :)

That was his morning worked out for him, then. And he was very glad, because he didn't think he could have done it himself. God, he was so tired — as if he'd not already slept the clock round. Would everything always be so much effort? He could scarcely bear to move.

* * *

The pile of paperwork Fran had taken with her to accompany her late breakfast lay untouched at her feet. Lina Townend, now dressed in white paper, with the little key they'd found last time resting in her right hand, was sitting as still as she was: simply sitting, as if listening to something. Or listening *for* something. The stillness was catching. It wasn't unlike being in church, during the silences between prayers — a similar shared concentration but also openness to something else.

Heavens, what a good job Kim wasn't here.

At last the girl got up and wandered over to the piles of furniture. Fran was desperate for her to explore the cabinet again, to take it down to its last piece. But she ignored it, heading instead to the piles of smaller items. Ah! A Victorian writing slope. That would have drawers a-plenty, wouldn't it? And a lock for the little key?

But it didn't have what Townend wanted. She moved aimlessly along, an index finger raised as if it was somehow guiding her. Amazingly, Fran knew what she was feeling. She'd had some of her best results by trusting a weird instinct, the sort you certainly wouldn't mention in the witness box, when her body had seemed to tingle with some below-the-level-of-consciousness electrical activity. In the past she'd had to fend off interruptions with a hand raised, traffic policeman style. At least the young woman didn't need to do that, but she had to shut out the sundry random noises of the building and its occupants.

Lina was drifting no longer. She had stopped and was almost frantically clearing items from the next pile. Whatever it was, was near the bottom. Finally, she sank to her knees.

Fran was desperate to stand and watch. But not for anything would she have disturbed Lina's concentration.

At last she was rewarded. There was the tiniest click. So the key had opened whatever it was. Now she could stand. And watch Lina reach into something and wave an envelope in the air. She crept over, fearful of disturbing the spell and having the whole lot disintegrate before her eyes.

'A dressing case,' Lina said, in her normal speaking voice. 'The obvious place really. Many of them from this era — it's pretty well contemporary with that lovely writing slope — have a secret drawer where Her Ladyship can conceal . . . *billets-doux* . . . from His Lordship.' Why the hesitation? But Lina was fluent again. 'All you had to do in this case was lift this manicure drawer and press this tiny lever. See? It's so beautifully made you'd hardly detect the drawer hidden amongst all the inlay. And here, as I said, may be what you've been looking for.'

Fran held out a tentative hand. So now it was time for the real, prosaic world of policing, with gloves, evidence bags and photos.

'I suppose,' Lina said mildly, 'that I'm not allowed to know what I've unearthed.'

'Have you got time for a cuppa? Until I find out myself? Because I really ought to examine this with someone like Kim Thomas, and although you're booted and suited, she might just feel . . . Sometimes one has to make compromises, Lina.'

'You've got to work with her,' Lina said, with a gentle smile.

'Exactly. On the other hand, the canteen will be full of handsome young men, if not their white chargers, and I could ask a nice lad called Tom Arkwright to shout you elevenses.' Tom — one of her nicest ever protégés. The son she'd never had. What if . . .

She made her calls, one to Kim — yes, rank must take precedence — and the next to Tom, already a most capable sergeant and ready to fly upwards. How would kids like him manage if she retired? No. With Mark sick, it must be *when* she retired. And the youngsters would just have to manage.

'Sounds good. Am I allowed to ask if the postcards were useful?' Townend emerged from the paper suit like a butterfly from a chrysalis.

'You are. We're working on them now. Did anything strike you about them?' Fran asked carefully.

'Your Ms Thomas asked me that. And then she phoned me to check. There was some problem about the order they'd been left in, wasn't there?' The question sounded innocent enough, but Fran suspected a mild case of grassing up. 'The answer to your question is the gravestone, of course. I'd have expected it to come at the end of the sequence, though, not at the start. All the other pictures were of places she'd visited or lived in, I suppose — I wouldn't have minded living in that place in France, would you? — and of course you'd end up in a grave. But not someone else's. It was as if the grave was the start of her story, wasn't it?'

'Carry on.'

'I suppose it wasn't her family's? No? Did something traumatic happen there?'

'Very good question,' Fran said, wondering why the hell she hadn't had the energy, and the others the nous, to find the answer already.

'I wondered if she wanted her ashes buried there, but Ms Thomas said there was nothing in her will about it.'

'Nope. She wanted her ashes scattered on Dartmoor, and I gather someone from the community she died in obliged when she went on her holidays.'

'No family to be near. Sad. Or perhaps it means she's a free spirit, with no ties at all, at home wherever the four winds will take her. Or that she's made good fertilizer,' she added with a prosaic grin.

* * *

'Don, I've got no time just now. I've got a witness waiting.' Fran jerked a thumb at the canteen.

Don Simpson looked over her shoulder. 'That her with young Tom Arkwright? Looks as if she's happy to wait a bit longer. And I thought you'd want to know. Everything's coming together nicely. First up, we've got an ID on the man young Cynd stabbed.'

'Allegedly.'

'Come off it, guv'nor — she told you she had. Turns out he's a Bulgarian.'

'Bulgarian? Ah! The Eastern European fillings. And what was our Bulgarian doing over here? I presume he had a name, by the way?'

'Andon Yovkov. How he wormed his way into the UK I don't know: he should have been stopped at the border, but with these cuts . . .' He shrugged. 'He was a career criminal starting at the age of fifteen — convictions in Italy and Belgium to his name. He's been on Interpol's radar, because — guess what? — his speciality is metal theft. He's got convictions for robbing everything from statues of saints to war memorials. He even nobbled a Giacometti bronze and got it melted down. So I'd guess a few church roofs will be the safer for his death. One of his mates fried alive a few weeks back up near Darlington while he was nicking the live wire from a railway line.'

'Poetic justice. You've told SOCA the good news? Excellent.' Despite herself, she was getting sucked into the narrative. 'But how did he come to get Cynd's knife in his ribs? And end up on his own near Bridge?'

He patted a file. 'You asked for a complete briefing: here it is.'

'So it is. Thanks, Don.' She tugged her hair. 'It's no good: I can't do two things at once. I know, I know — it comes with our job descriptions these days. What I'd like you to do — and I know you won't love me for saying this — is take it down to Jill and go through it together. She's got stuff; you've got stuff. Share it. You're both so damned territorial that I could bang your heads together. And then meet me in my office, the pair of you, in half an hour. When I get there I shall expect the latest on Janie Falkirk. I just hope we've got something reassuring to tell Cynd. Apart from anything else it might loosen her tongue. OK? I said OK, Don.'

'OK it is. I tell you this, guv'nor: that business with your old man hasn't put you off your stroke.'

She patted his arm. 'And you'd think the less of me if it had, wouldn't you? See you in half an hour, Don. Actually, make it an hour. So I don't have to leave you kicking your heels.'

To avoid further argument, she ducked into the nearest loo, reaching for her phone.

'Dave? I left your father asleep, but I can't imagine he'll stay that way. Now, the Pact women have enforced a news embargo on him — disconnected the TV aerial and hidden their radios.'

'I thought they were just painters, not psychologists!'

'The longer I do this job, the more I realize very few people are just anything. Anyway, if you contact him, just bear that in mind. Lots of your news from home, the latest on Phoebe's teeth, that sort of thing.'

'New train sets?'

'Precisely. Talk about the possibility of having one in the loft at the rectory — there's acres of space. Maybe you could even do a repeat of last night and take him out to lunch. But phone first — I know Caffy believes that walking's the best cure for anything and everything, and he may already have his boots on.'

'Will do. Maybe I'll organize a picnic, to keep him away from people. I hate the way all these lovely pubs have twenty-four-hour Sky news and no sound on. Just those endless Breaking News straplines continually repeating the same breaking news.'

'Get him started on that — he'll have a lovely chunter. And now I have to go — talk later. God bless!' Where had that come from? She stared at the phone for a moment before pocketing it. Then, of course, she had to fish it out again to call Kim.

She decided to collect Lina from the canteen herself, watching from the door for a few moments to see how she was responding to dear Tom Arkwright's obvious admiration. Between smiles, after laughter, even, her face fell into such wistful lines that Fran was reminded of Dilly, to whom she'd promised lunch. She'd meant to forget the tentative arrangement, but such sadness in the young maybe deserved an airing to older and confidence-keeping ears. Especially ones suddenly sympathetic to problems with one's lover.

Tom escorted Lina over to her. 'You OK, guv'nor, with all this going on around you?' He looked at her closely. 'You're not thinking of jumping ship too, are you? You'd be missed if you did — more than the ACC to be honest, for all he's a decent man who's done his best.'

'I shall have to go sooner or later, Tom, won't I? I'm eligible already. But maybe I'll let Mark find his retirement feet first.'

'Aye, especially as long as you're stuck in that caravan or whatever. You'd be falling over each other all the time, and there's nothing like that to cause the odd fight.' Where Tom got such homely wisdom from she'd no idea — the relative who always sent him cakes, maybe.

'Quite,' she said, with a smile, no hint of the snub a junior officer might have expected for venturing such an observation to his one-time boss.

'Don't forget: we all want that wedding to go ahead. I don't suppose you need an usher, ma'am?'

She gave a non-committal grin. Actually, she'd love the lad to be there, with or without Lina.

Would the youngsters fix another meeting? She pretended to check her phone to give them a moment. Perhaps they already had. She hoped so. But there was no sign of any arrangement, and she fought a strong impulse to suggest one. Maybe she'd ask Lina later. Meanwhile, there was more important stuff than affairs of the heart: there was the opening of the cache that Lina had found, which they and Kim would examine in the privacy of her office.

Doling out gloves to the others, and putting on her own non-latex, she put herself in charge of opening the packet and Kim in charge of recording each item. The first was a newspaper cutting.

CHURCHYARD RAPE

West Midland Police are searching for a masked attacker who sexually assaulted a young woman in a quiet suburb late last night. A spokesman described the attack as brutal.

No names, of course. But Kim was already jotting the meagre details — not a date, not even a year.

'Bet that's where the gravestone is!' Lina gasped. 'Wow!'

There was another scrap of newspaper: the death notice of Margaret Minton. No age, no details at all. More scribbling from Kim.

'She's still playing with you, isn't she?' Lina said. 'At least you know why she called herself Marion Lovage. The first names almost the same, the surname another herb — well, lop off the -on part of the surname,' she added with relish, clearly telling Kim that she could play her game, even if Kim couldn't play hers.

'However,' Fran said, 'this is not a confession by any means. Is there anything else?'

'Loads of newspaper cuttings,' said Kim, sounding more interested in them than she had in the furniture. 'One about a newcomer to Seahouses winning a prize at a flower show; another from North Wales . . . best jam in class . . . Ma'am, these might well tie in with the photos and with the name changes. Can I get someone on to them now? While someone else phones West Midland Police, of course.'

'Good idea. Use this to summon someone.' She passed her her phone. 'Meanwhile, I'm two minutes late for something else.'

She was already halfway to the door when Lina squeaked, 'Isn't that a death certificate? Shocking writing the doctor had. The name looks more like Margaret. So how can she have had her own death notice? Or has someone changed the name?'

Fran said, 'You're right. Absolutely right . . .' She ached to stay and theorize, but said firmly, 'The forensics people will help there. Call them as well, will you, Kim? And when you've done that, let's see if any of the dates you come up with tie in with Frank Grange. In any way, no matter how remote. Marion Lovage, I've had enough of your time-wasting — more than enough.'

CHAPTER TWENTY-EIGHT

Fran wished she could say much the same, in the same ferocious tone, to Cynd Lewis when she hastened into the interview room. But that would be to bully someone who was in every sense a victim. Jill joined her, sitting to one side, to make it clear to Cynd that Fran was taking the lead — and also, perhaps, to dissociate herself a little if the questioning became as fierce as Fran's often could. The solicitor beside Cynd was a mate of Janie's, a sleepy-looking middle-aged Asian woman wearing, to Cynd's obvious bemusement, a sari. One glance at Mrs Chandraseka's eyes, however, revealed an extremely alert brain. Even if Fran had wanted to catch the girl out, Mrs Chandraseka would be having none of it.

Fran smiled. 'How's Janie this morning?'

Cynd looked at her solicitor and at Jill, as if for permission. 'Jill says she's fine. The drains are coming out later, right?'

Jill nodded. 'Right.'

'Excellent. Before we talk about the night you went to Janie's to tell her about the rape and the stabbing, I want you to tell me why we couldn't find you last Sunday or all day Monday.'

Cynd smiled. That was easy. 'Hitched to the hospital to keep an eye on her. Got stuff to eat there. Slept in the A and

E waiting room. Same the next day — held her hand that night 'cos she was moaning in her sleep.'

Fran nodded encouragingly, not least because Janie would testify it was true. 'So you weren't running away from us? The police? For the benefit of the tape recorder, Cynd, can you speak up?'

'A bit. I didn't so much run away as want to be with Janie. She needed me.'

Fran smiled. The angel by the bed indeed.

'If you'd known we wanted to talk to you that evening, would you have run away?'

'Probably. But only to the hospital. 'Cos Janie needed me more, didn't she?'

'So how much did we need you?' Not a good question. 'And why?' Fran added quickly.

'Well, it wasn't to talk about me rape, was it? It must have been about sticking that bloke.'

'Quite. Now, I'd like you to tell me a bit more about the night you were raped. Tell me all about it, just as it happened. Who was in the room?'

'Just me. And a punter,' she added defensively. Her chin rose defiantly. 'Only, I didn't tell you about him 'cos he's married and a nice guy. I yelled at him to fuck off and say sod all if anyone asked. He was there, and this guy bursts in, starts shoving us around. High as a kite, he was. Not me punter, the other one. Gets his thieving hands on my gear, too. I'm afraid this punter's going to try to help me, but like I said, I told him to fuck off. He's got a sick wife, miss. Wouldn't do her any good to know what her old man's up to. Not that he's up to anything very much at all. Not these days. Often he just falls asleep, and I have to wake him up when it's time he shoved off.'

Fran asked, suspecting she knew the answer already, 'That's when his time's up — the time he's paid you for?'

Cynd looked blank. 'It's the time he should be home with his missus.'

'Right. OK, Cynd, carry on,' Jill prompted her.

'I know all about them CCTV cameras, so he comes and goes where the cameras aren't likely to pick him up. But you want to look for an old guy with a bit of a limp — I think his back's bad. Maybe from lifting her.'

Fran found herself tensing. Fifty per cent of her found the sentimental picture not just cloying but unbelievable. Then she remembered the waif-like angel at Janie's bed. One thing Cynd was good at — perhaps the only good thing, but maybe you shouldn't sneer at that — was patiently holding hands.

Meanwhile, Jill was nodding. 'Be nice to identify him, ma'am. Do you have a name for him, Cynd?'

'Yes, but it's not one I'm going to tell you. Part of the deal, see,' she declared ambiguously. 'Anyway, off he goes, and this guy — horrible breath, needs his teeth seeing to — jumps me. And he wants to take pictures of him doing it. No way. Fucking sick, I tell him. I got some self-respect. But I pretend to look at his sodding phone and say how brilliant it is, and while I'm doing that I reach for the knife I'd left on the table and go for him. Just enough to hurt, I thought. Hurt quite a bit — enough to make him fuck off too. So he grabs the phone and buggers off.' She opens her eyes wide. 'Find his phone, you'll find my prints on it.'

'We could do with your witness, Cynd. It'd really help you if you told us his name. Even the name you call him.'

Cynd shut her mouth ostentatiously. 'Help me or not, you're not getting shit from me. Not if it lands him and his missus in it. Dying of something nasty's bad enough without knowing your old man's seeing a tart. Sod it.' She looked from her to Jill, from Jill to Mrs Chandraseka. 'Even if I go to jail. And bugger the lot of you.'

Fran said quietly, 'Mrs Chandraseka, would you like a few minutes in private with your client, to see if she wants to reconsider anything she's said? For the benefit of the tape, the time is eleven fourteen, and DCI Tanner and DCS Harman are leaving the room.'

Don was hovering in the corridor, giving an impression of a man who was heading somewhere with a piece of paper of clichéd importance and had — quite by coincidence, of course — run into them. 'Any luck?'

'If you mean has she confessed,' Jill snarled, 'she has already. Right on day one. Remember?'

Fran didn't have time for their childishness. 'Don, have you got mugshots of Yovkov handy? And his usual mates? And get someone to check Cynd's claim that there are parts of her street or the street her flat backs on to that aren't very well covered by CCTV.'

'I can tell you that myself, guv'nor: in fact, I've already nagged the council about it.'

'Excellent. So it is feasible that a white van — I know you were looking for one — could have lurked without detection? And that he could have staggered that far before he collapsed?'

Don smiled, brightly and cheerfully. 'Indeed it is, guv'nor. Because I've just picked up some of the little scrote's friends, the ones that left him to bleed to death. At least, that'll be my line.' His chest puffed almost visibly.

'And it's conceivable that one of Cynd's punters could have used the equally ill-covered route?'

'I'll get someone to double-check the approach roads,' Jill said, with something of a flounce, and set off down the corridor.

'Excellent. Though I'd rather not have to haul in a carer with a dying wife who needs a bit of respite from time to time — even if it's not the sort for which social services would cough up. Then I think we should fix a swift meeting with the crown prosecutor, don't you?'

'Your take being, guv'nor?' Don asked.

'It'd be a waste of time to go ahead with a prosecution. Look at it another way, Don: she saved us a lot of trouble getting rid of young Andon Yovkov. If it wouldn't give you apoplexy, I'd be tempted to recommend she got some sort of crime-stoppers' award.'

'How about we compromise and fast-track her on to a drugs rehabilitation programme? You know if she got cash she'd only blow the lot and maybe kill herself in the process.'

Fran recalled the CCTV of her putting back stuff she'd shoplifted. 'I'm not sure she would.'

'You know what that vicar would say: *lead her not into temptation*.'

She threw her head back and laughed. 'You always could trump me, Don. I'll talk about it to Janie when she's fit. Meanwhile, I'll leave both the reward and the programme in your hands — you know you owe her a favour. Or two. OK, let's show her the mugshots and see if she confirms that Yovkov's the man who raped her, and whom, in self-defence, she killed. I just want absolutely everything tied up right and tight. And we'd better feed and water her too, or Mrs Chandraseka will complain.'

'I'd say,' Don said, surprising her, 'that she's put on a couple of pounds already on our grub. Let's hope the reverend will keep feeding her up.'

'You know what, I'd guess that when Janie's sister returns to Scotland, it'll be Cynd that takes over the caring. There's more to her than meets the eye, you know.'

'That's the trouble,' Don agreed with a sigh. 'There always is.'

* * *

By the time she, Don and Jill had conferred with the CPS and established that Cynd would not be charged, Fran was so high on adrenaline and lack of food that she almost forgot that she should have been worrying about Kim and Lina, still closeted in her office. On the grounds that she needed the loo and had a sick fiancé to think about, she decided to postpone her return for a few more minutes.

To her alarm, there was no reply from Mark's phone. However much she told herself it might simply be a matter of bad coverage, she wasn't convinced. She speed-dialled Dave.

'I was just going to call you. I can't locate him, Fran. I'm up here by the Winnebago, which was unlocked, but there's no sign of him.'

'Did you speak earlier?'

'Nope.'

'Have you looked inside the Winnebago? Any note or anything?' She couldn't stop her voice rising in panic.

'Nothing. I can't get any response from the house.'

'You've tried the flat at the back? Caffy's own place?'

'So there's another way in? I'm on my way. I'll call you back.'

She leant against the sink, fighting the nausea, the desire to scream, most of all the urgent need to do something — anything.

How long would it take Dave to get to the house? Into the flat? How long, for God's sake, for him to call her? And what if Mark wasn't there?

She'd made it to the loo before she threw up and was washing her face and mouth before the phone rang again.

'Can't get in. I've rung and banged the door but—'

'I'll call Caffy.' She cut his call unceremoniously and speed-dialled.

'I'm actually not far from there,' Caffy said. 'Don't panic, as they say. Just go and sit down. Do you hear? I mean it.'

And why not? At least in her office she was in a position to summon all the help going, from tracker dogs to helicopters. She staggered rather than walked back, trying to trot but hardly managing. She fell through the door.

'Guv? Are you all right?'

It took her a moment to register that Kim was in her chair, with someone else the other side. The Townend girl. Of course. And it was Lina who grabbed her as she swayed.

'I'm fine,' she managed. 'But there's a problem at home.'

On her feet already, Kim said, 'I'll drive you out there. We'll talk about all this later..'

'I've just got to wait for news. I'll be all right.' Dimly, she realized that Lina was holding her hand, making her sit but not letting go.

'Yes, you will,' Lina said, with strange assurance. 'Just wait for the call. Concentrate on breathing out. That's all.'

'I could do with a coffee.'

'Sure you could. Just close your eyes.'

From somewhere Sally materialized, with green tea and a slab of cake. 'Get these down you and tell me what I can do.'

'Nothing, Problem at home. Oh!' She snatched her ringing phone. Dave! In her anxiety she dropped it. Lina retrieved it and held it to her ear for her.

'He's OK. Hear that, Fran? He's OK. When Caffy got here we found him safe and sound. He'd only fallen asleep in the bath, for Christ's sake. He says it's his tablets. I've got him out and dried him off, and I'm about to ladle as much coffee into him as I can.'

'Nine-nine-nine, Dave. Just call an ambulance, for God's sake.' There was the sound of the phone falling. 'Hallo?' she screamed.

'Fran. Fran. It's me. I haven't tried to top myself. I just fell asleep. Promise. Seems the tablets don't suit me — Dave can make me a doctor's appointment when I've had this coffee and some of Caffy's muesli. I'll call you. Love you, Fran.'

'And I love you.' Even as she held back tears she wanted to hold the moment to her: Mark saying the L word, in front of his own son, no less. And she'd responded in kind in front of strangers. Maybe she wouldn't tell him about their audience.

Now she might have fallen asleep herself if she'd had a bath or even an empty stretch of floor handy, so huge was the wave of weariness that flooded over her.

Kim looked embarrassed that two senior officers — correction, one senior officer, one ex-ACC — could make such fools of themselves in public, but said, 'I could still drive you out there, ma'am.'

'I'll be OK. Honestly, I will. But thank you. It's OK now. And we've sorted the Cynd business.'

'Excellent,' Sally said, adding firmly, 'eat your cake. The tea'll be too hot. Now, I'm sure nothing's so urgent that these two young ladies can't give you a few minutes to sort yourself out.'

Obediently, Kim and Lina headed for the door.

'No, I'm fine. Maybe they need tea and cake too.'

'Tea they can have, but as for cake, they'll have to get their own. That was my lunch,' Sally said.

'They'd better get some for you too,' Fran managed.

'I'm on to it,' Kim said.

'And good thick wholemeal sarnies,' Lina added. 'Better for the blood sugar. My partner's got some pre-diabetic condition,' she added as Kim exited. 'So I know all sorts of silly things like that. Sally's right. You should sit quietly for a bit: when Kim gets back we'll have a lot to tell you, and you'll need a clear head. And no, I can't tell you anything without her here — it wouldn't be right.'

Fairly sure that Kim wouldn't have been equally scrupulous, Fran did as she was told.

* * *

She might almost have been dozing, the phone made her jump so much. 'Just an update,' Dave's voice said. 'He really is fine, Fran. I'll try to make him check in with that doctor later, but he's good. I promise. We'll go for a bit of a stroll and then have some lunch. OK? He wants to speak to you again.'

Mark's voice came through thickly. 'Still chomping muesli, sweetheart. How are you? Dave said you sounded weird.'

'You'd sound weird if you thought *I'd* slit my wrists in the bath, wouldn't you? Get on with your breakfast. Mark, I love you so much I'd have slit mine too if you had.' Unable to say more, she ended the call. Absently, she took the tissue that appeared from nowhere. No, she didn't have an angel like Janie's, but she did have Lina beside her.

'I'll keep Kim outside for a bit longer,' she murmured, leaving the room and closing the door quietly behind her.

And then the phone rang again. Caffy. 'Sorry, Fran — it was my fault. I should have warned him to jack the bathroom door open so he could hear the bell. Mind you, I didn't reckon on him playing Mozart so loudly he might not have heard the last trump. Fancy sleeping through Mozart . . . Anyway, Dave's taking him for a stroll, and I've told them a nice place for a picnic.'

'You're sure he's OK?'

'Fran, I promise you he didn't try to top himself. And unless he was a contortionist, he wouldn't have been able to drown: he's too tall to fit in it properly, for goodness' sake. And he only had a few inches of water. Such a puritan. Me, I like bubbles up to my chin. Look, I've got a load of emulsion to take over to the rectory. I mustn't keep Paula waiting any longer.'

'No indeed,' Fran managed. Laughing at this stage wasn't an option either: she knew she could become hysterical with no effort at all. So she sipped tea, ran a brush through her hair and touched up her make-up. There. Now she could invite the others to return. 'Time to look at all this paperwork,' she said as she opened the door.

'Not to mention the information my team's gathered together,' Kim said with a bit of a smirk.

'They've worked like greased lightning,' Fran said. 'Well done them.'

The first and most valuable piece of information came from the West Midlands Police: some thirty years back a serial rapist had attacked a young woman in a churchyard in Harborne, one of Birmingham's leafier suburbs. Margaret Minton had been found unconscious on a gravestone — the gravestone in the photograph. Perhaps the line *In God We Trust* was meant literally. Or was it profoundly ironic? Minton must have been exceptionally brave, giving clear and unequivocal information both during the investigation and being a superb witness at the trial. But then West Midlands Police came up with the rapist's chilling final words as he'd been sent down for twelve years. 'I've not finished with you yet. You need to watch your back. Because I shall get you for this one day.'

But he hadn't, because she'd died of cancer. Or had she? The handwriting expert in the forensics team swore the death certificate had been changed: it had originally been for Mary Ann Minton. And more phone calls to Birmingham had managed to glean the news that Mary Ann Minton had died in a hospice on the date on the death certificate.

'So in an effort to elude this guy, Margaret chose to "die", reinventing herself as her sister. But only for a short time,' Kim said. 'She kept moving location and changing her name. And she won prizes for gardening and goodness knows what else. We're still in the process of checking each step, but it seems she changed career. A couple of times too. Her sister was an administrator in an insurance office. Clearly, Marion/Margaret didn't feel up to that, but she started temping, and finally became a top-class secretary. That house in Carcassonne was almost certainly hers — probably she bought it with the proceeds of what looks suspiciously like insider dealing: she was employed as a PA by some drunk of a banker who lost millions; she didn't. She made a mint. She spent a lot on the rectory, and Lina says that cabinet would have set her back thousands—'

'A lot of thousands!'

'But she still had the funds to rebuild the school.'

'Then something about the school led Grange to her,' Fran said. She clicked her fingers. 'Hang on — wasn't she such a success as a head that some education minister went to see it? The government couldn't have used it as propaganda, could they? Got the footage on the national news?'

'If Grange'd seen it,' Kim agreed, 'then that would explain his trip to Verities and his insistence on getting a timed ticket as an alibi — which he never used, because of her killing him when he came to keep his promise. She walloped him on the head.'

'Poor woman.' Fran groaned. 'Why the hell didn't she do like that poor kid Cynd and give herself up? She's almost certainly have got away with it — self-defence. Not to mention the fact that he'd scared her so much he'd ruined her life.'

'Maybe,' Lina put in, 'she'd got so used to being devious, to pretending, that she'd almost forgotten what the truth looked like, felt like. But to give up that house, all her wonderful furniture — it's almost as if it broke her heart.'

'She certainly didn't last very long — and I've known bereaved people die like that for no apparent reason.' With a blush Fran recalled what she'd told Mark earlier. 'OK: we can take all this to the coroner and declare, hand on heart, that the case is closed. Well done and thank you, both of you. I'll expect an invoice, Lina — virtue doesn't have to be its own reward.'

Lina shifted awkwardly. 'OK. But there is just one more thing, Fran.' She touched a handwritten note on a single sheet of folded paper: *To whom it may concern.* To judge from their faces they'd already looked at the contents.

Gloves on again, Fran unfolded it.

> *Please take responsibility for selling all the effects you have found. Use the money to pay the outstanding storage bill — outstanding in both senses, I would imagine. Any left over should be donated to the charity Don't Badger Badgers, should it still be extant. Failing that, it should go to an animal charity.*
>
> *Since you obviously know your furniture, and have a considerable amount of ingenuity, I would like you to have first choice of some or indeed all of it provided you make an appropriate donation. Remember the theory that if you save someone's life you are responsible for him or her for ever. You saved my furniture, so now you are responsible for it. I would like you to have everything, but suspect that you will have to invite the Victoria and Albert Museum to look after the Italian cabinet.*
>
> *Sincerely — and, should anyone ask, in my right mind,*
> *Marion Lovage, née Margaret Minton*

Fran reeled. She literally couldn't breathe.

Lina hugged her. 'Please, please offer for what items you can afford. Then they can go back home — to their home.'

Kim said grudgingly, 'No one has done more than you to locate the stuff, and to make sure it yielded up what it has. But Ms Townend here—'

'Will renounce any remote rights she has,' Lina declared. 'Fran, you ought to sit down.'

Fran sat, to find her head thrust between her knees — Lina again, she suspected. Since a firm hand remained on her head, she had no way of finding out. At last the pressure was removed.

CHAPTER TWENTY-NINE

Acting Chief Constable Wren had certainly made the old chief's office his own, at considerable expense too — probably not his own! — but Fran sternly suppressed any nesting images that might force their way into her mind, especially involving cuckoos.

Why she had been summoned to see him she wasn't at all sure, but since she had been, she might as well take the chance to lay the Lovage bequest before him. Something with such moral and ethical implications could be dealt with only by someone at his level, though she'd rather have conferred with Cosmo first. And she'd much rather have seen him when she felt more herself: the day's events had conspired to leave her feeling weak and unfocused.

His face was impassive: surely, he wouldn't be bothering to sack her himself, even if she could think of any reason for him to do so, not after a notably successful couple of investigations.

Or was she somehow tainted by her relationship with Mark and couldn't be trusted to go quietly? If he thought that, it showed how little he knew of the ethos of loyalty and service. She might want to scream and shout if she were sacked unjustly, but for the sake of her colleagues and of the service in the abstract, she'd never risk their morale, never.

And what could explain the presence of a youngish man in the room with him? Dressed in a sober suit, the male equivalent of her own, he might have been anything, from a grudging bank manager to an overcautious accountant. His face was unremarkable, but for a pair of bright blue eyes, which might just humanize him and certainly radiated intelligence. 'Detective Chief Superintendent Harman has been with us for many years,' Wren told him. 'I'm sure you will benefit a great deal from her mentoring.'

Fran shifted the Lovage file to her left hand and held out her right, still standing at an approximation of attention. Her smile was genuine, however — this was going to be doing what she liked so much, after all, bringing on a young person and developing his or her talents. But introducing a new officer to an old was scarcely the role of the chief constable, more the job of Cosmo, or one of his functionaries. What did Wren think he was doing?

'Sean Murray,' the newcomer said, with a decently firm handshake.

'DI Murray has a particular interest in dead cases, and since Kent has had such national success with its cold case reviews, he asked to be transferred here.'

Fran's alarm bells rang strongly. But for the time being all she could do was smile and nod her welcome.

And that seemed to be that. Murray showed no signs of wanting to ask any questions, nor of leaving the chief's room. But her exit was clearly expected. However, she had her own business to deal with first.

'You are aware, sir, that I've been dealing with an investigation at Great Hogben rectory, now my own home.' She waited while he connected her with Mark. 'You'll be glad to know we wrapped up the case this morning.' Usually, she'd have lauded her team to the skies, but she still had reservations about Kim, however well she'd acquitted herself today. 'But there is a problem with Ms Lovage's bequest. Everything is summarized here for you. You'll understand, sir, why I can't action the bequest myself.' She plonked the file on his desk, saluted smartly, and left.

Now what? Several hours', possibly days', worth of paperwork. The synopsis of the case that she'd given Wren was no more that that, but maybe writing everything up in full was a task she could delegate to Kim. It would have her name on it, after all, an official declaration that for all Fran's interference she'd been the SIO and had carried the day. A big plus for someone newly transferred to the force. Which brought her back to the puzzle of Murray's arrival: no, no solutions presented themselves yet.

As for the Cynd's case, and the death of Andon Yovkov, they were Jill and Don's bags, though no doubt SOCA would suddenly and mysteriously claim the glory for the slight diminution in metal theft as a result of the latter.

She looked at her watch. Time to go home. First she'd better check if Mark had managed to see his GP. Had he risked driving? Or would he be relying on Dave for that?

She had a sudden frisson of fear — but told herself off: just because Mark was discovering he could love his son didn't mean he'd love her any the less. Did it? She could scarcely ask.

But Mark, picking up first ring, blithely informed her he hadn't bothered with a trip to the doctor. Dave and Caffy, Mark added with a wonderfully familiar chuckle, had only just managed to stop him flushing his medication down the loo.

'What?'

'I don't want to take any more pills. Not if they make me do that,' he added with a shudder.

'We'll talk about it later,' she said.

'Or not.' And he cut the call.

* * *

'I'm afraid my bath won't really fit you either, Fran,' Caffy said as she pulled up beside the Winnebago, 'but if ever a woman looked as if she needed half an hour with some essential oils, it's you. And I have to tell you your presence is not required in there.' She jerked her head sideways. 'Mark and Dave are preparing your supper. And you know what they say about too many cooks. I've spirited some clothes out for you too. Go on, they're so busy wondering how to peel onions without crying that they'll never have noticed you've arrived. I'm off to listen to the news and tell you when it's safe to restore your TV reception.'

They headed to the flat together.

'You've had quite a day, haven't you? What with one thing and another. And don't worry about Mark's pills — they're in my safe-keeping, so if he does decide he should take any more they'll be at hand. Mind you, I think counselling will work better — and he's agreed he does need that. He says it'll while away the hours that you're at work. Well,' she added with a smile, in response to Fran's open-mouthed stare, 'Pact isn't just about restoring houses — sometimes we have to restore the owners too.'

EPILOGUE

'We must be off our heads, standing here in this weather. I know we always talked about drinks on the terrace, but not in a full-blown blizzard.'

'Only a few flakes yet. And we have to celebrate properly moving in. No plumbers; no electricians; no decorators.' Much as he loves the Pact team, much as he owes them, it's good to have the place to themselves. 'I know hot toddies would be more appropriate, but it really has to be champagne,' Mark says, topping up her glass.

'Of course. And the cold's a good excuse to snuggle up together.'

Arms tight round each other, they sip in silence.

'It'll be cold in the loft for you, working on that train set,' she says at last.

'That can wait till Dave's moved back from the States. It's a neat solution, him renting the Loose house now it's been cleaned up. But Sammie—'

She puts a finger to his lips. 'Nothing you can do about her at the moment — we'll just have to wait till after her trial.' She won't mention social services, which still aren't very keen on their input. 'And in my experience, having even one child turn out as well as Dave has is a triumph,' she adds, with another hug.

'You don't mind having Phoebe as a flower girl?'

The wedding is still growing of its own accord. But perhaps in a good way. Their deaf vicar is all too keen to let Janie take the ceremony, and Janie has declared herself ready to officiate in the spring, when they all agree the garden will be looking better. The disappearance of rival fluttering tapes has helped, and Mark seems to be enjoying acting as unpaid under gardener to the dashing young expert Caffy — who else? — has recommended. From time to time he's joined by Bill Baker, who talks as much as he works, these days, and regards a trip to the Three Tuns for a quick half as an essential part of the job.

'Not at all. I just hope you can find a proper role for Dave and Mark junior — he must always have loved you, Mark, to name his son after you.'

He kisses her. 'Maybe you're right. Ready to eat? But I see you've brought home a pile of work. Tonight of all nights! Fran!'

'I know. I'm sorry. Just this once, I promise.'

'It's this new guy Sean Murray, isn't it?'

She nods. 'He seems to have Wren's ear in a way I really distrust.'

'Can you imagine anyone saying that of the old chief? Anyway — has Wren come to any conclusions about Lovage's bequest? Not him, I know — his legal eagles?'

'All in good time, he says. I know, I know — his time's no longer good but excessive. At least we have her real bequest. The house.'

'So we do. Let's go in and not talk about work — and especially about Wren and Murray — while we're eating.' He studies her face. 'They really are worrying you, aren't they?'

'Yes. But sod the files. Here we are, breaking our no-shop rule, and it's all my fault. Sod the files, sod Wren and sod Murray.' For now, at least. They both know she'll be up at five tomorrow to come up to speed. Meanwhile, she tucks her arm in his. 'I can think of something very nice to do in front of that lovely log fire.'

THE END

THE JOFFE BOOKS STORY

We began in 2014 when Jasper agreed to publish his mum's much-rejected romance novel and it became a bestseller.

Since then we've grown into the largest independent publisher in the UK. We're extremely proud to publish some of the very best writers in the world, including Joy Ellis, Faith Martin, Caro Ramsay, Helen Forrester, Simon Brett and Robert Goddard. Everyone at Joffe Books loves reading and we never forget that it all begins with the magic of an author telling a story.

We are proud to publish talented first-time authors, as well as established writers whose books we love introducing to a new generation of readers.

We won Trade Publisher of the Year at the Independent Publishing Awards in 2023. We have been shortlisted for Independent Publisher of the Year at the British Book Awards for the last four years, and were shortlisted for the Diversity and Inclusivity Award at the 2022 Independent Publishing Awards. In 2023 we were shortlisted for Publisher of the Year at the RNA Industry Awards.

We built this company with your help, and we love to hear from you, so please email us about absolutely anything bookish at feedback@joffebooks.com

If you want to receive free books every Friday and hear about all our new releases, join our mailing list: www.joffebooks.com/contact

And when you tell your friends about us, just remember: it's pronounced Joffe as in coffee or toffee!

ALSO BY JUDITH CUTLER

FRAN HARMAN MYSTERIES
Book 1: COME TO HARM
Book 2: DO NO HARM
Book 3: IN HARM'S WAY
Book 4: NO HARM DONE

DETECTIVE KATE POWER MYSTERIES
Book 1: MURDER THE BOYS
Book 2: MURDER BY THE CANAL
Book 3: MURDER BY ARSON
Book 4: MURDER BY FRAUD
Book 5: MURDER IN DEVON
Book 6: MURDER ON THE JOB

Printed in Dunstable, United Kingdom

72232572R10150